THE WHOLE OF MY WORLD

NICOLE HAYES

THE WHOLE OF MY WORLD

WOOLSHED PRESS
An Imprint of Random House Australia

A Woolshed Press book
Published by Random House Australia Pty Ltd
Level 3, 100 Pacific Highway, North Sydney NSW 2060
www.randomhouse.com.au

First published by Woolshed Press in 2013

Addresses for companies within the Random House Group can be found at
www.randomhouse.com.au/offices

National Library of Australia
Cataloguing-in-Publication Entry

Author: Hayes, Nicole
Title: The whole of my world / Nicole Hayes
ISBN: 978 1 74275 860 2 (pbk.)
Target Audience: For young adults
Subjects: Man–woman relationships – Fiction.
           Grief – Fiction.
           Love stories.
           Football stories.
Dewey Number: A823.4

Cover photographs: girl and bleachers © ~skye.gazer/Flickr via Getty Images;
clouds © iStockphoto.com/Raver32
Cover design by Christabella Designs
Typeset by Midland Typesetters, Australia
Printed and bound in Australia by Griffin Press, an accredited ISO AS/NZS
14001:2004 Environmental Management System printer

Random House Australia uses papers that are natural, renewable and
recyclable products and made from wood grown in sustainable forests.
The logging and manufacturing processes are expected to conform to the
environmental regulations of the country of origin.

For my daughters, Hannah and Emily,
whose stories are just beginning.

And to my mum, for always believing.

THE DRAFT

Dad always said we were lucky that there were two of us. Always someone to shepherd when you had the ball. Someone to pass to when the pressure was on. Someone to cheer when you kicked a goal.

But when it came down to it, when it really was just us two, that's not how it turned out at all.

PRE-SEASON

CHAPTER 1

THE WARM-UP

The mirror used to be my mum's. Her mum's before that. It's oval-shaped with a gold frame and patches of tarnish around the edge, like smudges of dirt that won't go away. Usually, I keep the mirror covered – I have a strip of black cloth just wide enough to tuck into the crooks of its gilded frame. I saved the remnant from Mum's sewing cabinet exactly for this reason. But today is different. I need to see what everyone else will see.

I study my reflection in the glass: mousy brown hair, blotchy skin, hazel eyes probably more brown than green if I'm honest. I'm short with a medium build – years of playing every sport I could are still visible in parts, even though everything seems harder to do now. I feel betrayed by my body. The lean muscles are looser, weaker. My chest has rounded out, full and obvious, despite my efforts to hide it. Hide *them*. It feels as though all the things that made me strong have become unrecognisable and soft. Of no use to me anymore. And there's nothing I can do to stop it. Dad says I'm a late bloomer. I should probably be grateful for that, except now I'm paying for it.

My school uniform doesn't help. The grey blazer sits huge on my shoulders; the bulky jumper under it two sizes too big. Dad liked the idea of not having to buy another jumper until Year 12. The navy-and-grey tartan dress with a touch of white turns my hips square, and the grey socks and black shiny school shoes make my calves look thick and stunted, robbing me of any hope of even *faking* average height.

I sigh, my heart squeezing. It's bad enough I have to go to a school where I don't know anyone without the humiliation of looking like a character from one of Mum's old English girls' boarding-school novels, with titles like *We're in the Sixth!* and *Second Form at St Clare's*. At least my breasts don't stick out as much with my jumper on. I stand a little taller, press my shoulders down. I'll get used to it. I have to. I mentally calculate how much is left of the school year. It's March now, so I have the rest of Year 10 plus two whole years to go before I can leave St Mary's Catholic Ladies' College. At fifteen weeks a term, that's one hundred and twenty-six weeks total.

And I haven't even started yet.

I draw the cloth back over the mirror and push it against the wall; its default position.

I hear Dad through the paper-thin walls even before he knocks. You can't breathe in this house without announcing it to everyone else – and probably the neighbours, too, on a clear day. 'Come in.'

Dad stands in the doorway looking anywhere but at me.

'Almost ready,' I say, a wide smile firmly in place.

He looks relieved. We've grown used to these moments without ever getting very good at them. Struggling to fill silences, looking at each other without our eyes meeting, talking about everything except what we should talk about. Or even what normal families talk about.

'I could go with you . . .' he begins, stopping when I shake my head.

'You have to work. I'll be fine.' I give him my best 'she'll be right' face as my heart pounds in my ears. 'It's not like a grand final or anything.' I laugh hollowly. It sounds fake even to me.

'No.' He smiles and studies the walls of my room as though he's never been here before. Shiny images of large brown-and-gold Falcons peer down at us as though preparing to swoop, dotting the spaces between newspaper pin-ups of Glenthorn Football Club premiership wins, team posters and other memorabilia. Wall-to-wall Glenthorn. Wall-to-wall football.

My dad looks old in profile, I note with a start. His handsome face is craggier than I remember it. His sandy-grey hair is brushed and smooth at the top, but the ends curl unevenly, and there's a ragged edge to his appearance. Although he's shaved for work, his face seems to be cast in a shadow. Smudges under his eyes, probably from his newest bout of insomnia. I glance at the family photo by my bed – all of us laughing at the beach, sandswept and brown from the sun. Dad's hair is blond-brown, the way mine is by the end of summer. He looks ten years younger, even though the photo was taken barely two years ago.

I feel Dad's eyes on me, watching me study the photo – our history shining up at us, taunting us, relentlessly cheerful.

I blush and look away. So does he.

'Did you see Hardie in the back line against the Vics?' I manage in the stifling silence that follows. I saw the highlights on *World of Sport*.

Dad's face transforms entirely – a mix of enthusiasm for the subject and relief at having something to say, the line of his mouth easing instantly. 'He's got it all right,' he says, shaking his head in disbelief. 'The way he can turn and spin – a cross between Compton and a young Barry Cable. He's got some mongrel in him, too. They'll come knocking, mark my words.'

'It's a different game in the West,' I counter. 'Nothing like here.'

'Geography,' he says, dismissing me. 'There's a Best and Fairest waiting for him, just as soon as he can make the cut.'

'If Killer can't win, your mate Hardie never will either. They don't give Charlie Medals to Glenthorn players – and they don't give them to redheads,' I say, only half-joking. I started this to distract my dad, to make him feel better, except it's working for me too.

'That's a myth,' Dad scoffs.

'Yeah? Name some.'

Dad shakes his head, eyes narrowing, pretending he's annoyed. 'Too smart for your own good.'

I shrug. 'Just call it like I see it.'

'You watch,' Dad mutters as he closes the door behind him, but not before I catch the edge of his smile. It never fails to elate me – that smile. I hardly see it anymore. I always think of it as Mum's smile since it pretty much disappeared when she died. Like he buried it in the grave beside her.

I let the warmth of that smile sit with me for a bit then return to my Mighty Falcons notebook lying open on my bed. I touch the page where I pasted a new article on Peter Moss this morning. It's still wet. A whiff of glue clings to the air. I'll have to wait to add my analysis beside the newspaper's. I run my eyes over the list of facts and figures compiled against his name – Best on Ground performances, trouble opponents, strengths

7

and weaknesses, an ever-growing injury list . . . Each number, average and tally printed carefully in my best handwriting. He kicked four goals on Saturday that I still have to add before I can work out his new average.

'Shell!' Dad calls from the kitchen, startling me back to reality. My heart does something acrobatic in my chest. There's no avoiding it.

I study Mossy's face in its pose for *The Sun* photographer. His blond hair and red moustache, pictured here in grainy shades of grey, are as familiar to me as my father's. Perhaps more familiar. I draw strength from Mossy's confidence, absorb the heat of his sunny smile and stand taller in my square blue-grey uniform. He's been playing with a dodgy knee and a recurring back strain for two seasons. If he can kick four goals despite all kinds of crippling pain, I can face a room full of strange girls and find a friend among them *somewhere*.

That's what Dad says when something looks too hard or you fall over from trying: *Pick yourself up, dust yourself off and get back to position.*

I shut the notebook, slot it neatly between my mother's leather-bound copy of *My Brilliant Career*, which she gave me when I turned ten, and the family photo from the beach, and pat them three times each for good luck. I grab my schoolbag and head out the door.

CHAPTER 2

THE FIRST BOUNCE

I stare at St Mary's Catholic Ladies' College as if the bricks themselves will tell me my future. Iron gates block the entrance, the points like sharp spears aimed at heaven. The red-brick building looms behind them, more like a jail than a girls' school.

Dad fought to get this 'good Catholic school' to accept my scholarship application after the deadline. He'd never seemed happy with Godless Glenvalley High, especially now I was a teenager. Or as he says, 'becoming a woman'. I guess he'd counted on Mum for all that. St Mary's probably saw me as a soft touch – no mum on the scene or anything they'd call a 'family' around to keep me grounded. A soul they could save. Of course they didn't *say* that's why they accepted me. They said it was because I blitzed the English test.

'You have to know when to draw a line,' Dad said that last extra-horrible week at Glenvalley High, when the silences had seemed longer and the loneliness beyond anything I could imagine, 'between last Saturday and next.'

I'd thought Year 10 would be better, not worse. But no one could forget, and neither could I. In their eyes Shelley Brown was broken. Half the person she used to be.

In my eyes too.

So I gave in to Dad, even though the school year had started, because I couldn't face another day there. That's what I'm doing halfway through Term One of Year 10 and already late for class.

I'm drawing a line.

I heave the new, creaky schoolbag onto my shoulder, weighed down with books I haven't opened. I pass the main entrance to follow the six-foot-high red-brick fence to an open gate further on, half wishing the fence barring entry would never end. *Sorry, Dad! I would have gone in but I couldn't find the gate . . .*

Not likely.

I keep going, my legs heavy as I make my way through the deserted school grounds. It's quiet. Eerily quiet for a school. I almost give up. Let the tide that seems determined to pull me home take me away, back to the things I know. But I don't. I keep wading, pushing against the force, knowing there's no point putting it off. I'm as ready as I'll ever be.

I follow a sign pointing towards reception, where a plain, pasty-skinned woman asks who I am and why I'm there. I give her my name and she directs me to a seat in the waiting room. After a few minutes a tall woman with burnt-orange hair approaches me, her lipstick a crooked pink gash across her face. She wears a skirt just like one I saw my mum give to the Salvos years before, and her cheeks each have a pink spot. This, I discover, is my new principal.

Mrs Brandt smiles and shakes my hand. 'We've been waiting for you, Michelle. I'm glad you could make it.' She keeps smiling but her voice has a briskness, a note of warning.

I'm late and she isn't happy.

'Um, the tram takes a long time . . .' I start, thinking about the blonde sun-tanned St Mary's girl at the tram stop. It took me five minutes to gather the courage to ask her for directions and I almost didn't, except getting lost seemed an even worse idea than looking stupid. But the girl pointed me to the wrong tram heading the wrong way, so I ended up feeling both lost *and* stupid. I picture her safely in class, telling her friends about the dumb new kid *who's probably halfway to the city by now.*

'Found your way all right then?' Mrs Brandt's voice is a mix of light and dark – ready to go either way. 'I know those trams can be tricky the first time.'

The blonde girl's smug directions throb in my head. I nod and smile, trying to think of something to say that won't sound idiotic.

Mrs Brandt waits for me to speak like she's deciding whether I'm simple, and she has a kind of ready concern in her eyes just in case I am.

'Has class started yet?' I rasp, burning with humiliation.

She gives me that same unsteady smile, as though she doesn't know what she's dealing with. 'Let's go and meet your new classmates then, shall we, Michelle?'

'Shelley.'

'Sorry, dear?'

'Shelley. I like to be called Shelley.'

'We don't much encourage diminutives here, Michelle. You were given that name for a reason.'

'Still . . .' I persist. I *really* hate my name.

'There's nothing wrong with Michelle,' she says, eyeing me up and down, measuring me. 'From Saint Michael, of course. A very honourable saint to be named after.'

I wonder if she thinks there are any *dis*honourable saints, and if there are, whether it would be okay to change my name if I were named after *them*? 'I don't like it,' I reply, smiling to make sure I don't seem impolite.

'Not for you to decide, dear. Your mother thought it

was perfectly suitable or she wouldn't have named you after him.'

'She didn't, Dad did. She used to call me "Shelley" with an "e", like the writer.'

'You're familiar with Shelley's poetry?'

'Actually, she's better known for her novels.'

'*She?*'

'Mary Shelley.'

Mrs Brandt sniffs a little, as though she's just smelt something unpleasant. 'When people talk about Shelley, they usually mean the poet, Percy.'

'Not my mum. She said Mary Shelley was a genius. Ahead of her time.'

'Yes, well. Be that as it may, I'm sure if that were her preference she'd have indicated so in your application.'

'She didn't write my application, my dad did. My mum's dead.' The words seem to leap from me without my permission, but they stop her in her tracks, her smile freezing on those bright pink lips.

'Of course. I'm sorry, your father mentioned that.' And while her face matches mine in its ruddy shade, I don't feel the satisfaction I should. Or want to. It still feels new, saying it like that, even after all this time. Because everyone knew. The whole of Glenvalley, anyway. That's the point of changing schools, I remind myself: I get to start again.

'Shall we go?' she continues, but gently now. Her whole attitude has shifted – the way she carries her head, how

13

she looks at me. It hits me then, like it always does, what I'm seeing: Concern. Sadness. Sympathy. A hard knot sits in my throat, the blood runs thick in my head. It actually hurts, sometimes, to have someone care.

I raise my chin, meet Mrs Brandt's gaze with a strength I don't feel and fight the tears that sting my eyes. 'Please call me Shelley.'

Mrs Brandt studies me as though deciding something important. And then, like a light has switched on, her whole expression shifts. 'Okay, Mich–' She stops herself and clears her throat. '*Shelley*. Let's go to class.'

Thirty girls' faces look up as one when we enter the classroom. Some look bored, some look curious, others just stare blankly. Thirty different girls with three different hairstyles. A lot like my other school except everyone is in uniform and no one with hair longer than their shoulder wears it down.

Sister Brigid stands by her desk, a small dark-skinned woman with large thick reading glasses and a plain green dress. She isn't wearing a habit – a lot of the younger nuns don't – and her hair is short, straight and neat. Her hands are clasped in front of her, and when she steps down from the platform, she almost disappears she's so tiny. But when she opens her mouth she seems enormous.

'Welcome to our class, Michelle,' she booms. 'I hope you're happy here.' She has the largest – not just the loudest, but the *largest* – voice I've ever heard on a woman, let alone someone the size of an eleven-year-old.

I'm about to correct her when Mrs Brandt steps forward and says, 'Shelley. She likes to be called Shelley.'

I smile at Mrs Brandt gratefully. She nods twice, pleased with herself, then leaves.

The door closes and silence falls.

I look at the class.

They look at me.

Then we all look at Sister Brigid.

I wonder if I'm supposed to speak. Then, because it's killing me, I find myself doing a weird kind of dipping curtsey to fill that space. Even as I'm doing it, I'm wishing the ground would swallow me up, but there's no way out, so I finish with a red-faced nod.

Everyone laughs. All thirty of them. Even Sister Brigid seems alarmed.

I stand there, scarlet cheeks probably visible from the moon, thinking, *Please let this end.*

Finally, Sister Brigid points to a seat near the back of the room, then turns towards the class as though nothing has happened, dismissing me in the same instant. 'All rise!' she intones.

There's a muffled scraping of chairs and everyone stands up. I take the moment to escape to the back of the room and slide into an empty desk.

'Heads down!'

As one, the girls bow their heads and wait in silence.

I watch from the corners of my eyes, doing my best not to be too obviously confused by this series of commands.

'Hail Mary, full of grace . . .' The whole class recites the 'Ave Maria', their voices blending into a flat, rumbling chant.

I can't remember the words. My blush has hardly faded before it creeps back right where it's most comfortable. I move my lips as vaguely as I can, my head dipped lower than everyone else's in an effort to hide my crappy lip-syncing. Dad started taking me to Mass more regularly after the accident, trying to play catch-up on all those years of neglect. But a few months later he stopped completely. He stopped doing a lot of things after the accident. That's probably the one I miss the least. I'm not sure he really believes in it all, anyway. Sometimes I think he just doesn't know what else to do with me.

'Amen.'

Everyone sits and Sister Brigid asks us to open our textbooks to page forty-two for 'quiet reading'. I scan the classroom, the buzz and chatter lifting with every passing minute. I try to concentrate on the chapter in front of me but there's too much happening – in the classroom and in my head. And I'm clearly not the only one struggling to focus. Within minutes, Sister Brigid's harsh voice cuts through the din and a girl I haven't noticed before –

'TARA LESTER!' – is sent to the back of the room, to the seat right next to me.

And in that instant I learn two important things about my new school: the back row of desks is a punishment at St Mary's, and Tara Lester has spent a lot of time in the desk I'm currently occupying. I know this because she's scratched her name into it. All the scribbles and scratches, indecipherable before, begin to take shape; far more interesting than the chapter I'm supposed to be reading on Australia's participation in the First World War. Beside Tara's name in small, crooked letters are the words 'Falcons for Premiers!'.

My heart does another flip. Only, this is the good kind.

I look sideways at Tara and catch her watching me. We both quickly turn away. For five long minutes we feign interest in the Diggers at Fromelles, carefully ignoring each other before she finally breaks the silence.

'I'm Tara,' she says, her voice low.

'I'm Shelley. Hi.'

Tara shrugs, meaning either she already knew or doesn't care. Or both. She's scribbling away on her folder, the contact paper disappearing under doodles of gold and brown stripes, squares and circles, with a football-shaped blob in the centre. There is no doubt what it represents.

'You barrack for Glenthorn?' I whisper.

'Obviously.'

'Me too.' Probably too loud for quiet reading, but I'm determined to be brave today. Dad once said I was 'terminally optimistic'. At the time, it wasn't meant to be a compliment.

Tara rolls her eyes. She's stopped doodling now, which I decide to take as encouragement.

'Who's your favourite player?'

'Killer Compton,' she offers, her voice matter-of-fact like she's said this a thousand times before.

Kevin 'Killer' Compton is probably the greatest player to have ever pulled on a boot. Dad says maybe the greatest player we'll ever see. Three-quarters of Glenthorn supporters would pick Killer over anyone else. Probably a good number of non-Glenthorn footy fans too, if they were honest. They'd never admit it, of course. They say they hate him – the other fans. But no one bothers to hate an opponent unless they're something really special.

Tara is watching me now. 'Who's yours?'

It feels like a test. 'Peter Moss.'

Tara snorts. 'Too showy. Besides, he's just about gone.'

I almost roll my eyes but manage to hold back. Nothing is more exciting than seeing Mossy go up for a mark, despite all his injuries. If you love football even the tiniest bit, you have to be impressed with his mighty leaps, if nothing else. Maybe it *is* showy but, boy, what a show. Still, I'm seriously thinking about adding to my favourites. Now seems as good a time as any. 'Chris Jury and Buddha Monk. Gavin Black, too.'

I want to add Mick 'Eddie' Edwards, but he's too new and a Western Australian. He's only played a couple of practice matches so far and he's a long way from proving himself here, but I have high hopes for him. I saw him in a Night Series match a couple of years ago – South Perth versus the Falcons. Eddie blitzed, kicking eight goals. We won the game but Eddie just about beat us all by himself. Even Dad was impressed. Eddie is probably closer to the end of his career than I'd like but he's got more football left in him than Mossy.

'You're not a bandwagon supporter, are you?' she asks, narrowing her eyes with suspicion.

'What – the Falcons?' I've forgotten about Sister Brigid now. This is way more important. *This* is where I live. 'My granddad barracked for them.' I want to add that my mum did as well, but I hate the past tense too much to say it out loud.

Those swimming-pool-blue eyes almost close as she assesses me. 'Even when they sucked?'

I shrug, happily on safer ground. 'I had to. They never gave me a choice.' I don't mention Mum's hand-me-down Glenthorn jumper that her dad had given her when she was a kid. She gave it to me when I was five, Mossy's number 24 stitched newly on the back. The jumper was easily four sizes too big but that didn't stop me from wearing it. Every single day. Mum used to sneak it out of my room at night just to wash it. I wore that jumper until the sleeves barely covered my forearms, and even then I tucked it away in my drawer. I still have it though I'm not really sure what I'm keeping it for – I have a new jumper that fits properly. But I just can't give the old one away. The new one doesn't have a number on it yet. I'm pretty sure I know who I'll choose but I haven't said it out loud before . . .

Suddenly I want to. The brand-new, line-drawing side of me *wants* to, just to hear the words. 'But my favourite is Mick Edwards,' I say, my terminal optimism refusing to shut up.

'He's a bit old for a recruit. Must be almost thirty.' Thirty-one, actually, which is pretty old, I admit, but he's got plenty of great football left in him. You can just tell with some players. I'm about to protest when she continues.

'Still, if he does what he did last year at South Perth, he could be a good buy,' she says slowly. 'Shame he's a sandgroper.'

'No one's perfect.' I try on a smile. Not a big one – that would only scare Tara off. Just a twist of the lips that I can easily cover up if I need to. Although I want to be brave, I'm not a masochist.

'I have his autograph,' Tara announces proudly.

I finally get a proper look at her as I gawp at this

stunning revelation. She has glossy brown hair, darker than mine and long. It hangs all the way down to the small of her back. It's neatly gathered in a ponytail, except part of her fringe kicks out in the opposite direction to what it's supposed to, as though in defiance of the rest of her haircut. Her skin is fair – sickly, even – except for the pinkest lips that look almost bruised. Her eyes are a startlingly crystal-clear blue. Individually, her features could be pretty but, somehow, in the process of constructing a face, the bits don't quite seem to match. I remember reading in Science that the human face is not symmetrical, but Tara's seems to be almost lopsided.

'How'd you get that?'

'Easy, just go down to Fernlee Park and watch them train. Sometimes you even get a sausage at the barbie.'

'No way.'

'Yeah. Really.'

'And the players are just wandering around?'

'At the start they are, then they train. What did you think they'd be doing?'

I don't know how to answer that. It had never occurred to me before. I watch the games on TV, and we used to go to Valley Park a lot. We'd play kick-to-kick on the oval after the game when Mum and Dad weren't in a hurry – ignoring the thousands of other kids recklessly doing the same thing all around us. But I've never seen a player up close. I've never *met* one of them. 'So anyone can go?'

'Of course *anyone* can go. It's just training. It's just around the corner from here, down Fernlee Park Road.'

I think about my accidental tram ride along Fernlee Park Road this morning care of the smug Barbie doll in St Mary's uniform, and wonder if I passed the oval without realising. I take a deep breath. 'Next time you go, can I come with you?'

'Maybe. I don't go *every* week.'

Sister Brigid shoots us a warning glance. 'I hope you two aren't talking!' she thunders.

We both smile weakly.

'Good,' Sister Brigid says, turning back to the blackboard.

We bow our heads and pretend to concentrate on our books. Time ticks over, the classroom hum grows, and soon I'm actually reading the words in front of me, the stories of the Diggers and the ANZACs, the war widows and the kids left at home. But all the while I'm praying that Tara will say something – anything – about watching the Falcons train.

And then, after I've given up completely, she hisses at me. 'Probably next Thursday,' she whispers.

I nod and smile, feeling something rise inside me. Something good. Something big. And I wonder if this is what it feels like to start again.

CHAPTER 3

THE MATCH REPORT

I don't get a chance to talk to Tara about Fernlee Park again after that because we're separated into different classes for most of the day, but I run into the sneering Barbie doll and her posse at lunchtime. There's nowhere to go in this tiny school – an open courtyard, a small quadrangle and some tired-looking tennis courts that also serve as netball, basketball and volleyball courts are my only options – so when I see these girls I have to stand my ground.

They don't say anything that I can hear, although there's plenty of whispering and nudging going on. I imagine their jokes about my weird curtsey in Sister Brigid's class, my complete inability to speak when introduced and my general lack of coolness all round.

But they don't speak to me directly, offering nothing more than hard stares and a deliberately wide arc of concrete between us as they walk past. I've discovered that the blonde girl's name is Ginnie Perkins, and that she's easily the nastiest girl I've ever met. Also, unfairly, the prettiest.

I barely open my mouth again after the conversation with Tara, except to lie to Mrs Brandt about how friendly the girls have been when she corners me in the hallway outside her office. I even remain quiet in English Lit with Miss Whitecross despite her announcement that we're reading *The Great Gatsby* next, one of Mum's favourite novels. The fact that the Perkins girl is in my best class is enough to nearly kill my enthusiasm for books and reading. But by the end of the lesson, I decide to never let her stop me from joining in again – not in English Lit anyway.

The trip home isn't much better. Tara disappears to catch the tram up High Street, opposite to where I have to go, so I'm on my own again. On the tram, a noisy group of Year 7 girls are giggling and exclaiming over each other and occasionally breaking into song. One girl starts singing 'Love is a Battlefield' at the top of her lungs, performing a theatrical mime of a shooting gun and fainting – cue explosive laughter from her friends – and I'm forced to sidestep her final lunging pose on my way through the messy pile of schoolbags that blocks my way. I manage to find a discreet corner in the back

24

of the tram and sink heavily into the last empty seat, the weight of the day's pressure finally lifting from my shoulders. I wish I could curl up and go to sleep right here but am afraid I would never wake up.

I get off the tram at Glen Malvern Station and am about to cross the street when I see the Perkins girl and her mates clustered on the Glenvalley-bound train platform. I try to measure my chances of slipping by them without being seen, but they're basically blocking the ticket barriers. There's no other way through. I consider my options – I'm so tired and just want to flop down on my bed and read. Or cry. Or read *and* cry. But that's not going to happen. I cross the street and disappear into a milk bar with a clear view of the station through its window, and wait as the train pulls up to take them away.

Except they don't get on. Instead, they join up with a group of Celtic College boys who leap off the train to meet them. The group virtually doubles in size, with a handful of kids from other schools I don't recognise appearing from other carriages. There's more than fifteen of them now, and none of them seems in a hurry to go home.

I look at my watch: 4.10. Another train comes and goes without the group thinning. I watch four more trains pass, the whole time pretending to study the bread selection as if agonising over white or wholemeal, evading the weird looks from the woman behind the counter. She asks me several times if there's anything I want, but when I finally turn to her, my eyes moist with the tears I refuse to shed, I see her hesitate then smile grimly. She nods, her expression softer, and I know she'll leave me alone.

Almost an hour later, the girls get on a train and the Celtic boys and their mates head off, and I'm left to face the long ride to Glenvalley alone. Which is what I wanted all along, really.

———————

The house is quiet as I approach the driveway. It looks empty in a way that it never used to before the accident. Even when Mum wasn't home, the house seemed to hum, as though her energy alone was enough to light the windows for hours after she left. Maybe it's the tired, neglected garden or the washed-out colour of the beige brick veneer in the dusky light, but it has the look of a place abandoned.

The heaviness presses in on me as I take the stairs one by one. I can hear the telly on inside. Dad's home after all. The flickering images reflecting on the front window, ghostly and erratic, tease me with glimpses of life happening somewhere else. Snatches of canned laughter deliver short stabs of something nameless inside me, stopping me from opening the door. It's just the TV, I remind myself. It's not even real. But these snatches of

26

sitcom happiness make the silent and lifeless house even more depressing than usual.

I stand there a long minute, wishing that the last couple of years hadn't happened. Wishing that the house could be warm with cooking smells and the sound of Mum humming along to *West Side Story* or *The Sound of Music* – it didn't matter which because they both sounded the same in her tone-deaf rendition. She used to sing loudly and passionately, so lost in the words and the music that she wouldn't hear us come in. And then she'd see us and her already-sparkling eyes would light up impossibly brighter, just because we were there. And she'd grin at my disgusted 'Mum! *Please!*' as though she knew that, no matter what I said, she could always make me smile.

I let myself into the house but avoid the living room where Dad is watching *Hogan's Heroes* repeats. He probably wanted to be home early because it's my first day. Before the accident I would have rushed in there to see him, let his arms enfold me and hold me tight. Hear his warm, deep voice tell me that everything will be all right.

'Hi, Dad!' I call out on the way to my bedroom, my enthusiasm as empty as the house feels. Not ready to relive the day, I'm counting on him to leave me alone until I come out for dinner. I shut my bedroom door and lean against it, careful not to catch my bag on the Falcons premiership flag draped across it. My whole body feels

27

heavy with the day's disappointments, as though they've been carved into each limb. And I don't know how to shake it off.

'Shell?' The sharpness of Dad's voice right outside my room startles me.

'Yes?' I manage weakly.

There's an impossible silence. 'Everything okay?'

I stand by the door, my breath loud and uneven. I don't have the strength to withstand his concern – not now. I need to warm up before I can face him. 'No big deal,' I say to the closed door. 'I have a headache. The train was packed, no room to breathe.' The lie comes easily enough – I just picture what might have happened had I stayed with the St Mary's girls and caught the train I was meant to. I can hear my heart thumping in the silence that follows. Surely he can hear it too?

'Okay,' he says eventually. 'Dinner will be ready soon.'

I can't imagine my stomach dealing with anything that even remotely resembles food right now but I thank Dad anyway, because it means I've bought a little more time until I have to face him.

———

'She barracks for Glenthorn, too?' Dad asks, chewing slowly on a piece of schnitzel. He has this thing about chewing everything twenty-one times. Literally, twenty-one chews per mouthful. I used to count him doing it, much to Mum's amusement. She used to defend him, saying it was good manners and excellent for your digestion. Her eyes used to sparkle when she'd say this though and he'd give her that quick, sheepish smile that meant he knew she was making fun of him but was also oddly pleased by it.

'Yeah. She invited me down to the club, too,' I continue. Now that the subject is open, I don't want to lose momentum. This isn't technically what she said, but it will make Dad feel better to think I've made a friend, and a small part of me believes that if you say things out loud often enough they have a better chance of coming true. 'She's really nice,' I add, tearing at the schnitzel like I haven't eaten all day, hoping to distract him. Faking enthusiasm for a school that clearly doesn't want me is harder than I imagined. I'll have to become a better liar to have any hope of being a good daughter.

Dad watches me closely. 'What's the point of going to *training*? Just a bunch of sweaty footballers running around an oval . . . Hardly worth the effort.'

This is the closest thing to a real conversation we've managed to have in days and it's so unexpected that I protest where usually I wouldn't. 'Isn't that what we do every weekend?' I say, tacking on a strangled chuckle, just in case. 'Watch sweaty footballers run around an oval?'

'That's a *match*, Shelley. A sporting endeavour,' he adds, as though that explains it all.

'But I could learn from their training methods. Their fitness and speed . . .'

Dad keeps chewing in silence. Seventeen, eighteen . . .

'I'm sure I could use it for athletics. St Mary's has a team.' I *think* they have a team. They must. Doesn't everyone?

Dad is chewing more slowly now. Maybe, maybe . . .

'I think it would be really cool. I've never been to Fernlee Park before,' I add, hoping the truth works.

Nineteen, twenty.

'I won't be home late,' I add. 'Promise.'

Twenty-one.

Dad eyes the remains of his schnitzel and mashed-up peas as though they're the cause of everything that's wrong with the world.

'I really want to go,' I say quietly, hating the weakness in my voice. 'More than anything.' It's all I've been thinking about since that first class. The one good thing that's happened all day. I don't know how I'll face tomorrow without something to look forward to.

Dad turns his eyes on me, studying me with such unexpected directness that I have to look away. It's hard enough to meet his gaze usually, and almost impossible after today's general crappiness. The one thing I've counted on since the accident is his silent acceptance of anything I tell him, no matter how untrue.

Dad cuts off a small piece of schnitzel and looks at

it speared on his fork. He turns it over, back and forth, then returns the fork to his plate. He takes his time to be absolutely sure he's got it right. It's a good thing too, as frustrating as it seems, because he never *ever* changes his mind.

'All right, then. See what it's like. But be home for dinner.' He returns to his schnitzel. 'This could do with more salt.'

Which means 'conversation over'.

CHAPTER 4

THE RECOVERY

'Not in your dreams!' Josh shouts, his voice whipped from his mouth as we sprint along the home straight. He's ahead of me, again, but only just. I feel the wind on my face, blood pumps in my ears, and my feet fly beneath me. I push myself so hard that my heart feels ready to explode in my chest. He's so close. I can't stand the idea of him beating me. He could never beat me before. He couldn't beat either of us.

Josh McGuire is the only friend I have left from Glenvalley High. I've known him since we were kids, even before we started school. He lives down the street, at number 39. We used to do everything together – our mums were best friends, basically forcing us to play together so they could talk about books and films and all the things they'd studied at university and never got to talk about with anyone else. I didn't mind the afternoons at the McGuires'. Mrs McGuire was always sunny and kind. She made me laugh, and Mum adored her. I try not to think about what Mum would say if she knew how long it's been since we've seen Mrs McGuire. It's not all my fault, I know. But some of it is.

Those afternoons were full of laughter and fun. Josh has always been a clown and brilliant at footy. We used to play for the Glenvalley Raiders together, and he was the only other kid who had any hope of catching me before I stopped playing. Josh never made me feel like I was less than anyone else, like I was less than a boy. He used to pick me first or, at worst, second for any team he captained in primary school, and would never let the other boys tease me, even when I beat them. Josh is the main reason I was able to stick with the Raiders for as long as I did, and his was the loudest voice protesting when I had to stop. Almost as loud as mine.

Josh is my best friend, if a teenage boy can ever be best friends with a teenage girl without hormones getting in the way. So far we've made it through okay, although recently the fact that he's a boy seems to be harder to ignore than it used to be. He's always been good-looking, like his mum, with tanned skin and curly brown hair that flops over his green eyes. A lot of girls like him. It

33

never used to bother me. Now, sometimes, it's all I can see. He makes me blush now, too, which is *ridiculous*.

I pump my legs harder, faster, gaining pace. There's no way I can let him beat me. I thrust my chest forward, lunging in an effort to pip him at the line. It's not like there's anyone around to clock us or referee the inevitable argument, but I need to feel like the gap between us isn't as big as it looks from behind. I lunge sharply – too sharply – losing my balance. My arms flail, reaching for anything that will stop my fall, finding Josh, who, I realise, isn't as far ahead as he was. As we both trip and nearly fall – him yelling, me laughing – I can't help but grin at the ground I made up in the last twenty metres. We collapse on the grassy track, laughingly trying to catch our breath.

Incredibly, I don't hurt myself when I land, and apart from possibly straining muscles from laughing so hard, Josh seems fine too. The track's deserted, being off-season. No one's mown it in weeks. The grass is already looking tired and worn, the strange mix of wet warmth and cold dry that makes up a Melbourne autumn doing its best to ruin the only official running track in Glenvalley. We lie there, our rasping breath the only sound between us apart from a handful of birds and the occasional roar of a truck passing along Summervale Road.

I roll over, grinning.

'I won!' Josh gloats.

I laugh. 'Another five metres and I would've had you.'

'Rubbish,' he says, but not with his usual confidence.

'You know I did. You just can't admit it.' He's quick for short distances, like I am. But I have stamina. That extra distance used to be enough to take him every time.

Josh shakes his head but doesn't argue, which is as good as admitting defeat. Josh never gives up when he's right. Or when he thinks he's right.

The grass is soft against my back, the air cool on my face. I haven't been running with Josh as much lately, not like we used to, and I can feel the tightening of my calf muscles at the very idea of how much they'll kill tomorrow. But I feel good, better than I've felt all week.

'How's St Mary's?' he asks, ruining the moment in a single shot.

'Fine.'

Josh props himself up on one elbow.

'What?' I say crossly. I don't want to talk about it.

'Fine?' The arch of his eyebrow adds an extra sting.

'Okay. It's crap. They suck. I hate it. Is that better?'

Josh sighs. 'Have you made any friends?'

I sit up, ready to snap. 'What sort of question is that? You're not my dad.' But the energy to be angry seems to slip away when I see the genuine interest in his face. And then I want to tell him about Tara and the invitation to go to Fernlee Park next Thursday. I want to tell him about *The Great Gatsby* and even Sister Brigid, who, while a nun – which is just plain *weird* – actually seems nice. I won't tell him about Ginnie Perkins, though. I don't want to think about her or her friends on my weekends. Monday to Friday is bad enough.

I lie back again, knowing it's always easier if I don't have to look at him. His green eyes. His floppy hair. 'One girl, Tara, is cool. She barracks for the Falcons –'

'Loser.'

I shoot him the required filthy and continue. 'We're going to Fernlee Park next week – to watch the Falcons train. She says they're just walking around like anybody else.'

Josh laughed, half snort, half chuckle. 'What, like real people?'

'You know what I mean.'

'Anyone else?'

'Geez, you want blood? No, there's no one else. It's only been a week.'

Silence settles naturally then. Our usual arrangement of him being annoying and me shutting him down is reassuring. Maybe not *everything* has changed after all.

'The kids at school asked about you.'

'Who?' I try to sound like I don't care.

Josh hesitates a second too long, like he's struggling to come up with some names. 'Julie . . . and Sam.'

A fly hovers near my eyes, my nose. I brush it away but

it refuses to give up. 'They didn't care much when I was there. Barely talked to them all last year.'

'Well, they asked. They wanted to know why you left – after . . . all this time.'

He means since the accident. Why it took almost two years to leave. I shrug and push my hair off my face. 'I have to have a reason?'

Josh shakes his head. I almost feel sorry for him. He's trying to say the right thing but there's no right thing to say. 'The boys at the club have been asking, too.'

This one cuts like he knew it would. My heart ices over and I don't feel sorry for him anymore. The fly buzzes and hovers, its fat body slow and lethargic as I try to wave it away. 'Bloody flies!'

'They asked if you were coming back.'

I roll away from Josh and face the edge of the track. The way the white paint bites deep into the turf, as though the weight of the paint flattened it and not the line machine that drew it.

'Jesus, Shell.'

'What?'

Josh nudges me to face him, fixing me in that green-eyed stare. 'You know what.'

'I tried, didn't I? Gave it a year – almost two. They didn't treat me the same. Like some of me was missing or gone. Like I was less than what I used to be.' I shake my head, the memory of it sitting like a rock in my chest.

'I'm done with them – with all of them, even the Raiders. Especially the Raiders.'

'How can you just be *done*? That's not how it works.'

'I've drawn a line, Josh. Between before . . . and after. Then. And now.'

'Is that you talking or your dad?'

I sit up, tuck my knees under my chin, tight and small. 'Me.'

'It doesn't sound like you.'

My shoulders lift and fall almost involuntarily. 'I've changed.'

'I can see that.'

I ignore the wave of panic that threatens to topple me. I want to claw it back, claw *him* back to where we were. Except there's that line, and I've drawn it. We all have.

After a long minute, Josh says, 'Mum wanted to invite you and your dad to our house.'

'She'll have to ask Dad.'

'I'm asking you.'

'Why? It's not up to me.'

'I guess she thinks it kind of is.'

I frown at him. 'Why? When is it?'

Josh is beside me now, forcing me to look at him. 'The eleventh.'

'Of what?'

Josh doesn't need to answer that. I already know.

'June.' He says it quietly, like something sacred.

It's weeks away. She's trying to get me ready for it. She knows I'm avoiding her – that Dad and I both are – and she's trying to break through before . . . it's too late.

I shake my head, no, unable to form the word, even though my whole body shouts it. Did he even need to ask?

Josh releases a dry, humourless laugh. 'I told her you'd say that.'

Sound still won't form in my throat. I take long, slow breaths, forcing moisture into my mouth, hoping my voice will come with it.

'So . . . what? You can't even celebrate your birthday anymore? Everything has to be different? Everything has to change?'

Yes, I want to say. Everything *has* changed. Even my birthday – especially my birthday. The idea of it, the shape of it. What it means. There's no one around and suddenly I'm conscious of the absence of noise, the emptiness of this place. The fact that it's just us.

'You only turn fifteen once,' Josh says quietly. 'You can't pretend it isn't happening.'

I should just go along with it but I can't. No one knows that better than Josh. 'No,' I manage eventually.

Josh sucks air noisily, his frustration almost physical.

'I can't,' I rasp, my voice stronger, though still a shadow of itself. 'Everything is different, whether you like it or not. I thought it would be okay by now but it's not. We just have to get used to it and start again.'

But it's more than this. Much more. How could he ask? *How could he?*

I pull myself up and brush my trackpants roughly. 'You ready?'

But I don't wait for him to reply. I'm already headed to the gate.

CHAPTER 5

THE ROOKIE

A cyclone fence stretches along Leafy Crescent, rusty and broken in parts. Fernlee Park is green and overgrown, with small billboards along the boundary. A long race leads into a brown-brick stadium. No one is out on the ground yet and the whole place looks deserted.

I follow Tara into the car park behind the stadium, loose pebbles rolling beneath my feet. Dust kicks up whenever a car drives by, and there are already other kids waiting at the entrance. They all clutch notebooks and pens, and a few have cameras slung around their necks.

'Hi.'

'Hey.'

41

Tara doesn't introduce me, but no one seems to care either. Or notice. 'Who's here?' she says to no one in particular.

A short, thick, redheaded girl, who, up close, looks much older than the others, answers with the tired voice of someone sick of having to know everything. 'Rocky and Jury came by. I haven't seen Blackie yet but his car's here.' She points to a dark green Toyota Corolla, a hotted-up two-door with a black spoiler and dark windows. 'I'm sure he'll come out to say hi.'

'He's in physio,' a boy says. 'He came early to see Barry.' He looks about sixteen and is sporting a blond-streaked mullet that I think is supposed to look like Bono's from U2, given his 'Under a Blood Red Sky' T-shirt, but looks more like Kim Wilde's.

'Did you see him?' The redhead isn't happy that some-one knows something she doesn't.

'No,' Bono Boy sniffs. 'But I heard on the news he's injured, and Barry's door is shut.'

'It's probably a hammy,' one says.

'Might be his knee again,' says another.

Either way, they all agree Blackie is with the physio.

The redhead sticks her hands in her jeans pockets and draws a semicircle with her toe in the dusty ground. If it wasn't for her lined face, you'd think she was a kid – thirteen at most. But then she smiles and tiny creases touch her eyes, and I wonder if she could be in her thirties. 'Buddha's had his hair cut,' she says, as if making an earth-shattering announcement – and it must have been, because she gets everyone's attention fast.

'Really?'

'What's it look like?'

'I bet it was his girlfriend's idea.'

'Yeah, Brandy must have made him do it.' They all laugh, nodding and smiling as though they're talking about their best friends.

I keep silent. So far no one has spoken a word to me. They don't look at me, not even a curious glance. I try to fight the churning inside, the frustration, even though I don't actually have anything to say.

As though reading my mind, Tara suddenly remembers I'm there. 'We're still early. Plenty more players to arrive. Did you bring your autograph book?'

Autograph book? I can't believe how stupid I am! *Of course* I should have brought an autograph book. I don't actually own one but it's suddenly so obvious I need one that I can't believe I've managed this long without. I don't know how I would have filled it, because I've never met anyone famous before, but that's not the point. I need one now.

'That's okay,' Tara says when I shake my head dumbly. 'I have some spare paper. You can have a few sheets,' she offers, and begins ripping pages from the back of her Geography exercise book.

'Thanks. If you're sure you don't need them . . .' This is the longest conversation Tara and I have had since that first day and, as I'm still not entirely sure she actually wants me here, I'm more than a bit relieved. I'd hung around her the whole day at school, waiting for a sign that her offer to go to Fernlee Park tonight still stood, or if it was something I'd just created in my head. But at the end of the day she came up to my locker and, with a shrug to suggest she didn't care how I answered, said, 'Are you coming?'

I'm unexpectedly pleased by the offer of pages from her Geography exercise book. I blink hard and focus on the paper, the whiteness almost too bright for my suddenly sensitive eyes. I blink again, furiously. Then I remind myself I'm about to meet my heroes and suddenly I'm fine, and I decide right then that nothing else matters. I feel bigger – *stronger* – just thinking about it.

Tara holds up a Glenthorn Football Club Official Autograph Book, opening it for me to see. Apart from the pages filled with scrawled signatures, it also has a section with rows of stats under headings like 'History', 'Premierships', 'Charlie Medals' (followed by a fat zero) and 'Goal Kickers'. I decide that I will definitely buy myself an official Glenthorn autograph book like this one and that Tara is suddenly the coolest girl I know.

A car appears in the driveway and everyone scatters. Every kid lines up at the doorway to the gym as though the whole thing has been organised and everyone has – and *knows* – their place. I find myself wondering if there's room for a newcomer. And how you qualify if there is.

'Eddie,' the redhead announces.

Tara shoves the loose pages at me and joins the others in the rush towards the new arrival. They all wave autograph books, club jumpers and brown-and-gold footballs under the player's nose, and bombard him with questions.

'Pull up all right, mate?'

'Not sore I hope?'

'Good game, Eddie.'

Mick 'Eddie' Edwards limps towards us, his left leg turned out like he doesn't want to bend it. He looks older than he does on telly, but handsome too. He is really tall. Lanky and narrow, except for his chest, which is a thick wall of muscle. His arms, too, seem heavy compared to his skinny legs. Basically, he looks like a full forward. Like he was born to be one. I can barely contain my excitement that he's playing with the Falcons this year. Of all the teams, he chose mine.

Eddie smiles and nods at the noisy fans as if this kind of thing has happened before, but also like he isn't really used to it yet and doesn't know what to say. 'Wow, you guys are keen,' he manages eventually, although he sounds more confused than impressed. He has a point.

The real season starts Saturday. So far, we've only played a handful of pre-season games that, luckily, we've won. They showed a few of them on telly. Dad always tapes them for me so I can update my scrapbook with the kinds of stats *The Sun* ignores: the goal assists, the shepherds and tackles – the selfless stuff that I'm sure wins games. Dad says the same thing.

Eddie signs whatever is pushed in front of him without slowing down, juggling pens and paper in one hand, his bag in the other, maintaining this balancing act all the way to the gym entrance. Then, giving up on any chance of escape, he drops his training bag and finishes signing everything that's handed to him. I stand back, wondering if my pathetic-looking scrap of paper will earn an autograph.

'You were robbed, mate, in the last quarter,' the redhead says, snapping her bubble gum and nodding. We played the Panthers at Valley Park Oval on Saturday and won comfortably. Doesn't mean much for the team – some players don't even try in the pre-season. But new guys or those coming back from injury are always keen, hoping it will be enough to earn them selection for Round One. Eddie kicked two goals but missed a few too. Not ideal but not terrible either.

Eddie smiles. 'You think?'

'He hit you way too high. Should have been a free.'

'Hard to tell from where I was,' Eddie says.

We all laugh. He'd ended up sprawled out in the mud.

'Seriously. And you were right in front, too. Would have been a goal. A definite gimme.'

'Actually,' I start, unable to keep quiet when someone's so completely *wrong*, 'you ducked into it.' I watched that game over and over, slowed it down, played it back. It was clear as day. 'Panoli went straight for the ball.'

'Really?' Eddie isn't smiling but he seems more curious than upset.

No point backing down now. 'He got you with his shoulder, not his arm. The ump was right. No free there.'

Eddie studies me, his face giving nothing away. 'I'll check the tape tonight,' he says. And then, like a bolt of lightning, Eddie smiles at me – right into me – like he's known me for years. 'You're new.'

'So are you,' I shoot back, blushing so deeply I can feel it in my shoes.

He laughs. A rich, low, strong sound. 'Fair enough.' He signs his name then pauses, his pen hovering over the page. 'What's your name?'

'Shelley.' I don't stutter but my brain seems to, and I'm not even sure I've spoken out loud. 'With an "e". Like the author.'

He looks up at me, amused. '*Frankenstein* fan, are you?'

Stunned, I shake my head. 'Not me. My mum.' I rush on, so surprised by this that I know I'm blabbing. 'It was that or Mathilde.'

Eddie laughs. 'I'm glad she picked Shelley,' he says. 'Probably my favourite name. I've always said that if I ever had a daughter, I'd call her Michelle. Shelley for short.' And he writes 'Dear Shelley, Best Wishes, Your Friend Mick Edwards'. He winks at me. 'Since we're both new here, I think that makes us friends, don't you?'

I can feel the other kids' eyes boring into me and I know my face is as red as a Sherrin. No one's ever said they like my name or have known what it means. 'Uh, thanks, Eddie,' comes out more like a grunt than any recognisable word, but Eddie smiles again and hands back my pen and paper.

'Call me Mick,' he says unexpectedly. I glance up to see who he's talking to, but he's looking right at me. 'The papers call me Eddie.' He runs his hand through his hair, his smile lopsided. 'But my friends call me Mick.'

My mouth is so dry I'm not sure I can form the words. 'Okay. *Mick*,' I croak.

'See you after,' he says with a wave to the group, then disappears into the gym.

I don't know what to do, so I just stand there while the others stare at me. Tara recovers first. 'New players are always like that,' she says. 'They try harder to fit in.'

The others nod at each other and return to their assigned posts outside the training-room entrance as another car drives towards them.

'Killer,' the redhead announces. And sure enough,

Kevin Compton climbs out of his car and makes his way to the gym entrance. He signs a few autographs and stands for a photo with Tara then says he's running late and disappears inside, all within about two-and-a-half minutes.

Bono Boy shrugs as we watch him leave. 'When you're that good, you don't need to be nice.'

Tara hangs her camera back around her neck.

'Cool camera,' I say, nodding at her Brownie. 'Do you have other photos of the team?'

'About a thousand,' Red chips in before Tara can answer.

Tara smiles proudly, the blush staining her pale cheeks. 'I've got a few.'

'They're all coming now,' Bono Boy informs us, as a parade of cars files into the car park. I watch the players arrive, one by one. Most of the players know the kids by name and answer questions about their post-game condition or their plans for next week's match. No one else speaks to me except to sign the bit of paper I offer them or to ask for my pen so they can sign someone else's book.

Mossy doesn't appear – he's had surgery and is still in hospital. But bit by bit, I see every other hero from the telly show up and follow the same routine. I'm in heaven. I never want to leave.

After most of the team has arrived Tara and I collect our stuff. I follow her around the outside of the gym, towards a tall pair of chain-link gates.

'Can't we go in?' I ask Tara as we wait for Red to fiddle with the rusted bolt. It seems stupid to wait outside the gym for so long and then not actually go inside.

'In the gym?' Tara yelps, as though I suggested we all strip naked.

'Well, yeah.'

'Not in the *gym*.' Tara stares in disbelief. 'Men only. Officials.' She keeps her lips together when she talks, as if she's holding back the words.

'Oh.' I decide not to ask any more questions in case I stuff up again. I follow Tara and the others into the stadium, where we squeeze onto a wobbly wooden bench along the boundary. The air is already cold and the sun is setting. The Fernlee Park lights are on low, but I can hardly see anything in the dusty twilight. After a bit, the lights come on full beam. The players run out onto the field, their bodies steaming in the still air, and I wonder if I've ever seen anything more thrilling in my life.

Everyone claps like they're thinking the same thing, although it isn't so much out of excitement as expectation, the way they applaud. I realise then that the crowd has grown since I first arrived. Men, women, families, people young and old have collected here like I have, numbering a hundred or so, all of them focused on the action on the ground. Some wear official Glenthorn Football Club clothes, others are in the usual supporter gear – tired-looking footy jumpers or heavy brown duffle coats decorated with players' badges, sewn-on name tags and large numbers emblazoned on the centre of their backs.

There are a lot of 3s, a good number of 24s and four or five 17s. No one is wearing number 5. Killer, Mossy and Buddha are popular, but no one has bothered with Mick Edwards. He might have been a star in WA, but that counts for nothing once you cross the Nullarbor. Footy fans love a sure thing, and we had a great year last year, winning the premiership after five years without making a grand final. There's every reason to be confident of winning again this year.

All except one: we've never done it before. We've never even played in grand finals back-to-back, let alone won them.

We need a star full forward. Someone like Peter Hudson, or even someone *half* as good as him. Dad says they broke the mould after Huddo retired. But Mick Edwards has something special too – an edge that could make the difference. If he doesn't step up, I don't see how we can go all the way.

For an hour and a half the players run laps, perform drills, polish their kicking and practise short plays, grunting and calling out in the quiet Glenthorn night. Their bodies flash across the ground, slick and smooth, gliding more than running. I can't believe these men are made of muscle and sweat just like everyone else. Their shadows fly under the lights and, even though I know they're tough and athletic, to me they look more like dancers than anything else. And the game is a ballet.

Every now and then a train passes by on its way to Yarra Valley and I keep thinking, *How can they go past like that and not get out to watch?* To miss out on all this just so they can go home to their boring lives to watch the boring telly. Who wouldn't love this? Who wouldn't want to join them? Right now I feel like the luckiest person on earth.

Tara and I head up to the press box, which, she seems surprised to discover, is empty. 'I usually have to fight the rest of the cheersquad,' she says. I glance down at the others who are all clustered on the boundary. I pick out Bono Boy, who is leaning against the cyclone fence, a boom box on his shoulder, U2 pumping at full bore. Red is on one side, and beside her is a bloke the size of a small house, with more tattoos than I've ever seen on one person.

Tara and I take a seat on a bench and watch the amazing scene below.

'There used to be games here,' Tara says after a while. Her face is calm, her whole body seems relaxed – different to the Tara I've come to know.

'Let me guess: the press sat here.'

She grins sideways at me, a real smile that changes

the whole shape of her face. 'I hardly ever get to sit here alone.'

'You're not alone,' I laugh.

She shakes her head. 'No.' But she doesn't seem to mind.

More and more people shuffle into the ground during the training session until there's a crowd of about two hundred, all yelling out to the players, the coach – whoever will listen – making suggestions, offering encouragement and generally just being here. Being part of it.

When it's over, the players head back up the race, their boots clicking on the cement, their voices joining with the rising chorus of encouragement that swallows them as they disappear into the gym. It's electric. The whole place is buzzing.

'Let's go inside,' Tara says. She opens the door to the stadium and leads me down a winding set of stairs.

'I thought we weren't allowed in the gym.'

She doesn't turn around to answer. 'After training *everyone* goes in,' she shoots over her shoulder in exasperation. 'The players are all in a meeting anyway.'

I follow her through the standing-room area and up the race and find myself inside the gym, the air thick with eucalyptus and liniment. The crowd is made up mostly of men but there are some women and kids too, all standing around drinking beer or Coke and eating sausages in bread. The barbecue penetrates all the chemicals so that soon it's all I can smell. The effect is mouth-watering. I'm starving.

'Can we get some food?'

'The barbie's in the trainers' room. You have to be invited, or someone can get one for you.'

'Like who?'

'A trainer, an official or a player.'

'Oh.' My stomach growls like something feral. 'What do we do now?'

Tara shrugs. 'Wait. The players will come out again. Usually, they announce the team.'

'Aren't you hungry?'

'Yeah. Wanna go to Greasy Joe's?'

'What if we miss the players?'

Tara looks around. One or two of the under 19s have already surfaced. 'Well . . .'

'Maybe someone will get us a sausage?' The barbecue is in full swing, and people everywhere seem to be eating.

'I s'pose we can see.'

We hover near the entrance to the trainers' room, watching men wander in and out, some with glasses of beer, others taking great hunks out of a sausage. After a while a few more players show up. One by one they appear from the dressing-room hallway, the younger reserves players first, then the senior players. Some of them slip into the trainers' room, disappearing into the cloud of barbecue smoke, standing shoulder to shoulder with trainers and spectators – all of them men. Some smile at us as they go by. The other cheersquad kids join us, and most of them have something to say to the players.

Mick Edwards appears after a while, his limp almost gone, his step somehow lighter.

'You in?' Red asks him as he approaches the trainers' room.

'Think so. Have to pass a fitness test on Saturday.'

I'm standing behind Tara, trying not to be too obvious but also hoping he will speak to me again.

As if he's read my mind, he looks up, smiles at me and winks. 'You must have brought me luck, Shelley. God knows I need it right now.'

This player is talking to me like I'm the only person in the room, and I feel myself grow taller, bigger, *better* just listening to him.

'Thanks for waiting,' he continues, swinging his bag over his shoulder, straightening to his full height, towering over me. 'You were right, by the way, about the free kick. I watched the tape inside. I ducked into it – it was all me.' He nods, impressed, and pats my arm. 'You've got a good eye.'

I can't believe Eddie – no, *Mick* – has picked me out of the crowd like this. I wish I'd changed out of my school uniform before I got here. It's so square and bland. So . . . *forgettable*. He'll never remember me next time. 'Um, thanks.'

'Hungry?' he asks, pausing at the entrance to the trainers' room.

I nod. He winks again then disappears inside the smoky room, returning a few minutes later with a steaming hot snag and a glass of Coke.

'Shhh. Don't tell anyone,' he says, although there isn't a single person nearby who isn't staring at me.

I smile, croak a thankyou and take the food and drink.

'Gotta go, guys!' he says to the group, giving us a small wave as he hoists his training bag on his back and pulls out a set of keys. Then he stops and swings his gaze right back to me. 'You live round here?'

'Um, no, not really. I catch the train from Stonnington.'

'I live near the station. Need a lift?'

I can feel Tara glaring at me. But this is a player – a *footballer* – offering to drive me home. Of course I'll go. I'd follow him to the moon if he asked me.

'I thought we were going to Greasy Joe's,' Tara says, her voice flat.

I stare at the food in my hand, look back at Tara, then smile sheepishly. 'You can have this,' I say, handing her the sausage and drink – the only consolation I can think of. Then I follow Mick out into the car park.

A streetlamp lights the way as we head towards his shiny blue Holden. It's a long way from the best car there but it's not the worst either. Dad says Mick would have been paid more to come a couple of years back, before his knee problem. More of a risk now – so late in his career. Still, it's a pretty nice car. Nicer than ours, anyway.

'Hey, I didn't get you into any trouble, did I?' Mick unlocks his car and yanks it open, the sudden noise sharp against the quiet night.

No one else is around and I begin to feel nervous. Not afraid, just uncertain. It doesn't seem real.

'Sorry if I caught you off guard. I thought, since you're new here too . . . that you're kind of a kindred spirit.'

And I know instantly that there's nothing to worry about – something in his eyes, how direct and clear they look. Honest. His eyes are *honest*. I suddenly feel very grown up, very *together* as I wait for him to open my door.

'They'll be okay,' I say, ducking into the front passenger seat. 'Actually, I barely know them.' But even as I say this, I know I've crossed a line with Tara without planning to. I don't know if I'll be welcomed back, but right now I don't care.

The Fernlee Park Road lights roll over us in waves as Mick's car moves in front of a labouring tram. The clattering racket fills the silence between us, trampling over the hum of Mick's Holden. I want to ask him why he picked me. Why I mattered more than the others. I long to ask him what it was that allowed me, in my square grey school uniform, to stand out from the other kids. Was it a moment I should treasure in case it never happens again? Or is it, as I hope, the beginning of something new and real? 'What's it like in WA?' I say instead.

Mick glances at me as though he forgot I was there. But there's an odd smile on his face that seems to look right into me. Maybe that's where his head was already – back home, on the other side of the country.

'Beautiful,' he says simply. 'Beautiful. Especially the beach.'

I nod, as though I have an idea what a Western Australian beach looks like.

'You ever been out there?' he asks, half watching the road, half turned towards me.

I want to be able to say yes, and a part of me is tempted to lie. But I can feel the heat in my throat moving up to my cheeks, guaranteeing that I won't get away with it. Even in the dim car, brightened irregularly by passing streetlights. I shake my head and shrug, covering my embarrassment as best I can. 'I've never been out of Victoria.'

He doesn't laugh or act surprised. 'You should go.'

And at that moment I know I will. 'Are the beaches different to here? Sorrento? Portsea?' I try to think of all the beaches my parents used to take us to – Anglesea, Torquay; even Port Fairy once, although I can hardly remember it. There were photos, of course. A lot of them. But they disappeared when Dad drew his line.

'No comparison. The sand is white and clean, fine

as sugar. And the waves are different. I can't explain it, but the way they tumble, clear and smooth, the colour of the water . . . Maybe it's the sky. Or the weather.' Mick's looking at me, his eyes as big as saucers. He fixes his gaze on the road again, carefully navigating the dribble of post-peak-hour traffic. 'No comparison,' he says after a minute, his voice unexpectedly hard.

As we approach Stonnington Station, the crossing alarm starts up and the lights flash with a grating urgency. Although we're safely outside them, and Mick has no trouble pulling over, something about their harsh ringing, the blinding red of the bulbs, pressures me to get away fast, as though the dark night outside is the only safe place to be.

I get out and lean into the car. 'Thanks for the ride,' I say. Still, the pressure, the ringing and flashing, the thunder of the approaching citybound train headed in the opposite direction to home . . . Why is it so hard to breathe? *What if this never happens again?* I smile at Mick. What if next time he doesn't recognise me or separate me from all the schoolgirls who make the trek up Leafy Crescent every week?

'It was good to meet you, Shelley,' he says in answer to my silent doubts, his voice enclosing my name like a perfectly fitting glove.

'Good luck on Saturday.' I offer a weird little wave that I wish I could take back, but stand there stiffly instead.

'Will I see you next week?' He seems to really want to know. My heart lurches in my chest at this possibility.

I clear my throat and brave a smile. I was planning to come anyway, but nothing will stop me now. 'Yes,' I say. And just in case he didn't hear me, I say it again, only louder. '*Yes.*'

CHAPTER 6

THE CENTRE BOUNCE

At school, Tara has been sulking all morning.

I make multiple attempts to get her to talk. I start with a couple of questions about the other cheersquadders – 'So the redhead is *how* old?' and 'Which one knows all the stats?' – but all I get are one-word answers and the cool, even stare that I was introduced to the first day we met. But by lunchtime, the push and shove of the schoolyard forces us to find shelter in a quiet corner, out of everyone's way. And slowly, slowly, the ice begins to melt.

'Do you think Mossy will play this week?' I ask, encouraged by the fact that Tara's last reply had come in the form of three words, not one.

She shakes her head. 'I hope not. Better he get right than risk another injury.'

I nod, opening my sandwich and pulling out the cheese.

'Can I have that?' Tara asks. We're leaning against the red-brick wall of the Art Room, our feet stretched out in front of us, our lunch boxes propped on our knees.

'Knock yourself out,' I say, and watch her slot the cheese into her Vegemite sandwich. 'Seriously?'

She nods vigorously, her mouth too full to answer. 'Bloody good.'

I shrug, relieved she's over her dark mood. I want to ask her about Mick – what he likes and doesn't like. The stuff I'll never find out on a footy card or even in her amazing autograph book. 'I hope Mick doesn't end up like Mossy,' I say, testing the waters before plunging in, realising too late that I might be mozzing Mick just by mentioning it.

Tara shrugs. 'Yeah.'

Not the encouragement I was hoping for but, as Dad always says, there's no challenge in taking the easy ball. *Real* champions want the hard ball. 'He seems really nice,' I add, watching her chewing mouth to measure the effect my words are having.

Silence.

I take a deep breath and am about to start again when she swallows her mouthful, turns those hard blue eyes on me and says, 'He's not your friend, you know.'

'I know that. I didn't say he was my friend. He just seems nice.'

'They're not like us. None of them are.'

'I was talking about Mick, no one else.'

'I know what you were talking about,' Tara snaps. And then she shrugs, as though the whole conversation is beneath her, and asks if I'm going to eat my apple.

———————

I wake early on Thursday morning, intending to catch the 7.08. I don't know why I bother. It's not like arriving at school earlier means the day will end sooner, but somehow it feels like it might.

Even in the dim, autumn light I can see Josh leaning against the waiting-room entrance on Platform 1, his messy hair and huge grin standing out against the dull, tired-looking businessmen and women around him.

'What are you doing here? Forget where your school is?' I ask, dumping my bag on the ground beside him.

He pretends to kick my bag, an exaggerated running kick like you'd see on a rugby field.

'Loser,' I say.

He laughs, stopping mid-air, then carefully straightens my bag like it's something precious. 'There, there,' he says, patting it.

I shake my head. 'No school today?' He's wearing jeans and a Billy Idol T-shirt with a black windcheater tied around his waist. It's freezing but Josh doesn't feel the cold like normal people. I tug at my blazer, pulling the collar high on my neck.

'Half day,' he says, not really answering my question. Half day or not, Glenvalley High is one block from the station. He doesn't catch the train to school. He walks. 'You're early, even for you.'

It's a Brown thing – to be on time or, actually, to be early. 'On time' is ten minutes early in my household. 'Big day,' I say. 'Going to Fernlee Park tonight.'

'Again? You moving in there?'

I shrug, bothered by his smirk even though I was expecting it. 'Tara asked me. She's my friend.' I say it like this is about her and not about me. 'That's what friends do. They do stuff together. All kinds of stuff . . .' I'm waffling and we both know it.

'Okay then,' Josh says, lifting his hands in mock surrender.

I can see the train from Mountvalley snaking its way around the bend towards us. Glenvalley is a terminus, which means that even when the train arrives we have to wait for the passengers to unload before it heads back into the city.

'Did you see Mossy?' He's pretending not to care but I know, even though he's an Eastern supporter, he loves Peter Moss. Josh thinks he plays like Mossy – high leaping grabs, kicking goals that defy physics, and that wild, scraggy hair that makes him look like a TV star.

'Nah, he's still out. But I met Killer, Blackie, Buddha . . .' I trail off, saving the best till last. 'Mick Edwards said I had a good eye.'

'Edwards? The sandgroper has-been?'

I bristle, despite knowing that Josh is only stirring. 'He's a star!' I snap. 'Better than Tinker and Fly put together!' The boys always used to wind me up like this when we were little, and it always worked. 'Dad says he's got the goods too,' I add.

Josh's eyes sparkle, and he nods, *fair enough*. No one argues with my dad's footy genius, not even up-himself Josh McGuire.

'See his goal in the second half?' I continue, pleased that he seems to be listening. 'Sheer brilliance.' It feels great to talk about Mick like this, free to gush and glow without having to be careful or in control.

'Nah, went to watch the under 19s at Glenvalley.'

'Did you get a game?' The senior coaches have let Josh play a few times – sometimes the junior stars are asked to fill in above grade when the older boys are injured. We used to all go and watch, too, lining the boundary to cheer them on, screaming like lunatics if our boys got anywhere near the ball. They didn't have to blitz – just making it into the action was impressive, given that the opposition and some of their teammates were twice their size.

'Not this time. But Brent is out – could be for the season. Sucks, but it means they'll probably need me again.'

'Poor Brent.' I step back a bit as I realise that Josh has grown a lot, even just this year. I study his face, the strong jaw and the protruding Adam's apple I hadn't noticed before. I can see, I think, what he'll look like as an adult. It's there – under all the smirking and pranks – the Josh of the future. Josh as a man.

'Anyway,' I say, hating the catch in my voice at this image, 'you should watch Mick's goal. It's an absolute beauty.' I manage a cool smile, hoping he swallows it. 'You could learn something.'

He snorts. 'Yeah right.'

The train shunts noisily, the hiss and grunt of the brakes drown out the Vic Rail announcer. We both watch it for a moment, the crowd on the station gathering and shifting as one towards it. I glance at my watch. A couple more minutes.

'Did you want to go for a run after school?' he asks, eyes still on the train. 'Next week some time?'

'I s'pose. When?'

'Wednesday or Thursday?' He shrugs like it doesn't matter but he's being weird, looking everywhere but at me.

'Thursdays are training nights. Wednesday?'

'You're going to Fernlee Park *every week*?' His eyes are narrow, but the smile remains. It's possible he thinks I'm avoiding him.

'Not *every* week,' I say, although I'd like to. I'm also going on Tuesday night but if I tell him that, he'll definitely arc up. Tara says the players have more time on Tuesdays – there aren't as many of them because it's not compulsory, but training finishes early so the players often hang around afterwards. But Josh won't understand. He just doesn't get it.

'Made some friends, huh?' he says.

I shrug. 'A few. I already told you.'

The train doors open and the station attendant announces that it's stopping all stations to Flinders Street.

'I have to go,' I say, heaving my swollen bag onto my shoulder.

'It's bigger than you.' Josh smiles, lifting the bag higher on my shoulder. His hand brushes against my neck in the process, and the heat rushes to my cheeks.

He grins, enjoying my embarrassment.

'Careful, *Joshie*,' I snap, desperate to put some space between us to catch my breath, my voice sounding harsher than intended. 'Don't want you to break a nail.'

He blows me a kiss, which – annoyingly – makes me blush even deeper. I stick out my tongue before I can stop myself, and just in case this isn't embarrassing enough, my blazer catches on the train door handle, yanking me back from a quick getaway. *Don't look back!* I tell myself. *Don't look . . .*

I look back. Josh is, as I feared, grinning stupidly. I'm tempted to yell something brilliant until I see a cluster of St Mary's girls zoning in on us, Ginnie Perkins' perfect blonde ponytail bobbing away dead centre, and I shut the door, praying they don't get on.

Despite my encounter with Josh, the buzz has returned by 3.30 and I feel like I've been floating all the way down Fernlee Park Road. Even Tara's moodiness seems to have lifted.

A few of the other kids nod at me when I arrive, which feels weirdly nice. I recognise only a couple of them, including Red, her quiet pride at knowing everything before anyone else securing her spot up the front. And a kid everyone calls 'Jim-Bob' because he looks like the boy from *The Waltons* – the mopey one who's obsessed with planes.

'Nice book,' Red says as I open my brand-new autograph book, flattening the pages for the first autograph. The cover is chocolate brown, and the new modern-looking Falcon emblem is large and bold on the front.

'Thanks,' I say, feeling ridiculously pleased.

'Eddie did well,' Jim-Bob says to the crowd, but it feels like he's talking to me.

'Yeah,' I say, pride swelling in my chest. It's starting to

feel a bit like I'm meant to be here. But when Mick's car pulls into the Fernlee Park car park, a lump lodges in my throat. None of this cheersquad stuff will mean anything if Mick doesn't care. Will he even remember me? Will he offer to drive me again?

'Thinks he's so hot in that ridiculous car.' Tara's voice is sharp like a dagger. She might have forgiven me, but she hasn't forgiven Mick for whatever she thinks he's done. I find myself torn between wanting him to talk to me and my dread of Tara seeing it.

The car door slams and Mick crosses the empty car park. He greets us all as a group, then the requests for autographs and photos start up. I join in with equal excitement.

Tara hangs back until the crowd has thinned. When her turn comes, she thrusts her autograph book at Mick, half watching him, half turned away, as though she's doing him a favour and not the other way around. He signs it, hardly noticing. And then it's my turn. I stand my ground, fighting the urge to push past the other kids. I hold out my shiny new official Glenthorn autograph book, its pages stiff and barely touched. The plastic cover had cracked when I opened it for Killer, who came through earlier. I'd turned it to the third page for him and watched him scrawl his signature with barely a glance my way. Kanga and Blackie arrived after him, signing their names on the pages following. I've saved the first page for Mick. I open it to face him, its surface flat and clean and new. He takes my book without looking up and the beginnings of panic tighten my chest. He doesn't remember.

He signs my book and goes to hand it back when he starts, as though only just realising I'm here. His smile is wide and open. 'Shelley! I didn't see you.'

Heat and pleasure battle with dread as I feel Tara's drill-like gaze. And I'm struggling to decide what's more important.

'Good to see you got home okay,' Mick says, oblivious to the silent battle happening in my head in front of him.

I smile and nod, trying to come up with something intelligent to say. I must look weird because he frowns at me in concern, raised eyebrows and all. 'Nice goal in the third quarter,' I say, reaching for the thing I know best.

'Lucky shot,' he says, shrugging. But it wasn't. It was a beauty, all the way from the boundary.

'Wrong foot too,' I add, forgetting about the others, who are staring at us in confusion and disbelief. Forgetting about Tara and her steely gaze. 'I like the two-step you did to push it out.'

Mick laughs. 'Thought I'd get pinged for that.'

I shrug, safe and warm in this space now. 'Nah, fifty-fifty. Dad says for every close decision you win, you lose two. So, be careful Saturday.'

The deep throaty laugh he lets out is the most exciting thing I've heard. He hands back my autograph book, shaking his head. 'Good theory. I'll keep that in mind.'

I stand with the book in my hand, the pages open to his broad, sweeping autograph, feeling like I could fend off bullets with this priceless thing. The other kids have disappeared to meet the latest arrival.

'See you after?' Mick says. To me, alone.

I nod. And nod again.

Mick disappears inside the gym, and I stand there for a full minute before I remember – Tara.

She's hanging back, not with the other kids as I expected, but right where she was standing before. She's no more than a long arm's reach away, and yet, the space between us is enormous. I see that in the stiff tilt of her chin. I want to confront her – confront *this* – to say something in my defence. But all I have are questions. Why is she angry with me? What does it matter if Mick and I are friends?

Before I can find the right words, she shoves her camera and autograph book into her schoolbag, which she swings onto her shoulder. Her smile is empty and light. 'See if the press box is empty?' she asks.

I smile hesitantly, then with more confidence. 'Yeah. Let's go watch some footy.'

71

CHAPTER 7

THE REPLAY

We live two kilometres from Glenvalley train station. During the week I catch the bus to the station, but on Saturdays the bus doesn't run, so when Dad and I go to the footy we walk to the station to catch the Valley Park bus. We could drive – *Dad* could drive – but he likes walking more than anyone I know. Sometimes he wanders through the whole of Glenvalley, all the way to Hunters Hill, covering miles without ever really going anywhere. Walking in an enormous circle, never choosing the same path twice, and always moving, like he's scared to stand still.

He used to walk when Mum was alive, but not like now. Sometimes he'll be gone for hours, returning with his cheeks pink from the cold air, the cuffs of his pants damp from the golf course or the grassy knolls at the back of the drainpipes.

I don't mind walking with Dad on a Saturday. I'm scared of dogs, and there's a particularly aggro Doberman that patrols the top end of the Finkler Reserve that Dad has rescued me from more than once. Plus, today's game is a big one. The Falcons are playing the Panthers at Valley Park and Dad said he'd take me.

It's a game we used to always watch as a family. We'd circle it on the fixture every year and make sure the day was set aside for the footy. But we haven't done it since the accident, so I'm surprised Dad's offered to come. He doesn't even barrack for Glenthorn. He doesn't barrack for anyone.

This is the weird thing about my dad: although he loves football, he doesn't follow a single team. He just wants to see a great game, fair umpiring and a high level of skill. Other than that, he doesn't give a toss. It's possible he's the only football fan in the whole of Victoria who doesn't have a team. Even people who *hate* football – in Melbourne, anyway – have a team. It's like a rule. The moment you're born in this city, or even if you move here, you have to choose a team to barrack for. You don't really even get to choose. It's handed down to you, like property or, if you barrack for Carringbush, a hereditary disease. No choice, no argument, no debate. If you're born into a Glenthorn family, you become a

Glenthorn supporter. Warriors breed Warriors, Panthers breed Panthers. That's why I've always felt sorry for Angels supporters – years of losing with no hope of success, but still they show up every week. Because that's what you do.

Marriage is the only thing that can mess with the system. We didn't have that problem, though, because Dad isn't normal. He let Mum win without putting up a fight. Still, once it was decided, he wouldn't let me bail on the Falcons even if they sucked. He says no matter how bad your team plays, no matter how many grand finals you lose or wooden spoons you win, you don't give up on them because 'You don't change teams mid-season.' But what he means is: you don't change teams *ever*.

Thank God Mum gave me the Falcons.

We make it most of the way through Finkler Road and are just about to pass the Christies' house when we run into Josh on his way back from school. I try to ignore my pounding heart and remind myself it's just *Josh*. No one special. It's not like I haven't seen him lately – we've gone running together twice since I saw him at the station three weeks ago, and he's called a few times, too. So this should not be a big deal. But still my hands are clammy and there's a lump the size of a golf ball in my throat.

I can see the purple and blue stripes of the Glenvalley High footy jumper under his tracksuit, which means he's come straight from their game. He still has a smear of dirt on his face where he's pushed the hair out of his eyes with muddied hands. Josh plays for the Raiders too – Saturdays are the school team, Sundays are the Raiders. Our whole family used to spend every Sunday throughout the footy season watching the Raiders; the Browns and the McGuires almost part of the furniture at the club. But Dad and I haven't been back since the accident, not even to watch Josh play. You'd think Josh would be sick of it – the same people, the same clubs, the same coaches, but there's no such thing as too much footy in Josh's world. Probably in my world, too, if I could still play.

'Hey, Josh,' I say, while Dad shakes Josh's hand with that awkward gravity he saves for anyone who knew us before the accident. The old us, when we were still a proper family. I notice Dad glancing over Josh's shoulder to make sure he's alone. I do too. It takes an almost physical effort to deal with Josh's mum – for both of us – and once again we've dodged a bullet. She's nowhere in sight.

Josh's grin is as wide as a Mack Truck. Seriously, you can spot it a mile off. And it's infectious, too, that grin. Even Dad gives in to it once he relaxes a bit. 'Big one today,' Josh says, nodding at my Glenthorn scarf. Although he barracks for Eastern Panthers, I don't hold it against him. His dad played for the Panthers' reserves for a few years and would've made the seniors if he didn't

75

destroy his knee on a swampy Punter Oval during one particularly brutal game. So of course Josh barracks for the Panthers – it's a McGuire family tradition. But that doesn't mean I don't love watching the Falcons thrash the Panthers senseless every time they play. What I'm praying will happen today.

'You want to come?' I offer.

'You should, Josh,' Dad says too quickly. 'The Panthers are due for a big one,' he adds, nudging Josh stiffly, cajoling him with too much enthusiasm for the careless offer it's supposed to be. Dad needs him as much as I do.

Josh has the good grace to shrug it off and laugh. 'Love to, Mr Brown. Can't think of anything I'd rather do than watch the mighty Panthers flog the willies out of those brown-and-yellow losers.' He winks at me, daring me to bite.

'Gold,' I correct him, unable to resist. 'Brown and *gold*.'

'Right, right. Brown-and-*gold* losers,' he says, cracking himself up and earning a grateful grin from my dad. 'Can't though – got to help Mum with some stuff.'

I know mentioning Mrs McGuire will hurt Dad even before I see his face crumple. A wave of pain washes over his face but it's gone almost before it appears, and if you weren't watching and knowing it would hurt, you'd never know it happened.

Josh blanches and forces a brittle laugh. He saw it.

76

'I mean, I have to do homework,' he says, as if that would undo the pain.

With a heroic effort, Dad manages something like a smile, shakes Josh's hand again and says goodbye. 'Say hi to your parents for me,' he adds, like he's any other dad and the McGuires are any other friends.

'Sure, Mr Brown.'

'See you, Josh,' I say, ready to get my head back into football.

'Shell?'

I stop, ignoring the flip my stomach does when he says my name. 'Yeah?'

'You promised you'd come to a Raiders game,' he says, his steady gaze giving me nowhere to escape. 'You haven't made it to one all season.' I haven't made it to one in almost *two* seasons, actually, but the details are kind of irrelevant right now. Fact is, I promised I would.

I watch Dad continue his walk – shoulders hunched, head straight. In his own world. So completely alone, it aches to see it. 'Sure, okay,' I say to Josh, knowing that I'll find a way to get out of it easily enough when the time comes. Josh will understand.

As I turn to go, Josh catches my hand, and a hot stream of electricity shoots up my arm. 'Sorry,' he says. For a second I think he knows what I'm feeling, but then he nods at Dad, and I realise he's apologising for the weirdness before.

I smile it away, too confused to speak, unable to look at our hands even though it's all I can think about. Josh lets go, and my whole arm seems to go cold. For a long second I stand there, incapable of speech. Then he winks and walks off, the grin on his face all the proof I need that he knows exactly what his touch did to me.

Shame surges through me, hot and thick. It's enough to get my limbs moving again, and to kill any desire to watch Josh leave. I chase after Dad, who seems almost to be running, those long, powerful legs outpacing my short nimble ones. I'm so out of breath by the time we get to the station that I don't give Josh a second thought. Not once.

————

'The better team won,' Dad says as we head home, his obsession with sportsmanship robbing me of a chance to whine. We take the stairs to the front door, side by side, his steps long and determined, mine slow and heavy, loaded with disappointment. Eastern Panthers crushed us by thirty-nine points. I'm so glad Josh didn't come.

'Hold your head up, Shell,' Dad says as we enter the cold, dark house.

I wish he'd left a light on, and the heater. The fluorescent lights flicker in the kitchen, blinking quickly before catching. I go straight to the kettle to put on some tea, hovering over it to warm my hands.

He disappears into the family room and turns on the telly. I know what that means and feel the dread building at the thought. I stand in the doorway, gathering the courage to object. Dad eyes me from his chair across the room, eyebrow raised, expectant.

The music to the replay kicks in, its cheerful tones about as depressing as the final siren was today. The pain of losing is still sharp in my chest. Everything feels raw and open. And now I have to watch the whole thing all over again.

When we win, I love it. When we lose, I'd rather have a tooth pulled.

'Come on, Shelley. A true sportsman takes the wins *and* the losses. No point investing unless you can lose respectably.'

Easy for him to say – he doesn't care who wins. 'Do I *have* to watch?'

There's a flicker of something in his eyes. Sympathy? Concern? But it's gone too soon to be sure.

The kettle starts whistling and I glance hopefully back to the kitchen.

Dad's beside me before I realise. 'Anyone can win, Shell. It's losing that makes you strong.' For a second I think he's going to hug me. Instead he squeezes my shoulder then heads into the kitchen. 'I'll make the tea.'

I've heard all this a million times before. Losing builds character. Anyone can win. Blah, blah, blah.

79

The commentators start the introduction to the show – the Falcons and the Panthers are up first. Brilliant. No time to warm up.

Awkwardly, I sit on the arm of the couch, as far from the telly as I can be. Dad reappears, hands me a steaming cup of tea then returns to his chair, where he puts up his feet and gets comfortable. I slide into the couch properly, set my tea on the table beside me and take a deep breath. Resigned to my fate.

Dad nods his approval and smiles that mischievous smile he hardly ever uses anymore. 'You never know,' he says with a wink, 'you might get up and win this time.'

And even though I know the result and have heard this tired old joke a thousand times before, as the game draws to an end for the second time today – the same kicks, marks and goals replayed before me – my chest tightens and a lump forms in my throat all over again. It's like, somewhere in my heart, I hope Dad's right about winning the second time around, even when I know it's impossible.

If that's what it takes to build character, I'm not up to it.

CHAPTER 8

THE RULES

'Contact!' Mrs Hodge cries out as Anna Barnes slams into Melanie Hauser, giving Melanie a clear shot at goal. I suck in air and rest my hands on my knees, struggling to catch my breath before the ball comes back into play.

Tara is watching from the sidelines because she has a sore ankle and can't play netball. Or that's what she told Mrs Hodge, who raised her eyebrows and nodded curtly, having heard this a hundred times before. Tara never does P.E., no matter what sport we're doing or when we're doing it.

'I don't know why you bother,' she says to me at the half-time break. Despite the cool air, I'm sweating bullets and my lungs ache with the effort to breathe. I'm playing on the wing and against Ginnie, who, to add to her already stupendous number of accomplishments, is a state-level netball champion. I've managed to avoid netball until St Mary's, and my footy skills are only able to take me so far. She's beating me and I hate that.

'It's fun,' I lie, returning to my position. It's anything but.

The whistle blows and I leap forward just as Ginnie's foot catches mine, knocking me off balance. 'Sorry!' says Ginnie, as I stagger for a step or two, just managing not to fall over.

'Tripping!' I call out, and point to Ginnie, who smirks discreetly. 'She tripped me.'

Mrs Hodge does the eyebrow lift. 'I didn't see it.' She doesn't believe me. She thinks I'm a bad sport. Between Mrs Hodge and my dad, I'm starting to think they may be on to something.

I shake it off and get ready to go again. Ginnie knows the game, but I'm faster. So I think through how to make this work. I fall back from the centre line and hang outside the ring, on my toes, circling a bit as we wait for the centre pass. Seconds before Elena Irving releases the ball, I jog towards the line, then sprint at it, breaking through a split second after the whistle blows, timing it perfectly. The ball slams into my chest and I've left Ginnie several paces behind play. I pass it forward, run to meet the next pass on the top of the circle, then slot it into Kathy Doyle's waiting arms. She shoots and scores, and Ginnie is left panting behind me. Tara cheers like it's the footy.

I wink at Ginnie, rubbing it in. Somewhere deep down I'm ashamed of my gloating, but it's pretty deep and easy to ignore.

After the game, which, despite a slight improvement at my end, we lose, Tara and I head to the lockers to get our lunch.

'So Saturday morning at the Burke and Wills statue at eleven?'

I look over my shoulder. Is she talking to me? Tara's face is buried in her locker and I'm the only person around, so she must be. Except I have no idea what she's talking about.

'I can only wait fifteen minutes max because we have to catch the eleven-twenty up Elizabeth Street.' Tara closes her locker and looks at me. 'Saturday trams are dodgy,' she adds, as though I've asked her a question.

'Are they?'

She nods. 'I always watch the reserves first. That's why I go so early.'

And then I get it. She's asking me to the footy. Not just training but to an actual game. On the weekend. *This* weekend. 'Okay,' I say, shock doing a very nice job of flattening my voice despite my excitement. I've never gone to the footy just with a friend before. It's always been a family thing – with my parents or Josh's or both. Going with Tara alone feels important, somehow, for all kinds of reasons.

Dad seems pleased when I tell him that night and offers to drive me to the station. But as I get dressed to go on Saturday, the doubts kick in. Will Tara even turn up? Or what if she does show up and ignores me for the whole match? I let all the horrible and excruciating possibilities pile up in my head even as I rush Dad to get to the station early.

Josh is on the platform when I get there, but the train isn't. Vic Rail is as bad as the trams on a Saturday – actually, every day. I take a seat beside him on the bench. 'We need to stop meeting like this,' I say, yanking my scarf out from under my leg, where it threatens to choke me half to death.

'Go Gorillas,' he says predictably.

'Loser,' I reply. He'd already called to gloat about the Panthers' win so at least I've got that out of the way. 'You got a game?' He's wearing his tracksuit and there's an Adidas sausage bag by his feet, its corners frayed and torn.

'No,' he grins. 'Thought I'd go fishing today.' He digs out his footy, raising it like a trophy. 'My fishing rod,' he says, spinning it in his hands.

I knock it out of his grip and we both leap up to grab it before it falls off the platform. I get there first.

'Idiot!' he says, laughing.

'What?' I offer an innocent smile and handball it to him at close range. Hard. He fakes injury, coughing and spluttering, then handballs it back, neat and straight.

The train finally pulls up and we find seats in the middle of the third carriage. I always choose the third carriage from the front – for good luck.

'So much for running after school,' he says, not looking at me. He's called twice this past fortnight to organise a run, but I've fobbed him off. The whole hand-tingling thing is messing with my head. I think he knows I'm avoiding him but he probably thinks it's about the Raiders. I feel bad about that, but better he think it's about football than the other stuff. Everything would be easier if we kept it all about the footy. 'Mick's up for a big one today,' I say, changing the subject.

'Bloody Edwards again?' Josh says. 'What's so special about him?'

'He's cool.' I shrug. 'And really nice.'

Josh tilts the footy onto the tip of his finger, spinning it before it falls and lands on my lap. I grab it before he can. 'Nice? How would you know if he's *nice*? He could be a mass murderer when he's not playing footy.'

I laugh. 'Yeah right.'

'Or a devil worshipper. Or a . . .' Josh looks around for inspiration. 'A secret Warriors supporter on his days off.'

It's really hard to hate Josh. Seriously, I've tried. 'I talk to him at training,' I say, unable to stop the chuckle that escapes. 'They're all nice.'

'You get all that from how they sign your autograph book?'

'We talk a lot. About all kinds of stuff.'

Josh grabs at the ball, but I baulk, holding it just out of reach. 'What stuff?' He looks away, acting all cool, but I can tell he's mad.

I don't know why exactly, but it feels good. 'You know . . . footy, of course. And WA. School. Lots of stuff.'

'So instead of training – the reason they're actually there – they hang around chatting with the fans. About school. And *stuff*.' His tone has changed, and suddenly it's not funny anymore.

'It's no big deal,' I say, lying. It's easily the most important thing that's happened to me all year. The best thing.

'Does your dad know you're mates with these guys?' Josh snatches the ball back from me with more aggression than needed, if you ask me.

'What?' I rub the back of my hand theatrically, making sure he knows he was being too rough. It didn't hurt. But it *could* have.

'Sorry,' he says, looking like he means it.

I nod but am too annoyed to ease the moment.

'You didn't answer my question,' he says eventually.

'What question?' I refuse to help him.

'So your Dad's fine about you hanging out with these . . .' He trails off, searching for a word. 'These . . . *men*?'

His attitude reminds me of things I don't want to remember. 'Of course he is,' I snap. 'Mick's just a friend. They all are.' But my voice is unnaturally high and thin. I look out the window, hoping he'll get out soon.

We pass two stations before anyone speaks. 'Shell?' Josh says softly.

I slowly face him, prepared to fight even though the kindness in his voice almost undoes me.

He opens his mouth like he's about to say something, but seems to change his mind. 'Just . . . be careful, okay?'

'I have no idea what you're talking about, Joshua.' And even though it means I'll end up at the wrong end of Flinders Street Station, I get out at the next stop and switch carriages. I keep an eye out in case Josh comes looking for me, but when I see him get off at Yarra Station, he only briefly looks back at the train before disappearing into the swell of disembarking passengers.

———

The City Square is basically empty but for Tara, who is standing under the Burke and Wills statue, clearly waiting for someone. I cross my fingers, hoping that someone is me. The first thing I notice is that she's wearing the most amazing duffle coat. It's dark brown with gold trim and is covered top to toe in Glenthorn colours. All the players whose faces are now so familiar to me smile in the same stiff pose they save for our cameras, their faces pressed into round, shiny badges. But it's not just all those badges that impress me. It's the whole thing. Her total and absolute *dedication*. Every centimetre is devoted to brown and gold in all different forms: name tags sewn neatly in rows, premiership insignias for each year we've won, rosettes and ribbons and flags in the gaps between. I have to stop myself from gushing at her when she notices me. 'Cool coat,' I say, as evenly as I can manage.

Tara sticks her hands in the coat pockets and stands a little straighter. 'Dad got it for me,' she says.

I struggle to picture her dad. She's never mentioned him before. But the idea of a dad sewing badges on a duffle coat amazes me. I like him already. I wait for her to say something, encouraged by the fact that she seemed to be looking for me only moments ago. She raises her eyebrows and frowns. 'You right?'

'Um, yeah. Just . . . Ready to go?'

'I was here first,' she says, deadpan. 'Obviously *I'm* ready.'

I'm not late. In fact, it's five to eleven, so technically I'm *early*. Not by the Brown clock, of course, but maybe Tara follows the same system. 'So where do we get the tram?'

Tara leads me across to the tram stop, ignoring the looks her coat attracts. Other people don't seem quite as admiring of it as I am. We take a seat on the tram in silence. It's clear Tara's stressing about something but I know I can't come right out and ask her, so I make conversation about the one thing we share. 'Can't wait to cream the Gorillas and put our stamp on the season now that we're on top.'

Tara thwacks me on the arm with her scarf.

'What the . . . ?' I say, genuinely irritated.

Tara closes her eyes, as if summoning some greater power to help her deal with this imbecile beside her. Slowly, she opens her eyes and fixes me in her stare. 'Never *ever* say we're going to win before the game, okay? *Never*. You'll jinx us.'

'Okaaaaay . . .' I'm as superstitious as the next footy fan, but I also can't completely dismiss the power of positive thinking. 'Still, if you say it like you believe it, it might just come true.'

She shakes her head. Those greater powers aren't enough, apparently. 'When you say we're going to win, you sound cocky and then all the good luck disappears. Or worse, goes to the other team.'

'Right.' I'm not convinced, but at least she's talking to me and we're on the way to the footy – together – so I'm prepared to go along with it. 'Anything else I should know?'

'You can't say we've won until after the final siren, when there's no doubt.'

'What if we're slaughtering them?'

She's thought about this. 'The only exception is if we're more than sixty points up at the twenty-five-minute mark of the final quarter. You can say it then, but anything less than that and you'll have to find somewhere else to sit.' She pulls out her ticket, nodding at the conductor who's making his way through the packed tram.

I hunt around for my pass as the connie calls for our tickets. He stops before us and takes in our gear – my Glenthorn jumper with the number 5 still shiny and new on the back, and Tara's duffle coat – and says, 'Think the Gorillas might get you today.' It's only then that I notice the red, blue and yellow fringe of a Smithwood scarf poking out from under his M&MTB blazer.

Tara eyes the conductor steadily. 'May the best team win.'

The connie smiles and moves on to other passengers.

I turn to Tara, waiting for her to laugh or make a joke about the tram conductor, but her eyes are serious and flat. 'And *never* argue with the opposition before the game.'

———————

Tara told me to join the cheersquad because they have the best seats, right behind goal and, during the finals, they get a separate allocation of seats exclusive to members. It virtually guarantees you a ticket for the grand final, assuming the Falcons make it, of course. Plus, you get a free copy of *The Falcon's Nest* mailed to you every week. A no-brainer in my mind.

When we get to Queens Park, Tara points me to David, the cheersquad president sitting in the front row. David doesn't look like the other cheersquadders. He has pointy shoes, slicked-back hair and wears a tweed jacket and slacks, rather than the usual jeans and footy jumper. He looks closer to thirty than twenty. I've never really spoken to him before – the committee members keep to themselves at training while the rest of us hang out on the other side of Fernlee Park, near the press box or the Mayblooms Stand.

I hand David five dollars and he gives me an Official Glenthorn Cheersquad badge, a receipt and a small flogger to wave at important moments. 'When we're lining up for goal,' he says, 'you wave it like this.' And he shows me the happy wave: up and down in a steady rhythm, like a salute. 'But when *they* are,' he says – which I take to mean any team that isn't Glenthorn – 'especially when they're up our end, you do it like this.' He holds the flogger up to eye level and waves it from side to side in what seems an unlikely attempt to distract the opposition players. A lot like the players do when they're on the mark, and what kids do in the under 9s, minus the cries of 'Chewy on your boot!'.

To be honest, I highly doubt the players would be able to see the difference from where they're standing, but

I nod my understanding and thank David for the advice. Armed with my flogger and badge, I make my way back to Tara, who's found a seat in the fifth row alongside two of the cheersquad regulars: the tattooed monster of a bloke, 'Bear', who looks more like the Hulk than the teddy bear he's supposed to resemble; and Danny, the Bono lookalike.

'Jury's up for a big one,' Bear says as I squeeze into the seat between him and Tara. Up close, he's even bigger and more intimidating. To look at, anyway. I can just make out some of his tattoos creeping out from the sleeve of his Glenthorn jumper, a trail of teardrops decorating his left hand. 'Milestone game,' he continues, 'and he's been working on his upper body.'

Bear has finished school, though I don't think he stayed for Year 12. Tara says he works as a brickie and is as strong as an ox, which makes him really popular after training when they load the truck. He can carry three of the big floggers at once and the entire run-through banner all by himself. He's a bit of a bogan but has memorised every single player's stats, including their height and weight, which comes in handy way more often than you'd think. Despite his appearance, he's probably the gentlest bloke I know.

'Fingers crossed,' I say, not really paying attention. I can't help staring at the way Tara's talking to Danny, like he's the only person at the ground – or in the universe.

She hasn't even noticed I'm here. She's turned away, her attention entirely on him, so I can't really hear what she's saying except for bits and pieces that float up from the noisy crowd – '. . . *so* funny . . . nearly *died* laughing . . .' And something about a shower curtain. She's talking a mile a minute and grinning a little crazily. This is not the Tara I know or think I know. Nowhere in sight is the painfully self-conscious and prickly girl I spend most days trying not to annoy. Instead, there's this flirty, giggly schoolgirl who keeps throwing her head back with an energy I didn't know she possessed.

In contrast, Danny isn't saying much of anything. Actually, he looks bored, only occasionally nodding and running his fingers through his Bono mullet. Is he even listening? But Tara doesn't seem to mind, blushing and babbling loudly, her laughter coming out jerky and harsh because no one else is joining in.

It hurts to watch. I try to get her attention to distract her, hoping she'll stop or just slow down a bit. But she won't even look at me. I find myself torn between wanting to stop her and just staring in fascination at this Tara I've never seen before. I sit there, absorbing the mind-blowing news that Tara Lester has a major crush.

Danny is studying the ground now, but Tara barely skips a beat. I feel a sharp twisting in my chest. Either he's clueless or he's not interested. And it's looking like the second option.

'I haven't seen you at the games before,' Bear says, pushing Danny's boom box along to make more room for me.

'Huh?' It takes me a second to drag my attention away from the disaster playing out beside me. 'Uh, yeah. I usually go with my dad,' I say, too distracted to realise my mistake until it's too late. That was the least cool answer I could have given and it's out there for Bear and the rest of the cheersquad to hear. 'I mean, when I was a kid,' I add quickly.

But Bear doesn't seem to care. He just nods and says, 'Cool dad.'

There was a time I would have agreed with him.

Out on the ground, the cheersquad leaders are fighting to hold the run-through banner steady, the wind and gravity doing their best to defeat them. But as though summoned, the Falcons burst out of the race, and are met with the crowd's roar. In the lead, Chris Jury, who really does look stronger up top, breaks through the middle of his '100 GAMES!' tribute, and suddenly none of the other stuff matters. To anyone. The players run around a bit, forming a group in the middle before starting a slow warm-up while we wait for the Gorillas to show.

Three rows down, Jim-Bob and his girlfriend, Sharon, are trying to get a chant started. Sharon's voice could probably break glass if she put her mind to it – but Jim-Bob is too distracted by two scrappy kids between them whose tight black ringlets are identical to Sharon's. They couldn't be more than eight, but they're brawling over a packet of Twisties like their lives depend on it.

'I reckon he's pushing eighty-five kilos,' Bear says, admiration thickening his voice.

He's still on about Jury. 'Yeah,' I say, 'could be.' The little girl looks like she's strangling her brother. Jim-Bob is physically pulling them apart, while Sharon gives her chant one last go.

'Give us an "H"!' she cries, her broken pitchy voice already cracking under the strain.

A half-hearted 'H!' ripples across the crowd.

'We can't be too strong up forward,' I continue, unable to look away from the bickering kids who should seriously consider careers at the World Wrestling Federation.

'Or down back,' Tara adds, her attention back where it belongs.

I smile at her, genuinely relieved she's given up on Danny for the moment.

'Let's go, Falcons!' Danny yells as the players take position, grinning at Tara for the first time since I sat down, prompting Tara to squish even closer to him. Maybe he likes her after all.

In the front row, David stands up and, as though directed telepathically, the entire cheersquad rises to meet him. Dad says some people are born leaders and that John Kennedy Snr and Allan Jeans are perfect examples. People always seem to be waiting for them, ready to act without being asked. I think I know what he means now.

The chant picks up and soon we are clapping and cheering, breaking up into individual calls, yelling instructions or advice – to our team and theirs – about what we think will happen and what we think *should* happen. All of us self-appointed experts, directing play from the sidelines even though the players can't hear us and probably wouldn't listen if they could. But no one seems to care. It's not for them anyway.

I sit there, surrounded by these people I barely know, wondering what my place is here. Wondering if this will do, this thing that's happening. My heart flutters, my palms are clammy. Tension and expectation form knots in my chest. And then the Gorillas run out onto the ground, bursting through the banner, their supporters screaming just like we did, and the first pangs of panic take hold. As the Falcons players find their opponents I take a moment to look around: brown and gold stretches as far as I can see – on the oval, across the stands, all around me – and I know that it will be okay. A wave of something I can only call happiness passes over me. I think that's what it is, because it's warm and smooth and fills me completely.

I can just make out Mick heading to full forward down the far end. He bounces the ball a couple of times before kicking it back to the centre, waiting for the first whistle to blow, ready to take on the world – or the Gorillas anyway – and I know suddenly that it will be enough.

This, right here, is enough.

When Mick kicks the last of his amazing seven goals, minutes before the final siren is due, he pumps the air. And a split-second later the rest of the forward line mobs him. Tara and I are screaming and hugging and high-fiving everyone around us. I turn back to the ground in time to see Mick leap onto the fence right in front of us, into the arms of the madly cheering cheersquad. They adore him, finally, and he's loving it.

He stands up, looks into the brown-and-gold mob and catches me in his gaze. For a long second I can hear nothing. The whole world has fallen silent, and I'm only dimly aware of the chaos around me. He points his finger at me and smiles. I feel the weight of the cheersquadders looking at me, including Tara, who, incredibly, doesn't get angry but is leaping about in sheer delight. Bear hoists me onto his shoulder like I weigh nothing. Danny is grabbing Tara, then Bear, and reaching across the seats to perfect strangers who are clapping each other on the back.

The siren blasts in the middle of this and the crowd explodes. And everyone around me is glowing with the sort of elation that only winning can bring. I grab Tara in the tightest hug I can manage, not caring if I've broken one of her rules or if I'll have to pay for it later. The last couple of years it's felt like I've been split in half, the better part of me gone alongside Mum and what used to be my family while I'm stuck with what's left over: the smaller, weaker, broken version of me. Always alone and less than I used to be.

But that feeling is slowly starting to fade. Something good and strong is building up around me and it's here, right now. Today. I have a friend beside me who's feeling every ounce of the same excitement, the same joy, pure and simple. There's a whole crowd around me who are as delighted – as *completed* – by the experience as I am. And there's Mick out on the ground, sharing it with me.

I'm surrounded by happiness and it's infectious. No thinking. No reasoning. Just passion and feeling, like how I imagine falling in love would be. I had no idea it would turn out like this. I don't have to measure my words or analyse the game, highlight the errors of our opponent, assess what needs to be done next. I don't have to list the Gorillas' best players or identify Glenthorn's weakest. Not yet – not until I'm home with Dad. Today I am free. No guilt for who's missing, who should be here, what's been left behind. Apart from Fernlee Park, there isn't a single place I'd rather be right now. My face aches from smiling in the wind and my voice rasps from all the screaming, and I know that it's been forever since I've felt so completely alive. No longer half of something left behind – suddenly I feel whole.

GAME ON

CHAPTER 9

LITTLE LEAGUE

By the time the last week of first term comes around, I've visited Fernlee Park thirteen times – every Thursday since that first time and six Tuesdays too. I've marked each trip in my scrapbook and have recorded all my observations about how the players train, who looks good and who doesn't, unreported injuries and any new game strategies I've identified.

I've also set aside a new section just for Mick and have written down every conversation we've had, because sometimes it feels like I've dreamt the whole thing. All the kids love him now; everywhere I look neat, shiny number 5s have been stitched on to Glenthorn jumpers, old and new. And yet, every time I see him, he still looks me straight in the eye and speaks to me like I'm more important than anyone else.

I got to training early today. Sister Brigid was sick and we had a substitute teacher who didn't bother to take the roll. Tara didn't show up at school, and I haven't seen her all night. She does that sometimes – disappears from school for a couple of days, only to turn up at training or at the Burke and Wills statue before the footy like nothing's happened.

I asked her once why she'd missed school.

'Didn't feel like it,' she'd said, like it was a perfectly normal reason.

Bear was early today too – an RDO for brickies, apparently – so I've been testing my memory against his. I told him about my scrapbook and about all the stats I've been keeping, the stuff that no one else cares about. I was nervous telling him in case he thought my scrapbook was lame – I haven't mentioned it to Tara because I *know* she will – but he was so impressed he made me promise I'd bring it along to training one week. I just have to make sure Tara doesn't see it.

By the time training ends, Bear has provided me with a breakdown of every single senior player's fitness level and potential to improve, and I've given him my predictions for Best and Fairest and leading goalkickers, first, second and third. (Mick Edwards winning both, obviously.)

'You ready?' Mick asks across the heads of the other

cheersquadders as Bear and I finish our sausages. It's been raining on and off since I got here, and the damp, musty smell of wet carpet is thick in the air.

'See you later,' I say to Bear.

'See you Saturday.' He says it naturally, like we've been friends for ages, and he doesn't even blink when I leave with Mick. No one does. This ritual is so accepted by everyone now that I don't have to explain it. And with Tara away today, I don't have to feel guilty either.

Mick takes the usual route down Fernlee Park Road, weaving quickly in and out of traffic. He's really rushing, and has to brake suddenly to avoid running a red light at Riverglen Road. We're halfway across the pedestrian crossing, and two men in business suits have to avoid an oncoming car to walk around Mick's Holden. One of them yells something at us on the way, but thankfully keeps walking.

'You late for something?' I ask, loosening my grip on the car seat to stretch my sore fingers.

He glances at me like he's forgotten I was there. 'Sorry.'

When the light changes, he accelerates gently and we resume something closer to a normal speed. 'We were meant to be going out to dinner,' he says, his eyes squarely on the road. I think he means with his wife but I can't be sure because he's never mentioned her before.

'I can get out here if you like?' I twist around to see how far we've travelled from the Riverglen Road tram stop. Not even a block. I could easily make it before the next tram.

'We're almost there,' he says lightly. 'I don't mind.'

I'm relieved. I hate waiting at the tram stop alone. It's always empty this time of night and the one by the oval is right outside the Fernlee Park Hotel. Drunk idiots yell stuff out the pub window or stagger past, slurring insults. I know they won't do anything, but I hate the way they make me feel. All exposed like that with nowhere to hide from their sleazy jokes and leering eyes. It's not so bad when Tara's there. She tells them where to get off or just turns that hard stare of hers on them and they shrink before our eyes. But I can't count on her showing up. Not like Mick.

'School holidays already, hey?' he says, as we pull into the Stonnington Station car park. There are hardly any cars left but I can make out some people waiting on the platform.

'Yeah, thank God.' I say this because I know I should. It's what everyone expects. But being alone at home for endless hours every day, those big empty rooms large enough to swallow me whole, is awful. Finding a way to keep busy when Dad comes home on top of that . . . I shudder just thinking about it.

Mick laughs. For a second it's like he's read my mind. But then I realise he thinks I'm horrified by school, not home. 'Brendan keeps asking if he can visit his teacher,

104

like he's worried if he disappears for a fortnight, they won't let him back in.'

'Brendan's your son?' He's never told me their names.

Mick nods. 'He's in prep. First year of "big school", not kinder. He loves it.'

'I did too,' I say, trying to picture what Mick's son would look like – a tiny version of Mick, I suppose. But I draw a blank. There are some people it's impossible to imagine were ever children. My dad's like that. Mum used to joke that he never got to be a kid – he was born a miniature adult and just grew into it. 'Everyone loves school at first,' I continue. 'But he'll get over it.'

Mick laughs.

I see a flash of something young and childish in his face, and a picture of Mick as a boy emerges. I bet he was cute. And tall, too. Scruffy hair and those warm brown eyes. 'What school does he go to?'

Mick hesitates. 'It's near the house . . .' He does a half shrug, half smile. 'His mum takes care of that. With training straight after work and matches every weekend . . .' Mick falls silent.

I'm not sure if I should leave or say something else. I slip the shoulder strap of my schoolbag over my head and open the car door. I've got a minute or two before the train's due. It will probably be late – typical Vic Rail – but I like to have time to pick the right carriage. 'Where are you going?' I ask as I get out.

He frowns, confused.

'To eat?'

'I don't know.' He checks the clock on the dashboard. 'It's probably too late.'

'I'm sorry.'

He shakes his head. 'See you next week?'

'Of course.'

He nods, like he's thinking hard about that.

'Okay, bye.' I shut the door and wave before I sprint across the bitumen, towards Platform 2. A string of passengers arrive from the tram stop across Fernlee Park Road. I peer along the tracks as far as I can see but there's no train in sight. Late as usual.

Finally, several minutes later, my train pulls up and everyone boards, leaving the platform empty and quiet. As I take a seat by the window, I notice a young family in the aisle across from me; a mother and father, and two little girls, the youngest asleep in a pram. The father has a pretty pink doll's bonnet propped absurdly on his head, while the older child, clutching the doll that presumably owns the bonnet, is lost in a fit of giggles, squirming so hard she can barely stay in her seat. Her dad acts like everything is perfectly normal while her mum shakes her head in amusement.

I tear my eyes away to focus on the passing houses, my attention drawn to those with brightly lit windows. I picture similar scenes to this one playing out with different families inside, a little boy here, a teenage daughter there, and wonder what it is they wish for at night in those last moments before they fall asleep.

CHAPTER 10

THE DRILL

The next week, Tara and I arrange to meet on Monday at the footy clinic at Punter Oval. The clubs run the clinics during the school holidays, so when we get there the crowd is huge. There are kids from all over Melbourne, although, as the games kick in, it's obvious that only the boys actually participate. There are a handful of girls among the littlies, but no older girls playing at all. They mostly hang around to watch the players, taking photos of the better-looking ones and flirting with them over the top of the other kids' heads.

I recognise two of the girls from the cheersquad. Tara calls them 'The Lovely Ladies' because they always have immaculate hair and fingernails that are long enough to be registered as lethal weapons. They're more interested in the players after the game than during it – or that's what Red says. Kimberly is the leader – the prettiest and most popular, but Lisa, the only one not here today, is definitely the nicest. I'm not sure what Renee is – she's actually a Carringbush supporter, which is unforgiveable, but says the Glenthorn players are better-looking.

We've chatted to all three girls at training before, but they're so focused on the players that it doesn't seem worth the effort. Tara and I have decided to avoid them, which isn't difficult because all they do is follow spunky Irishman Brendan O'Reilly everywhere he goes. Mick's the only other Glenthorn player at the clinic, so Tara and I follow his group to a corner of the Punter Oval.

I hardly play footy anymore, except some backyard mucking around with Josh, and even that's happening less and less. It's been two years since I last played anything that resembled a real game, back when I was still playing for the Raiders. The club hadn't taken me seriously at first. But it all changed when I took a mark at centre half-forward over Cam Evans, who was twice my size, and suddenly I wasn't just Josh's friend or 'the Brown girl' but was one of the team. Or as much a part of it as I could be. Girls aren't allowed to play in any real games so, instead, I trained with them twice a week and played in all the practice matches and light-ning tournaments that I could get away with. Stealing every minute of game time the coach, Jacko, would give me. He always included me in drills and even gave me an award at the end of the under 10s' season, after the Raiders lost the grand final.

At first I thought he was just being nice, but then when I was about to turn thirteen, Jacko asked Mum and Dad if he could go to the tribunal to challenge the rules on my behalf. He said I was almost as good as any of the A team on my best days and way better than all of the Bs. There was no reason I shouldn't play, he'd told Dad, as long as I wanted to.

And I wanted to, more than I could say.

Josh wanted me to play, and Mum too. But Dad didn't think it was a good idea until Mum gave him a nudge, and he eventually agreed. Then the tribunal said no, offering all this 'scientific evidence' as proof that it was dangerous for girls to play in real games. Anyway, it freaked Dad out. He'd said it wasn't right for me to play football now that I was 'becoming a woman', that I could get hurt, as though my body was suddenly softer and weaker than it used to be. Josh stuck up for me, but he was the only one. Even Mum stayed quiet.

So I had to quit playing footy, even though I still had to do the family thing and watch the Raiders play every single week. It hurt in a way that nothing else had until then. Josh got it. But everyone else – my family, the rest of the team . . . It was like I'd never played at all.

And then our world ended, and none of that mattered anymore.

Tara and I lean against the low boundary fence as they divide all the kids into age groups. I watch the kids mill about having no idea what to do, my feet itching to get into it.

'Stuff this, I'm playing,' I say abruptly. I wave to get Mick's attention and am about to head over when Tara steps between us.

'What?' I say.

'If you play, I'm leaving.'

'What's the big deal? We're here, aren't we?'

'You're not twelve.'

'There are other girls playing.'

'They're all in *primary school*,' she mouths, through gritted teeth.

I think about the tribunal, Dad's words and the silent acceptance by the one person I thought I could trust the most, and shake my head. 'I'm not going to stand around and do nothing.'

'Why not? Why can't you just ... be normal like everyone else?' People are staring at us now.

'You can do what you like,' I say, my voice as even as I can make it.

'Okay, I will,' she says, and leaves. Just like that.

I watch her back fade into the distance with a strange mix of anger and awe. That's the thing about Tara – she

111

always makes good on her promises – *and* her threats. She does everything she says she's going to do *exactly* like she says she's going to do it. A part of me appreciates that, while another part of me wishes I'd picked an easier friend.

I walk over to Mick's group of boys, who are all about my age. Some of them are small like me, others look like miniature men with square jaws and gangly limbs – all elbows and knee joints and shoes like tennis racquets. On a pure strength test, they'd cream me. But they'd have to catch me first. I still have pace.

'I'll play here,' I say, louder than I mean to.

Mick looks surprised, like he doesn't know if I'm joking. 'Maybe you should go with a younger group. Those kids over there,' he says, less gently than I'd have liked, pointing to a bunch of ten-year-olds. What he means is *somewhere else.*

'No,' I say, aware that everyone is standing around watching. 'Here's good.'

'Fine.' Mick shrugs and handballs the brown-and-gold football to me. I think he might be angry until I notice he has a bit of a smile near his lips. Not quite on them but right around the edge.

We go through all kinds of drills, from handball target practice to marking, tackling and sprints. Each time Mick sends the ball towards me he deliberately keeps it softer, slower, like he's worried I won't get it. But it doesn't take long before he stops treating me differently to the boys. I'm not the best kid playing anymore, but I can hold my own. Whenever it comes to running or ball handling, I manage to beat most of them, though nothing feels the way it used to. After the accident it felt as if I'd lost a limb, like the fearless and capable part of me was amputated in an instant. But today it feels like I've got a completely different body. A slower, heavier one that won't do what it used to.

'Okay, listen up!' Mick is pacing in front of the kids, like a schoolteacher taking a class. Or a dad who's used to handling little kids. I'm surprised. He's actually pretty good at this. 'Goal drills. Defence and attack.'

Dread settles low in my stomach. I'm a terrible kick, even worse when goalposts are involved. The Raiders boys knew it. They made sure I knew it too. In fact, if I'd been a better kick, I reckon Jacko would have tried harder at the tribunal.

There are temporary goalposts set up about twenty-five metres away. We're supposed to work in pairs but of course nobody wants to go with a girl, so Mick takes me.

'All right, know what to do?' he asks me.

I sigh, long and deep. 'Yeah, I *know* what to do . . .' But knowing isn't the same as being able to do it. Then it hits me. 'I'll defend,' I offer, even though any normal kid wants to be in attack.

Mick squints at me, confused. 'Nah, my knee's a bit tender. You shoot, I'll defend.'

I don't answer. I can't. For a tiny second I watch the goalposts shrink before my eyes at the same time that my dread grows large enough to smother me. Then I picture Tara smirking at me. I got what I asked for, and this is exactly what she wanted to avoid. I shrug, like someone's asked me a question. I stare into the yawning goalmouth and set my body into the starting position.

'Ready?'

I nod, and Mick waves me free. I bolt from the starting point and manage to get to the ball ahead of him. He isn't kidding about his knee. I turn, avoid his tackle, then go for goal without much resistance at all. I know he's playing it down for me, but he's definitely favouring the dodgy knee again, and half of me feels sorry enough to let him win.

Well, maybe not *half*.

I twist and shoot, but the worm-eater that comes off my foot undoes all the beauty of my turn as the ball dribbles pathetically until it stops in front of goal.

We all look at it for a second, none of us quite believing what I just did. And then a pimply boy with hair that looks like steel wool says, 'Nice kick.' And laughs.

For confidence, I cling to the memory of my magical blind turn, which was easily the best one all day, but I'm obviously the only one.

'Wow, that really sucked,' the boy behind me says matter-of-factly.

Mick shoots him a warning look but doesn't argue. 'You need to work on that,' he says after an excruciating pause, then moves on to the next kid.

After the clinic, I'm wishing Tara had hung around. I think I see Danny across the oval, but I don't feel like I know him well enough to call out. He's never been as friendly as Bear. I'm even regretting my decision to avoid the Lovely Ladies, because at least they'd be someone to talk to.

On the way to the station I notice Mick waiting by the gate, his bag on his shoulder, keys in hand. I stop and wave, but he doesn't see me among the crowd. He's searching for something or someone. I watch him scan the faces of the people in front of me, the cars that move through the car park, then the crowd again. He looks lost. Or lonely.

I make my way over to him, zigzagging against the crowd. 'Hey. Did you lose something?'

Mick looks up, distracted. 'Hey, Shelley.' He shifts about uncomfortably, moving his bag to his other shoulder and crossing his legs as he leans back on the fence.

'Are you okay?' I wonder if his knee is worrying him and decide that's probably it. He's clearly got something going on there.

'You going home?' he says, ignoring my question.

I nod and force a smile, hoping he didn't notice I was on my own. 'O'Reilly left already.' Who else would he be looking for? There's no way he's friends with any of the other players – the opposition – and he's not important enough for the Lovely Ladies. Not yet, anyway.

'What? Oh. No, I saw him.' He looks away, searching with less energy. Whoever it is, he's not expecting to see them.

'I have to catch the train,' I say, turning to go.

'My kids were going to come . . . with Wendy.' He smiles but it doesn't reach his eyes. 'She said she might bring them down.'

I put my bag down and make an effort to help him look. I'm not sure why because I have no idea what they look like. But we stand there for a few seconds, watching the tail end of the footy clinic crowd make their way out of the park.

'It's okay,' he says, shrugging like it's no big deal. 'I don't think they're coming.'

I nod. 'Next time, maybe.'

He offers a half smile that disappears before it settles. 'Yeah. See you at training.'

The first drops of rain fall, round and fat and cold. I swing my bag over my shoulder and tug my collar high against my neck. 'See you Thursday.' I head off again, the rain coming down heavier. I start to jog towards the station underpass, my feet squelching in the soft, never-quite-dry mud, catching up to some of the others on the way. I see Jim-Bob and Sharon wrangling their squabbling kids on the Frankston line platform, and the Lovely Ladies picking their delicate way up the platform ramp just ahead. I'm tempted to approach them but have no idea what I'd say. I reach the cover of the underpass and am about to head up the ramp to Platform 9 when I feel an overwhelming need to look back.

Across the oval, in the wet, muddy car park, Mick is still leaning against the fence exactly where I left him. Even though he's getting drenched in the steady rain, he seems to be scanning the last few faces around him just in case.

CHAPTER 11

EYES UP ON THE FOLLOW-THROUGH

I arrive at Thursday night training before everyone else. Dad's been working late a lot the past two weeks, and apart from an Australian History essay that's giving me grief because I can't decide on a topic, I don't have any other homework. There's only so much TV and stats-keeping I can do to pass the day. With the McGuires away for the holidays I don't even have Josh to hang out with.

It must be quiet in the Promotions Office at Fernlee Park, where Mick works, because he's already in the gym in his training gear and it's barely half past three. I'm now an expert on Glenthorn training rules: as long as you arrive in the gym before Geoff the sign-off guy gets there you can hide at the back without anyone bothering you, while the players begin their warm-up exercises. I love to do this because it means I'm on my own for much of the practice until the players go outside, so I can talk to them without the other kids around. The players are a lot friendlier when there aren't heaps of us clinging to their every word, and I often overhear a trainer discuss a player's injury or their performance – sometimes even with the coach, Stretch Davis.

'You're early,' Mick says when I walk into the gym. Every time I see him, I'm struck by how tall he is. How strong he looks.

'Better than doing homework,' I say.

'Just can't get my head into anything at the moment. The boss sent me here to clear out the cobwebs.' It still feels weird having him talk to me like this. Like he trusts me and expects me to have something important to say.

'Is it working?'

He laughs. 'Not really. How's the kicking going?'

I want to ask if his family ever showed up after the clinic, but then I think about how lonely he looked standing in the mud and the rain, the car park emptying around him, and I know not to. He looks so different today. It's hard to believe he's the same person. 'Okay,' I lie. Even if I wanted to deal with the embarrassment of my footy clinic effort, with Josh away there's no one to kick with and it's not like I can ask Tara to go through

119

some drills. Plus, Mrs Hodge asked me to join the school athletics team, so I've been along to some early practices this week to check it out. I guess athletes at St Mary's don't get holidays. I actually enjoyed it – running laps, sprinting in short, fast bursts; the cold morning air fresh in my lungs. If it wasn't for the fact that they're moving training to Thursday nights once the holidays are over, I'd probably have joined by now.

'Did you try that drill I showed you?' Mick asks, his tone suggesting he knows the answer.

'I haven't really had time,' I mumble, hoping he'll change the subject.

'You have time now,' he says, and passes me a ball from the large bin behind him.

The ball seems to find its way into the correct position in my hands, without any help from my brain. 'Do I have a choice?'

'Are we talking or are we practising?' he asks with a raised eyebrow.

I line up and send him a hard short pass right at his chest. Or it was *supposed* to be a hard short pass right at his chest. Instead, it hits a good three metres to the left of him. It isn't as ugly – or as public – as my shocker at the footy clinic but it's a long way from good and is made worse because, despite laughing like I don't care, it's pretty obvious to both of us that I was really trying.

'Not bad,' Mick says generously. He handballs it back.

'Keep your eyes on the ball this time. Line up the seam with your target.'

I kick again. It's not very different to the last one but at least it's closer to the mark. Straighter. Steadier.

The thing is, I *know* all this. I know how I'm supposed to kick. I could tell him all of this – step by step – like a walking football textbook. In fact, I think I already have. A couple of times.

I just can't *do* it.

He comes over and hands me the ball again. 'Fingers on the seam, tip the ball forward . . . Good, good. Now, without putting any power into it, follow through as though you're going to kick.' I practise the motion of kicking. He nods, straightens my leg then nods again. 'Now for real.'

We practise together for half an hour and, incredibly, my kicking shows small signs of improvement. We finish up as the other players begin to arrive. Some of them yell out comments like 'Is it all right if I go out with your kid sister, Ed?' and 'Isn't that illegal?' But none of it sounds mean or serious, and Chris Jury even compliments me on my style, telling me to keep my eyes up on the follow-through.

'All right,' Mick says, eventually, 'lesson over. I need to warm up. See you after training.'

I go outside into the bright afternoon light to take up my position at the gym entrance, behind Red and Tara.

I've been promoted ahead of a number of other kids who have been going to training much longer than me, almost definitely because of my friendship with Mick. I smile at Tara. Neither of us has said a word about her leaving the footy clinic, but I'm beginning to understand the way things work with her. If it doesn't blow up at that single moment of misunderstanding, it won't blow up at all. Or be mentioned. Ever.

'Where've you been?' she asks, frowning.

'Inside,' I say.

'Who with?'

'Mick.' I can hear the defensiveness creeping into my voice.

'What were you doing with him?'

I can feel everyone's eyes on me but they all look away when I stare back. Except Red, who has her arms crossed in front of her like she has a right to know.

'Well?' says Tara, looking at me like I've done something wrong.

'Nothing. Just hanging around. I got in early.' I shrug, trying to act like it's no big deal when I know that somehow it is. How does she do this? How does she make me feel like I've betrayed her when it has nothing to do with her?

'What does that mean?' she asks, her tone suggesting she already has an answer.

'What's your problem?' I ask. I've done nothing wrong. But if that's true, a stubborn voice inside my head says, why haven't I told her the truth? I feel the ground beneath me shifting.

'You haven't answered my question,' she snaps, moving towards me.

I force myself not to step back but, inside, I'm flinching. 'He's showing me how to kick.' This sounds weak even to me, although it's the truth.

'What's the point of that?'

'He's just being nice.' There is no point, I realise. Which makes her words sting even harder. It's not like I'll ever get to kick for goal again – not in a game, anyway.

'You think hanging out with him and calling him Mick makes you special? *Everyone* calls him *Eddie*. Even the other players. You're just embarrassing yourself.'

My whole body burns with humiliation. 'No, I'm not! He likes me!' I protest, hating that I sound like a six-year-old. The other cheersquadders are all acting like they can't hear, looking everywhere but at us. Even Red has decided the arrival of an unknown under 19s player is worthy of a photo. 'We're friends,' I add lamely. 'That's what he told me to call him.'

For once Tara doesn't care who's listening or what the world thinks. She's not shouting, nor is she making any effort to keep this between us. 'He's married, you know.' She spits out the word 'married' like it's something rotten, and everyone within hearing distance – which is pretty much everyone in total – decides maybe we're worth another look after all.

'What?' I croak. Why is she saying this? Why is she trying to ruin things? My heart is racing like I've just finished a set of wind sprints – and beaten Josh in every one. 'I know he's married. What difference does *that* make?' It doesn't make a difference. I'm not doing anything wrong. And yet, when she talks to me like this it feels a lot like I am. I can't look at her – at anyone.

I won't give in to this. I won't. I force myself to meet her gaze, determined to show my innocence. But when I do, the accusation is gone and I see something sad there, in her eyes. Something like loneliness or grief. But bigger, deeper. I soften, my embarrassment forgotten. I suddenly don't care about the other kids. 'Why don't you come too?' I offer. 'Maybe next week? Mick won't mind,' I add, clutching at the only thing I have to give her. I have no idea if Mick will mind or even if he'll be there next week, but it's a bit late to think about that.

'Why would I want to do that?' she snaps, her face flushed. 'I couldn't give a shit what Edwards wants.'

Just like that, the softness – the loss – I saw in her before is gone. I don't know how to fix this. And for the rest of the night, whenever Tara thinks I'm not looking, I can feel her eyes on me, burning away, like she's trying to peel back the layers to see what's really inside.

Though, honestly, I don't know what she'd find if she could.

CHAPTER 12

ONE WEEK AT A TIME

The phone cuts through my sleep, its shrill ring merging with the strange dream I was having. Dad must have picked it up, because the sound cuts off and then the house is silent again.

I take a moment to orientate myself. And then reality strikes with all its might and I remember why today is . . . *special.* It's my birthday. With practice, I've gotten used to saying it like other people do, as though it's the simplest and most normal of things to say. I allow myself a quiet moment of pride that I can say it. *My birthday. My birthday. My birthday.* It's my second since the accident and it already feels a bit different to the last one. I take heart from this for a moment and then, just as quickly,

I'm appalled. This day used to feel like the centre of our world, the thing around which my family revolved, year after year for as long as I can remember – right up until it was ruined forever.

My birthday.

I say it again and again in my head, believing that there will be a time when it might even sound normal, and hating the idea at the same time.

I drag myself out of bed and hesitate at my bookshelf. My hand hovers over *My Brilliant Career*, tempted to retrieve it. To draw strength from Sybylla Melvyn's indomitable spirit, her refusal to give up on her dream, even in the face of that bleak and dusty landscape.

There's a knock on my door and I freeze. 'Come in,' I say, letting my hand fall awkwardly by my side.

'Hey,' Dad says, opening the door without actually coming inside. He leans in but stays safely in the hallway. The smile he forces looks like it could crack at any moment.

'Hey.'

'Happy . . . birthday,' he says, pausing between each word as though they don't usually follow each other, as though they don't completely contradict each other. The birthday bit is right, but how in the world do we make it *happy*? I always had to share my birthday, but it's only been the past two years that I've had to share it with something as enormous as this. 'Josh called.'

I nod. 'I'll call him later.'

I can blow Josh off without guilt because it's my birthday. I say it again in my head. I shout it silently. Turn it around in my mind, back to front, round and round. My birthday. *My birthday.*

Except, it's not just my birthday. It never was just that to start with, though I'd wished for it often enough. But it's worse now. The past two June 11ths have been something entirely different as well: an anniversary. *The* anniversary. The accident was two years ago today.

Life. Death. Life. Death. The two have become one for the Brown household. I turned thirteen and my family was destroyed; all in a single unforgettable day. And for the rest of my life I'm supposed to find a way to celebrate it. We both are.

'Going to the game?' Dad's voice is hopeful. He wants me to go. It will be as difficult for him to look at me all day as it would be for me to stay here with him.

'Yeah, should be a big one.'

He nods. 'Big crowd too.'

Normally we'd go together. Falcons versus Carringbush at Valley Park would be a season highlight for us. Normally. But there's nothing about today that's normal.

'Did you want to come?' I'm supposed to meet Tara at Glenvalley Station at 11.15 to catch the Valley Park bus together. I have no idea how I'd break it to her that Dad's coming, but that doesn't seem so important right now.

Dad shakes his head and looks away, unable to answer. He shakes his head again, then turns to face me. 'Not for me. You go.'

It's an order and I'm happy to accept. He'll go out to the crematorium, like he did last year, like he does on his wedding anniversary, at Christmas, Mum's birthday, his birthday . . . He'll leave flowers, walk for miles around the grounds, talking to himself. I don't go anymore. I can't connect those cold, brassy plaques with anything that resembles my family. With anything that used to be alive. He doesn't make me, either. I think he prefers to go alone.

The silence settles. Dad has moved forward, coming out from behind the door. I see now that behind his back he's holding a package wrapped up in metallic purple wrapping paper with 'Happy Birthday' printed all over in bold white font. Dad holds the present out to me. 'Just a starter,' he apologises. 'The main one is for later.'

Later – at dinner. My heart lurches at the idea. 'Thanks!' My voice is as shiny and bright as the wrapping paper. I cross the room quickly, glad to be distracted by the gift, thinking through my possible responses – how to get just the right level of appreciation and pleasure, expectancy and surprise, no matter what it contains.

The softness of the contents suggests clothing of some kind. A lump forms in my throat, knowing what's inside but hoping for something different. I unwrap it at the door so Dad doesn't feel compelled to come further inside my room. The paper falls away and I pull out a Glenthorn beanie and matching socks, almost identical to the ones he gave me last year. 'These are great, Dad! Thanks. I'll wear them today.' I step towards him. He stands there stiffly, letting me encircle him with my arms, like he used to, except now there's a space between his chest and mine – a careful, polite gap to allow for my breasts and my changed body. To make sure there's no contact. 'Thanks, Dad,' I say again, stepping back.

'Pizza tonight?' he asks, the flush in his cheeks a perfect match to mine.

'Yum-mo!' I say, sounding like an idiot, but he doesn't react or seem to notice.

'Breakfast is ready,' he says, and leaves without waiting for a reply.

'I'll be out in a tick,' I say, shutting my door again. I place the socks on my bed, thinking about the three other pairs I have balled up in my sock drawer. I get dressed, pulling on my socks, then black jeans and my footy jumper. I spend a few minutes debating what to do with my hair before deciding to tie it back with a scrunchie. I pick up the beanie and carefully stretch it over my head, hoping my hair won't be completely destroyed in the process, and head to the kitchen for breakfast.

At the train station, I drop two pairs of Glenthorn socks – the two oldest pairs – into the Salvation Army bin in the car park, then slip into the toilet block while I wait for the train. I can barely see in the metallic mirror on the wall for all the rust stains and dirt smeared across it. I take off the beanie and pull the scrunchie out of my hair. I drag a brush through its unsatisfyingly short length and tuck my beanie into my backpack. I'll have to wear it at least for the next few weeks until Dad forgets about it, but there's no way I can wear it to the game or I'd never hear the end of it. Finals time, maybe, but not for a Home and Away match. You can wear anything crazy to a finals match – the daggier the better. But for the rest of the year beanies are for little kids. I just have to remember to put it on again before I get home.

I'm halfway to Valley Park with Tara before I realise I didn't call Josh back. What would I say anyway?

———

The crowd was huge and the game fantastic. We won by thirty-two points; the gap in percentage between us and the Warriors now looking smaller with every week. I just wish they'd lose again so we can move ahead.

But I refuse to let the Warriors' ridiculously good run these past weeks ruin the day. I haven't told Tara it's my birthday. She could probably work it out if she really wanted to, but Danny sat with us all game, stealing her rapt attention and allowing me to drift in and out of her awareness, free to focus on the footy.

I love Valley Park games because it means there's no rush for me to get home before the replay starts, and since we've won, that's about the only thing I'm looking forward to. Dad will let me watch it while we eat, taking some of the sting out of the heavy silence that my birthday brings. 'The elephant in the room', Mum would have called it. It makes me think about the scene from *The Great Gatsby* – in the Buchanans' parlour with the open French doors and the billowing white curtains, and Jordan and Daisy's dresses blowing up like balloons. Like white elephants. I think I'm mixing up my metaphors – are the elephants in the room white elephants or is that something else? But the image of those enormous balloon-like women, all light and airy and ghost-like, reminds me of the space Dad and I have put between us, a space loaded with silence and the unspoken. The unspeakable.

When I open the front door, I hear a woman's voice and I recognise it instantly.

I note the pizza on the kitchen table, the box unopened and propped on a platter like some steaming centrepiece – too much for two people, too small for four – and arrange my expression into the best smiling welcome I can manage. My lips are dry against my teeth, my mouth stiff with the effort to smile. I'm sure I look like a clown – the creepy kind, like in *Poltergeist*.

131

'Happy birthday, Shelley,' Mrs McGuire says gently, all kinds of emotions bundled up in the two simple syllables that comprise my name.

'Hi, Mrs McGuire,' I reply, my heart in my throat. It feels like something heavy is pressing against my chest. I don't have the energy to fight the blush that rises to my cheeks. Mrs McGuire. Here. In our house. Tonight of all nights.

'Josh wanted to come,' she says, her eyes trapping me in their warm and kind depths. 'But I told him that wasn't polite. It's your birthday. If you wanted visitors, you'd have asked.' Which apparently doesn't apply to his mother.

I think about her invitation, care of Josh, all those weeks ago and how I'd killed it off so hard and fast. Now I wish Josh was here to at least act as buffer so I don't have to face that endlessly forgiving and knowing look in her eyes.

'Thanks.'

No one moves for a long time. The TV is off despite the fact the replay is due to start, and the only sound is the suddenly stark ticking of the grandfather clock in the hall.

Tick.

Tick.

Tick.

'Mrs McGuire has invited you to Josh's hundred-and-fiftieth game,' Dad says finally, his voice rasping and thin.

He's standing uncomfortably by the TV set, his hand resting heavily against it as though preparing to leap into the screen if the situation demands.

I hate seeing him like this. So awkward and unnatural, so . . . *small*. When Mum was alive, Dad was tall and strong, certain and smart. Now all I see is this shrinking shadow of a man who can't even face his wife's best friend because . . .

Because.

Who am I to criticise? I can't face her either. I am my father's daughter, after all.

'It's just been too long,' Mrs McGuire says, stating the obvious and yet somehow conveying her surprise and hurt. Her eyes are damp and her face is soft and mushy like it was at the funeral. Every moment of hurt and pain is etched into that pretty face, so kind and welcoming but also so terrible. She knows everything. *Everything.* Mrs McGuire. Dad. And me. That's it. An entire circle of knowledge. Conspirators. Protectors.

Liars.

The truth has never been safer than it is with the three of us.

'I have homework,' I say weakly.

'You don't know when it is,' she says, smiling so gently I feel something break off my heart.

It shouldn't be this hard. This isn't the first time I've seen her since the accident. We saw her a lot those first

133

long and empty days. Days that stretched into weeks, months, years – two years. As time went on, the pain of her knowing and seeing all that she saw became something so enormous and unspeakable that Dad and I seemed to come to the same silent realisation – that we had to avoid her at all costs. We couldn't face her, eye to eye, because Mrs McGuire had become the last thing that connected us to my mother that wasn't, quite simply, each other. Everything we couldn't say to each other somehow shifted onto her. She stopped being a person and became Death. Our family's death. And also, most terribly, the witness.

She seemed to understand this, too.

'When is it?' I whisper. I'm sure Josh has told me but my brain isn't functioning like it should.

'All being well, first week of the finals.' Mrs McGuire studies me for a long, difficult minute, seeming to read all of my thoughts in that careful look. Her pretty brown eyes pierce my heart like no one else's can. *Could.* Mum could do this to me. My mum could trump anyone's ability to see into my soul in a way that Dad never could. He still can't, even though I've never needed it more. It must be a maternal thing, that penetrating, heartbreaking stare. If there was a championship for this, Mrs McGuire would be second on the ladder, right beneath Mum.

'Please,' she says quietly. '*Please.*'

That's it. That's all she says. Not the long, excruciating

argument, reassurances of innocence, the promise that no matter what I believed it wasn't my fault. Just that simple, ordinary word we're taught to understand long before we can say it. The first of the three big ones that mean so much or mean nothing at all.

Please.

Thank you.

Sorry.

I've been blaming Mrs McGuire all this time for being there; for seeing and knowing . . . *everything*. Now that she's here in my living room, I can't pretend that avoiding her is any kind of answer. I realise it's not about Mrs McGuire at all. It's about me and what I've done.

I nod. 'I'll try.' My voice catches in my throat. I don't trust myself to argue or refuse; it's too hard and I'm too tired. 'I'll try.'

Before I can say another thing, before she can say another thing, I tell them I have homework, knowing that none of us believes it, and escape into my bedroom, quietly shutting the door behind me. I need to block out the look of sadness and loss carved permanently in Dad's and Mrs McGuire's ageing faces, working together to accuse me of this unspeakable betrayal.

I survived. My family didn't. And it's all my fault.

MID-SEASON BREAK

CHAPTER 13

CHEWY ON YOUR BOOT

Miss Whitecross's English Lit class is always insane. She seems to think it's because we're so engaged in the activities, bubbling with excitement and enthusiasm for *The Great Gatsby* or Robert Lowell's 'Skunk Hour'. She might have been right about me – if I had anyone to bubble and enthuse with, I'd be quoting great chunks of *Gatsby*. But I've got a feeling that if I so much as hinted to Tara that I love books, she'd never invite me to the footy again. I want to not care about this. But as difficult as our friendship is and as prickly as she can be, she's the only friend I have in this whole school. I tell myself that the other girls are all limp, squealing airheads who cling together, who flick their hair and twirl their skirts with the fakest kind of confidence, too busy obsessing over the pimply boys from St Ignatius Boys' School next door to talk about anything important. To *think* about anything important.

That's what I tell myself.

But it's a tricky thing to tough out, day after day, without a single one of them talking to you, except when they have to for class activities or under direction from a teacher, and still maintain the belief that *they're* the idiots. Not you. After long enough, you start to suspect you've got it backwards.

So I need Tara for all kinds of reasons.

I watch her across the room, stuck at the back as usual – what the teachers call 'Siberia' – exiled for staring out the window or scratching the Falcons symbol onto a desk, or both. Tara's whole body is hunched over the desk, shutting out the world. I have no idea what she's doing but an intense energy radiates from her. She's like a clenched fist, all balled up and closed off.

'Shh! Girls, too noisy!' Miss Whitecross's voice barely registers with the class. The main problem is Ginnie Perkins and her clique. They're squealing and laughing like Miss Whitecross isn't even in the room. There seems to be a revolving door into this group, swinging between four or five girls who change depending on who their boyfriend is or who's having a sleepover in the near future, or even what their horoscope says. I can hear them arguing the merits of Jason Donovan's straight blond hair against the sandy curls of the Year 12 Wesley boy who catches the number 6 tram on Tuesdays and Wednesdays. It's a toss-up, apparently – the consensus being that the Wesley boy is better looking, especially when he has a tan, but Jason has the advantage of having a famous father and probably access to every TV and film star in town – even Mel Gibson, who's easily the best-looking bloke in Australia. Cue squeals of agreement.

Miss Whitecross raises her voice again but it's lost in the sea of laughter, and she seems to finally give up. I don't know if she's decided that her absence has a better chance at attracting our attention than her feeble voice or if she's desperate for a ciggie from all the stress, because she suddenly gets up and walks out, slamming the door behind her.

My money's on the cigarette.

For a long second there's a shocked silence and it looks like Miss Whitecross's exit might have actually worked. But a few brave giggles break the quiet, followed by a less brave chorus of muffled laughter and, bit by bit, the noise returns to its impossible level.

The singsong passion of the girls' easy friendship stabs at my heart. The careless way their hands brush against each other, the squeezing of shoulders, the linking of arms, the easy hugs. I've never had girlfriends like these, not even at Glenvalley High. For a second I let myself imagine what it would be like to be a part of it. Just for a second. And then I see Tara frowning at me with a startling intensity. Her clenched body has opened now yet none of the tension seems to have relaxed. Something has shifted, but I'm too far from her to hear what or why. I know Tara hates these girls with a passion only equalled by her love for the Falcons, like a mutant yin and yang. I don't know who spoke first, but Tara is suddenly standing over them all, shouting unintelligibly at a smirking Ginnie Perkins, who is safe in the centre of her flock.

'Shut the fuck up, you slut! Just shut the fuck up!' Tara shrieks.

Now I can hear her. Now *everyone* can hear her.

I watch, immobilised, knowing I should do something, equally positive that this can't end well – for Tara or for me, no matter the outcome.

'Maybe if you weren't such a frigid lesbian, *Lesbo Lester* – maybe then you'd understand,' Ginnie sneers, to the strains of pealing laughter from the gaggle around her. Someone opens the classroom door – Justine Deckland, I think – and sticks her head outside before shutting it and nodding the all clear.

Panic rises in my chest. I don't know what this will mean or what I'm supposed to do, but standing there with my mouth hanging open is probably not it. I want to be the sort of person who steps into the middle of this to defend my friend. I think of Mum and what she

142

would have done, of Dad and what he would want me to do, and then I'm moving forward, my head empty of anything that resembles a plan.

The small group has grown. The stragglers from the corners of the classroom have clotted together in the middle. I can't see Tara or Ginnie anymore. I push my way through the crowd. I'm smaller than most of them and not especially strong, but years of tackling practice with the Raiders has paid off. I move steadily through the girls and make my way to the front.

Tara is glaring at Ginnie, her face white with fury. Or hurt. She looks like she's been punched, the wind forcibly knocked out of her, and the energy that radiated from her only moments before has vanished. The impenetrable, invincible Tara Lester looks defeated, while Ginnie has a victorious grin on her face.

I hate that grin. Every part of me wants to wipe that nasty smirk off her face.

I watch as Tara backs away, tears running down her face. She turns and runs out the door, almost tripping over her desk in the rush. I stare after my friend, stunned by her retreat and embarrassed for her too.

'What have you done?' I shout at Ginnie, turning squarely on her.

'The lesbo lover, I presume?' Ginnie says, smirking. She doesn't even look at me, her words intended exclusively for her audience. Her skin, tanned from weekend tennis, is smooth and perfect. Her teeth are square and even from her freshly removed braces, and her hair is a silken blonde – the natural, almost-white blonde of a Scandinavian.

I know that among this group, in this class, there are girls who hate Ginnie as much as I do. Girls who are not mean or cruel or eager to impress her. But not one of them speaks up. No matter how I turn this around, I know it's up to me.

'Wow. So eloquent, Ginnie. Let's see how you go with more than two syllables . . . You are the most disgusting, repulsive excuse for a human being. It's a shame the Wesley boy and Jason Donovan don't know you exist because I'm sure they'd be really turned on seeing you gang up with your gutless bimbos against a girl on her own.' I swing around wildly, scanning all the faces for a sign of support, but instead I see fear and, among some of them, shame. I want to shout at them to say something, to help me, to help Tara, but that's not how it works. It occurs to me then that I have nothing to lose. 'You think they're your friends?' I ask, my arm sweeping widely to indicate the stunned girls. 'No one here likes you, Ginnie. No one. They're scared of you. That's all.' I suck in air, stepping away from them just so I can breathe. 'One day, they won't be,' I say quietly, 'and you'll be the one on your own.'

I don't have to look at the girls' faces to know I've completely isolated myself. The air is suffocating, and the silence hangs thick and heavy. So I run out just like Tara did, feeling the weight of my words drive me further away from the other girls than any slammed door could. I hurry through the length of the building, trying to make as little noise as possible. I don't know if I'm more afraid of running into Miss Whitecross or running into Tara.

But as I put the long corridor between myself and the classroom and I remember Tara's tear-streaked face, her silent retreat, I know absolutely that I'd rather have to deal with an indignant Miss Whitecross any day.

CHAPTER 14

NEW RECRUIT

It's a week before Tara comes back to school. I still don't know what Ginnie said but Tara obviously took it to heart. She finally showed up yesterday, right before Sister Brigid called the roll. She walked in and handed a note to Sister, then took her seat at the back of the class.

She didn't talk to me all day, disappearing to the toilets or the office – anywhere that I wasn't – first at recess and then again at lunchtime. So I let her do this, and didn't attempt more than a half-smile when we passed each other at the lockers. I don't know what she did the week she wasn't at school. I'd tried to call her a couple of times but no one answered the phone. Apparently she was at the footy on Saturday. I waited at the Burke and

Wills statue for half an hour before deciding she must have gone on ahead. Jim-Bob said he saw her at half-time outside the girls' toilets, so I know she's all right. She just doesn't want to talk. She'll speak to me when she wants to and not one minute sooner. I can wait. I'm good at waiting.

At least Ginnie Perkins has backed off. She hasn't apologised or tried to talk to me but she's stopped laughing every time I speak in class. In fact, she doesn't even look at me, like she's decided I don't exist. It's kind of a relief. Apart from being nasty, she's also very creative in ways that go well beyond the limits of my imagination. But if I think too long about it, it makes me nervous. I can't match her, not that I'd want to. I know it's not over.

Incredibly, some of the girls from Miss Whitecross's class have been really nice to me. Rose DeLillo and Elena Irving walked with me to the tram stop that night, and Anna Barnes asked if I was planning to stick with the athletics team. I told Anna I won't know for sure until after the footy season ends, which is still a couple of months away, but suggested we meet for the morning sessions just in case. At least Tara seems better today. She nodded at me on her way to Siberia this morning, and after recess she sat next to me during the library research session for our Australian History project. She hasn't really spoken to me properly, but her mood is shifting. I can feel it.

In the meantime I've decided on a topic for my project – I'm going to write about the history of the Glenthorn Football Club. We're supposed to choose a Melbourne institution, so it seems as good a topic as any. I'm supposed to have spent all term researching it, so making the deadline will be tricky. I haven't even asked Sister Brigid if I can do it yet. But at least it's a subject I care about.

Tara actually smiles when I show her. 'I wish I'd thought of that,' she says.

'You can do something about footy too,' I offer. 'As long as it's your own story.' But she just frowns at me as though I'm an idiot. Rather than be offended, however, I'm secretly pleased. It feels a lot like things are back to normal.

When the bell goes at the end of the day, I know they are. Tara grabs her bag and waits for me to get mine and, without a word, we head straight for the 69 tram, sprinting the last bit to get there in time. Just like any other Thursday after school.

With Tara beside me, I watch Fernlee Park Road pass by at varying speeds – slow at the beginning, the tram wheels shrieking and whining, then faster as we top the hill down past Riverglen Road. Mansion after mansion, some old and pretty, some new and square. Enormous plane trees line the side streets off Fernlee Park Road, their vast branches hanging heavily across the width of each street and their roots breaking through the footpaths. The weird mix of old and new, nature and architecture, jostle for space, neither winning outright but neither ready to surrender. The boring geometric streets of Glenvalley couldn't be further from this place if it were another country. I look at Tara and smile without having any reason other than I'm glad she's back. I can't wait to disappear into the sweaty chaos of the Fernlee Park gym.

We get off at Fernlee Park Station and walk under the bridge, our bags knocking against each other as we make our silent trek through the Coles car park. We haven't mentioned Ginnie once. It's like nothing has happened, even though it feels like, in some way, everything has. This is as good as it's going to get. I doubt she'll ever tell me what Ginnie said, and I haven't mentioned what I said to Ginnie, either. There's a reason we all keep secrets. Sometimes it's safer that way.

The regulars are all waiting in their spot, and after the arrivals and autograph-signing has taken place, the players run onto Fernlee Park. Tara and I find a seat along the boundary, tucking our Glenthorn scarves tightly around our necks, their brown and gold stripes clashing horribly with our blue-grey tartan winter uniforms. My grey stockings itch like crazy and the cotton blazer is too thin for mid-August in Melbourne. I wish I'd changed into comfortable clothes, but that would mean arriving late and explaining it to Dad.

The weather is miserable as we huddle on the boundary line. I'll have to make my own way home tonight because Mick had to visit the physio. He told me after Saturday's game that he was a bit sore. He didn't score any goals and was pretty stiff around the ground, but at least we won – we beat the Devils by thirty-two points at Queens Park, ensuring we keep second spot. We can't drop any more games, though. Mick has to get his knee right – and soon.

After training, Tara and I find a corner of the gym to sit down and eat our steaming hot sausages care of Blackie. There are only two players apart from Mick who'll do the sausage run for us: Blackie and Brendan O'Reilly. I don't know if they're just being friendly or they're too nice to say no, but they never blow us off and have taken to grabbing extras snags when they get their own.

I slurp my Coke and wipe my mouth with a torn serviette, then notice that Tara is watching me strangely, like she wants to say something but doesn't know how to begin.

'I could easily go another,' I say, finishing my last bite of sausage.

'I hate going to Errol Street,' Tara says eventually.

'Seems a bit of a hike,' I agree, although I've never been there and only have a vague idea of where North Yarra is. Other than, well, *north*. Of the Yarra. My hand

150

is like a block of ice from gripping the can of Coke. I tuck my fingers between my thighs to get the feeling back.

'You could stay at my house after the game. Maybe go to the social club straight from the ground.' It's not a question exactly, more an observation. And yet the words seem to require a response.

'Um . . . yeah? Okay.' Dad will let me sleep over. I used to do it all the time before the accident – with Sam and Julie, and even at Josh's. Another thing that stopped after that day. I'm not sure how Dad will feel about the social club part, but I don't really know what happens there anyway, so he probably doesn't either.

'Bring your clothes to the footy. I've got a sleeping bag and a spare pillow.'

'Cool, thanks.'

Tara shrugs. 'I'm going. See you at school.'

I watch her walk away, her schoolbag slung over her right shoulder, a slight stoop in her back to account for its weight. Her stockings have a small hole along the back seam and her skirt is hitched up unevenly on one side. She looks tired, as if she's had a long day. Or a long life. I'm struck by an unexpected stab of pity as I watch her leave the gym and disappear into the darkness behind the double doors. I wonder about her family. She barely mentions them – apart from her dad giving her the duffle coat, I don't think she's said a single other thing about

151

them. I have no idea what to expect at Tara's house, even from Tara.

I breathe in, long and slow. Too late now. I squash my empty can and toss it into the bin beside me, already full with discarded strapping tape, serviettes, beer bottles and soft drink cans, and decide that whatever happens at the social club, I've always got Mick for back-up in case Tara flakes. Like Josh, he's never let me down.

I can't even say that about myself.

CHAPTER 15

AWAY GAME

Errol Street Oval is a hole. I mean, literally a hole. Firstly, it's damp and old, with rotting wooden railings and wobbly seats that seem to inflict splinters just by looking at you. Secondly, it looks like it's been built in a pit. The sides rise up, elevated slightly over the tired-looking oval, giving it the appearance of being below ground.

Like I said, it's a hole.

Or maybe it's just that it feels like the depths of Hell because the North Yarra Redbacks – our archenemy in the seventies but now barely worth mentioning – have given the Mighty Falcons an absolute shellacking. I mean a humiliating, excruciating walloping. To the tune of seventy-one points. Even saying it out loud stings.

Tara and I gather our bags and coats as the siren goes, our hearts heavy with the loss. Top spot on the ladder is nearly impossible now. Although we're second and safe there, finishing on top sends a message. The Warriors are two games clear now and, with only three matches to go, there's no way they'll drop. My only consolation is that, since Mick didn't play, losing means there's some hope he'll be selected next week. Plus, everything changes once the finals race begins. It's like starting again. Clean slate, new page, whatever cliché you want to use, finals football is in a league of its own, and what happens during the season doesn't guarantee you anything on grand final day.

That doesn't change the fact that I hate losing to North, made worse because Tara and I were virtually abandoned by the cheersquad at three-quarter time. Danny was gone once they hit fifty points up, and Bear left at ten goals. Another of Tara's rules – one Dad enforces too – is that we never leave before the end of the game, even if we're being slaughtered.

We're in no hurry to get to Fernlee Park, knowing our loss will kill any party atmosphere at the social club, so we decide to go to Tara's house first. But as we lug our flogger and a backpack full of clothes for the sleepover on that long trip home, surrounded by victorious

154

Redbacks supporters, I almost wish we'd left early too. Screw the rules.

I'm so dispirited by the time we get off at Flinders Street Station to change trains that I'm tempted to split from Tara and just go home. But she doesn't feel any better than I do and I can't face Dad's relentless determination to make me a good loser. I can't watch the replay tonight. I can't suffer this disappointment twice. Surely losing is enough of a lesson on its own? At least Tara understands how I feel.

We catch the damp, smelly train with a few stragglers from the game in the same carriage, and get out at Silverdale Station. I follow Tara across the busy High Street intersection to a side street not far from the station. As we round the corner she says with a stiff kind of sarcasm, 'Home sweet home.'

I don't quite do a double take but my jaw drops a little. Her house is a mansion. As we enter through the side fence, I see a tangle of garden and a swimming pool resembling a tropical rockpool. I feel like we've stepped into a jungle. The house is huge – three storeys – and sticks out high above the neighbouring buildings. I think of my single-storey, beige brick house, the plain patchy lawn and the wobbly wooden letterbox, and wonder why in the world Tara's home isn't the centre of St Mary's party calendar.

Inside, it's like something from an American sitcom. It looks like it's been recently renovated – outside is traditional and *historical* somehow, but the inside is modern and new. Everything is so pristine and tidy it looks like no one lives here, like the kind of house featured in *Home Beautiful*. It's so different from any house I've ever been inside that it takes some moments before I realise why I'm so taken aback by it, and the fact that it belongs to Tara . . .

She's rich. Tara Lester – or her family, anyway – is *rich*.

Tara leads me straight to her bedroom. In complete contrast with the rest of the house, Tara's room is more than lived in. It's *possessed*. I can see Tara's imprint in every corner and space in sight. The wall, like the walls of my room, are lined with every Glenthorn picture and poster I've seen and even a couple I haven't, including a shiny full-length photograph of Killer smiling at the camera, ready to kick the ball. Her doona is in Glenthorn colours, her bedhead is covered in stickers and ribbons, all of them featuring brown and gold, so that there really doesn't seem to be any other colour in her bedroom. Even her bookshelf is filled with brown photo albums trimmed with gold ribbon.

I am completely in awe. 'I love your room,' I gush.

Tara shrugs and flops down onto her bed as though it's no big deal. But there's a shadow of a smile on her lips and I feel good that maybe I put it there.

I drop my bag on the floor and take a seat on the fold-out bed she's already set up beside hers.

After a long silence, during which neither of us seems to know what to say, Tara jumps off her bed. 'Hungry?'

I follow Tara into the kitchen, taking in the tall ceilings, and the shiny, polished floorboards. The walls are lined with paintings that look like they belong in a gallery.

'In here,' Tara says, leading me into a huge kitchen. She immediately heads to the fridge, which is one of those double-door models you see on *The Brady Bunch*. I'm about to follow when I hear a voice behind me.

'Hello, girls,' Mrs Lester says, seeming to float into the kitchen to join us. When she looks at me, her gaze sits just above my left ear. It's as if her body is here, but her head is off visiting someone else.

Tara barely looks at her mother. 'This is Shelley. From school.'

'Hi, Mrs Lester,' I say, standing straight and tall like Mum always told me to.

'Tessa, dear. Call me Tessa.' She looks a lot like Tara, but where Tara's features don't seem to match, Mrs Lester's fit perfectly. She looks older than Mum did but you can see she was really pretty once. She's gazing at the space right beside me now, like there are two of me, and she's focused on the wrong one.

I smile nervously. My dad would freak if I told him Mrs Lester wants to be called 'Tessa'. Which is *so* old-fashioned, but that's my dad.

'Got a cigarette?' Tara asks her mother boldly. Mrs Lester doesn't seem surprised, in fact, she looks as though Tara's just asked her for a Tim Tam.

'Of course, darling.' Mrs Lester waves a packet of Alpine Lights in front of her daughter. I can't stop staring at her nicotine-stained fingers as they tremble violently. Neither Tara nor her mum seem to pay any attention to those quivering hands. Mrs Lester waves the pack in my direction.

'N-no thanks,' I stammer, blushing. I'm pretty sure Mum never gave me instructions on how to refuse a cigarette from my friend's mother.

Mrs Lester continues to stare at me in that dizzy way. It reminds me of when a cartoon character has been turning around in circles and their eyes turn into crazily spinning spirals. 'Thanks,' I manage again. 'But really, no.' I don't want to offend her and I really don't want to piss off Tara, but I don't smoke. Dad would kill me if he found out I'd even tried it.

Mrs Lester drifts past me towards a cupboard, then back again, her eyes searching. I smell alcohol – not the faint trace of beer I used to smell on Dad after Christmas lunch, but more like how a pub smells.

I watch her navigate the kitchen table with deliberate care then ease the kettle onto the stove, as though frightened of dropping it. Her whole body is tilted to one side and her head seems to loll under its own weight.

My blush is spreading outward, not retreating at all. I'm so embarrassed for Mrs Lester that I briefly forget Tara is there. Mrs Lester takes out three mugs from the cabinet above her, her whole body swaying from the effort of looking up. Her hands move at a glacial speed, her concentration taking all of her energy. She's not just drunk – she's blotto.

Tara stomps towards her mother and grabs two of the mugs from her hands. 'I'll do it.' She looks mortified.

I hover near the doorway, wondering if I can come up with an excuse to go back to Tara's room or even to go home – anything to get away from Tara's humili-ation. And then I remember the image of Tara walking away from me that Thursday after training; her skirt uneven, her back stooped from all it had to carry, the weight of the world, it seemed . . .

I can't leave her.

I force a smile. 'What time do you want to go?' I ask Tara, desperate to ease the tension in the kitchen.

Mrs Lester is blissfully unaware. She swings around at my words, her smile vacant and enormous. 'She's so good to me, my girl. Isn't she?' Mrs Lester says, her words running together. She's talking to me, looking at me, but I'm pretty sure her question is rhetorical.

I smile and nod, just in case. Hedging my bets, as Dad would say.

Tara pours hot water into two mugs, deliberately leaving the third one empty. It doesn't matter, Mrs Lester's forgotten anyway. She's propped up in the corner of the kitchen with her back to us, humming something that would make Mum's tuneless singing sound like Dame Nellie.

Tara walks right past her mother as though she doesn't exist and hands me one of the cups of coffee, the cigarette tucked behind her ear for later. She takes a packet of biscuits from the pantry and leads me back to her bedroom.

On my way out, I turn back to say goodbye to Mrs Lester. She's facing me now, that same absent smile on her lips. She stops singing, smiles brightly and waves, as though I've just walked into the room. I wave stiffly and shut the door, hoping I can wipe that picture from my head just as easily.

CHAPTER 16

THE FIFTH QUARTER

We scoff down half the packet of biscuits while getting ready to go out. I pull on a pair of clean bubblegum jeans and a grey shirt, while Tara chooses stone-washed denims and a lemon scoop-neck blouse with puffy shoulders. We both wear boots – mine are grey suede pixies while Tara's are black patent leather. She doesn't mention her mum and I know better than to say anything, so I lie on my bed while I watch her do her make-up. Tara traces her startling blue eyes with a black pencil before adding mascara. She has one of those mirrors with the lights around them, the kind movie stars have in their dressing room. I remember watching Mum put on make-up when I was little, and feel a strange pang at the memory.

'You ready?' she asks, returning her mascara brush to its bottle.

I get up and study my reflection in the mirror beside her. My grey shirt is tighter than it used to be. All that effort to distract people from my breasts – the loose jumpers and the oversized school uniform – undone in a single look. I stretch it out as much as I can, tugging under my arms and around the collar, hoping it's caught on my bra or is just sitting wrong. I tug at it again. It's a bit better.

'Did you bring make-up?' Tara asks, dabbing her lips with pink gloss.

We're not allowed to wear make-up at school – the nuns scrub it off with alcohol if they see it, leaving your skin raw for the rest of the day – so I've never seen Tara with make-up before. And I've never worn it myself. Mum always said I had to wait until I was fifteen. Which I am now, but it's not like I can ask Dad to help me. I can just picture how *that* conversation would go. I shrug. 'I don't have any.'

Tara barely blinks. I'm guessing by the slow and careful turn of her wrist, her tongue half stuck out in concentration and the make-up remover right by her hand, she's pretty new to the process. 'You want some of mine?'

I hesitate, not sure I know what to do. I'd probably just mess it up on my first shot. 'Nah. Thanks.'

Tara studies me. Then, without a word, she stands up and guides me to the dressing table. 'Sit.'

I take a seat at the dressing table, immediately feeling altered somehow just by having all those lights framing my face. Is it possible to look different in different mirrors? Because somehow my reflection doesn't resemble the one I usually see in my mirror at home.

Slowly, with the hint of a tremor in her hands, Tara touches the mascara to my lashes, paints my lips a creamy pink then rubs some blush on my cheeks. At the beginning I sit stiffly, uncomfortable at having her so close to me, taking control like this, like an older sister. Like a mother. But she doesn't once meet my eyes, so set on the task at hand that eventually I relax and let her go.

Tara steps back and pulls the chair out so I can get a clear look at my reflection. I don't look terrible. I look . . . nice. Older, too. My eyes look big and stand out from my not too pimply skin. My mouth looks fuller with plump lips I didn't know I had. 'Thanks,' I say quietly.

She shrugs, dismissing me, then runs a brush through her long hair and ties it back in its usual ponytail. 'We should go.'

She grabs her jacket, and I follow her out through her enormous house and into the busy street. The air is damp and the grey clouds overhead have brought a heaviness to the wintry night sky. The tram trundles down High Street, half empty yet seeming to labour under the weight

163

of its passengers. Before we get to Fernlee Park Road, Tara stands suddenly, flicking my leg for me to follow. We're in Glen Malvern – nowhere near the club. I catch up to her in the doorway as we pull up at the stop. 'We're not there yet,' I say.

'I need to get something first,' she answers airily.

This has to be bad. I wonder if she's going to buy some grog or cigarettes – though why would she when she can bum them off her mum? – or maybe she's been lying the whole time and has no intention of going to the social club at all.

Tara is already leaping off the tram so I figure we're safer having this conversation on the footpath.

'Hey! Where are we going?' I pull up beside her as she lights up a cigarette.

Tara blows out smoke in answer and jogs across the busy road. It's not until we cross the side street next to a Chinese restaurant that I recognise where we are. School. I haven't walked along this part of High Street before and, in the darkness, lit only by uneven streetlamps, everything looks different and strange – even the increasingly recognisable shape of St Mary's Convent and the school buildings beside it.

'Forget your homework?' I joke, catching up to her.

Tara just keeps walking, slower now because she's crossed into the car park beside the convent and is heading towards the church next door. St Michael's Church is shared by St Ignatius and St Mary's, and is the usual venue for school masses and the occasional R.E. lesson. The church is filling up for the Saturday night service. Cars nose their way through the crowded car park, carefully avoiding the stream of pedestrians heading toward the church building, who seem oblivious to the danger.

Tara takes the front steps to the narthex in twos. I stop at the bottom, wondering what the hell she's doing. I don't go inside churches anymore if I can manage it. Not just because I don't believe the stories they tell us at school – although I don't – but because I'm a little nervous about setting foot inside, knowing I've made this decision to reject my religion.

I wait nervously for Tara to reappear, trying to decide how long to give her before I head back to her drunk mother and ask her to call my dad to pick me up. I don't have enough money for a taxi all that way, and Dad would freak if I caught public transport by myself so late on a Saturday night. But when I picture Dad's face meeting a blind Mrs Lester, I decide I really don't have a choice. So I wait, untying the pink V-neck jumper from around my waist and slipping it carefully over my newly made-up face. After a few minutes I spot Tara as she makes her way through the thickening crowd, pressing against the tide on her way down the stairs. She hands me a St Michael's newsletter and folds her own copy before slotting it into her duffle-coat pocket.

I stare at her, perplexed.

'For Mum tomorrow,' she says matter-of-factly as she heads back through the car park towards Fernlee Park Road.

I stand there, confused.

She turns back and stretches her hands in the universal gesture of 'What the hell is your problem?'.

'Why do I need a newsletter?'

'It's proof,' she says, then shakes her head at my apparent stupidity. 'Mum will ask us what the Reading was.'

I look at the newsletter and back at Tara, who's still frowning at me like I'm an idiot.

'She thinks we're going to Saturday night Mass,' she says.

'Why would she think that?'

'Because that's what I told her,' Tara says, shrugging.

Bemused, I follow her back to the tram stop, feeling the weight of the many lies we're telling dragging behind me, wondering why Tara even needs to lie to her mother, given that Mrs Lester was so sozzled when we left the house that we could've told her anything and she'd never remember.

It feels a lot like I've moved into something more than a new friendship. I've moved into a whole new world. And although I'm a little terrified by all that can go wrong, I'm also unexpectedly excited about it, too, in almost exactly equal parts.

There are only a handful of cheersquad regulars at the entrance to the social club – Jim-Bob and Sharon, for once without their kids, plus a couple of committee members I never talk to. None of them are members of the social club, nor have they found anyone to sign them in, so they're hanging around, waiting for likely soft touches.

Tara nods at the Lovely Ladies – all three are glammed-up and shiny, their long necks weighed down by all that foundation and hairspray. I sense Tara holding back big time, the desire to mock these girls crouching inside her ready to pounce. But she has to be nice. They're our way in.

'Hey,' Tara says, transforming her usually tight smile into something resembling friendliness. 'You guys going in?'

It's a stupid question. All three are at the top of the stairs, rummaging through their matching Glomesh purses for membership medallions and fake IDs, their feet halfway across the threshold between the Great Unwashed and the Signed In and Paid Up, their giggling chatter punctuated with names of the likely targets of their affection for the night. Players, of course.

'Yeah,' Lisa says, without looking up. Lisa is blonde like Kimberly but her hair colour looks natural, while I'm pretty sure Kimberly's comes straight from a bottle.

'Can you sign us in?' Tara asks. 'We'll buy you a drink,' she adds, even though this is the first I've heard of it. Not only do I have no fake ID and look like I'm barely through puberty let alone eighteen years old, I have a total of fifteen dollars in my wallet and face the very real possibility that I'll need every cent of it in case I need to catch a taxi alone.

Lisa shrugs noncommittally while Kimberly completely ignores Tara and goes through the glass doors without looking back. Renee rushes after her friend and it occurs to me that this is how it always works for these two. Kimberly does what she wants – decisive, unthinking and absolute – while Renee simply follows, always two steps behind. Renee is pretty but not *as* pretty, smart but not *as* smart. She's the Clayton's version of Kimberly – the girl you have when you're not having The Girl.

Tara and I watch the bouncer through the doors as he stops them inside the foyer, their mouths moving mutely, their hands flying. They giggle and squirm as they provide evidence of their legitimacy or their ability to fake legitimacy (they can't be more than sixteen, seventeen at best). I'm amazed as I witness his whole attitude shift in response to their extra flirty smiles, the subtle way they tilt their heads, the gushing apology for holding everyone up . . . All the ways their bodies convey to this man that while they are both gorgeous and out of his league, there's still the tiniest chance that if he's *really, really* nice and *really, really* helpful . . .

How do they learn this? I wonder. Does someone teach them? Or is it something present from birth, like the colour of their eyes, or the shape of their chin?

Lisa, still looking for her ID, glances at Tara then at me, clearly frustrated but doing her best not to take it out on us. 'How long before Mick's back?' she asks, sifting through the junk in her purse.

It feels like a test. I weigh my answer. 'A couple of weeks, depends on the scan.'

She nods, taking this in. Sounds reasonable, that nod says. Believable. 'When's the scan?'

I don't know. Mick doesn't even know. But I understand I have to answer, and for reasons that escape me, I pluck this fiction out of the sky. 'Tuesday morning. They have to wait for the swelling to go down.' The lie comes easily – disturbingly easily. I wonder where it was hiding that it could emerge so perfectly formed.

'We really need him,' she says.

'No kidding.' I'm relieved to be back on safer ground, the kind made up of truth. I offer a dry chuckle even though the sting of the North Yarra loss is still raw. I'm performing, I realise; faking cool to this girl who will or will not be our ticket into the social club tonight, depending on how I do.

'Yes!' she cries, holding up her social club medallion and the errant ID victoriously. 'Come on,' she says, and Tara nods her approval at me as we follow Lisa inside.

The moment we enter the safety of the social club, Lisa turns and flashes her nearly perfect teeth in a seamless dismissal. 'I'll see you later,' she says, before heading towards the back of the room.

'Where's she going, do you think?' I ask Tara, glad Lisa's gone on one level – the cool Shelley takes enormous effort and focus to get right – but also disappointed because I kind of like her. Or I like *me* when I'm with her, which is a new experience. That this seems largely one way is not something I want to spend too much time thinking about.

'The players' room probably,' Tara says, leading me to the bar.

'Where's that?'

'At the back.'

'And it's for players, I'm guessing.'

'You think that's why they call it that?' Tara asks, rolling her eyes.

'My point is – she's not a player.'

'Nothing gets past you, does it?'

I wait at the bar beside her, wondering what she'll say when I order a soft drink, hoping she's thinking what I'm thinking and not what I'm afraid she's thinking.

'Vodka and passionfruit UDL,' she says to the bartender.

Damn. There goes that idea.

The bartender sizes her up. Although Tara's barely eleven months older than me, she has a way about her – the hard set of her mouth, the way she stares into people without letting up – that makes her seem older than she really is. A lot older than me, anyway.

The bartender asks for Tara's ID. She shows him a fairly unconvincing photocopy of a complete stranger's learner permit and, without checking that it's her or even that it's real – she's been practising her date of birth and star sign just in case – he plonks a UDL and a glass of ice on the bar, then turns his attention to me. Just as I feared. 'Yes?'

I'm not going to get away with this the way Tara has. I don't even want to. 'Beer?' I ask, hating the tremor in my voice.

Incredibly, he sloshes a pot of beer on the bar towel, winking at me. My co-conspirator. Two problems face me now. One, I don't drink – at all. Two, I hate beer. I hate the taste of it, the smell of it, even the colour of it. I have no idea why I ordered it.

I take my foaming beer, already queasy at the idea of it, and follow Tara into the darkest corner of the club, where she's found a table and one chair. I look around for somewhere to sit, spy a stool by the back bar and drag it over.

I'm still wearing the pink V-neck. It's too heavy for the overheated club but I'm not keen on the grey shirt underneath – what it shows and how it makes me look – not to mention the very tricky business of not horribly smearing my make-up in the process of taking the jumper off. Someone turns the back-bar lights on, and I feel the heat of them on my face. I sit on my stool and tower over the table, feeling pink and enormous on my high perch, and also a little trapped.

'Seriously?' Tara asks, eyeing my pedestal.

I think she's disappointed that Danny isn't here. He said he might come, but so far there's been no sign of him. I wonder if that's why Tara invited me. I want to ask but I know better. Even hinting at her crush is dangerous. The first time I tried, she shot me down with a look that would make Freddy Krueger cringe. And all I'd said was something about moving seats to sit with him.

'There aren't any other chairs,' I say defensively. I sip my beer without throwing up and decide that maybe this experience isn't going to be as excruciating as I feared. I sip again. Each mouthful is a little less awful than the previous one. We watch the crowd slowly build. It's turning into a normal pub now, with a smaller Glenthorn crowd and more people from off the street – still members or friends of members but without the brown-and-gold scarves and duffle coats of the footy faithful.

The music suddenly gets louder as the lights dim again and I feel a bit disorientated. It's ten o'clock and the place is switching from bar to club. My jumper looks even more out of place than it did before, but my confusion is increasing with every extra mouthful of beer and I can't deal with anything else right now.

'Aren't you hot?' Tara asks, watching a trickle of sweat run down my cheek.

I nod, exposed. The room has taken on a slight tilt, a slow swirl. I'm suddenly so hot that I can't stand it another minute. With a deep breath and a careful steadying of my seat, I take my jumper off. Incredibly, I don't tip over. I brush the grey shirt down, straighten it and attempt – again – to loosen it around my breasts, then slip the jumper over the back of my stool.

Red comes over, still wearing her footy gear. 'Anyone here?'

'Not yet,' Tara shrugs. Red means players, but it's possible Tara means Danny.

'They'll be out soon,' Red says with that authoritative voice.

We listen to a couple of songs and when Billy Idol comes on, I suggest we dance.

'I don't dance,' Red says flatly, and I believe her.

'I need a drink,' Tara says, and disappears to the bar.

I sing along quietly to 'White Wedding', until Tara returns with another UDL. I watch her take long slugs of the can. It won't be long before she'll need a refill. My drink is disappearing, finally, although Tara's almost caught up to me again. I hope she doesn't notice.

173

When George Michael's 'Careless Whisper' comes on, I can no longer resist. 'I love this song,' I say, ready to go and dance on my own. But before I can navigate my way off the stool, Red nods towards the back of the club and says, 'Players.'

The doors to the players' room are now open, and several of the seniors have come out, all clean-shaven and dressed up for a night out. They look so different compared to when they're at Fernlee Park. I have to completely readjust my image of them to fit these neatly dressed, cologne-wearing apparitions – men, just like the ones you see anywhere else, only much better looking and stronger. Not quite real but real enough – like movie stars or celebrities. It's not just that they're handsome, although most are. It's more than that; something about how they carry themselves, how they look at us – at everyone – reminds us they're something special. They're stars – *superstars* – paid to play the very game the whole city worships. They know they're being watched. And admired. This is the thing I'm trying to name – this thing they wear like a badge. Confidence? Arrogance? No, it's more than this. It's ownership.

I think about Dad's awkward stiffness, my own difficult isolation at St Mary's and, well, everywhere that isn't Glenthorn. I think about Mrs Lester's drunken afternoon, Tara's sullen silences and even Josh's nervous backtracking in the face of his accidental reference to our life before . . . The players couldn't be more different from the world and people I know than if they were born on another planet.

The Lovely Ladies emerge from the darkness of the players' room, as though summoned. Kimberly first – always first – then Lisa and Renee, each of them sipping on brightly coloured cocktails, their ridiculously high heels and short skirts the focus of the players' attention.

Kimberly leans against the bar, her pretty smile glowing across the room. It's entrancing, even to me. Even to Tara. I steal a look at Tara, her glass poised ready to drink – or ready to be hurled – and the steel in her gaze surprises me. I follow Tara's line of vision to Brendan O'Reilly, who moves in towards Kimberly. O'Reilly's teammates grin their approval as he approaches Kimberly and drapes his arm across her shoulders, startling her apparently, as she lets out a brittle laugh. She recovers quickly and offers him an inviting smile.

Something hard lodges itself in my throat. I look at Tara, whose attention hasn't moved from this scene. Her fist is clenched tightly around her drink, and her mouth is grim. I worry that she'll break the glass, she's bearing down on it so hard.

I look at the couple again. What's she seeing that I'm not?

O'Reilly leads Kimberly out of the main bar and back into the players' room, without a single word exchanged between them. The other players observe this without raising an eyebrow. A surge of something hot and unsettling rushes through me, and I don't know what it means.

Lisa watches nervously. For a second she looks like she might go after her friend, but Renee starts talking to her and Kimberly is soon forgotten.

'Slut,' Tara mutters under her breath.

'Huh?'

She breathes in deeply, the colour draining from her face as she seems almost to hold her breath. Then she releases it slowly and faces me square on, her expression flat and unreadable. 'Nothing.'

'Where are they going?' I ask.

Tara turns on me sharply. 'How should I know?' She sips her drink, facing the players' room again. 'Wherever it is, I'm sure his wife won't be there.'

'What? Oh.' I should be appalled. I should feel the same anger Tara obviously feels. I think about this, and decide that I do. Deep down, buried under a whole lot of other things I don't understand. Like envy and . . . *possibility*. What would that feel like, I wonder? To be looked at like that?

'They always do that,' Red says, shrugging.

I look at this girl-woman, who could be thirteen or thirty, depending on the light, her tight cap of red hair and her lined, pale face sitting so oddly on the rest of her.

Does she do 'that' too? Does she want to? Does Tara? Or Lisa and Renee?

Do *I* want to?

Before I can process it all into anything more than an uncomfortable idea, Mick hobbles out of the players' room, his dodgy knee heavily bandaged, his arm thrust out in front of him as he struggles with a single crutch. He sees me across the room. For a second his eyes graze me and move on, like he doesn't know who I am, and then he does an almost-comical double take. Recognition, then uncertainty.

I'm suddenly aware of how my grey shirt is stretched tightly across my chest, how my jeans hug my thighs. I smile awkwardly, embarrassed.

He doesn't smile back. He begins to – and then he doesn't. It's like he's never seen me before. He stares at the beer in my hand, anger etched into his frown.

I shift in my seat, regretting the beer because of how it's affecting my balance. I have to talk to him, to find out why he's angry.

I carefully slide off my stool and make my way towards him. He glances away, then turns back to face me, his expression cold and hard.

I stop, confused.

He turns away, and then I notice a woman behind him. Pretty with long blonde hair and jeans so tight I wonder how she can breathe, she comes out of the players' room, carrying Mick's other crutch. Her hand moves naturally to cup his elbow, guiding him towards the exit. Although I've never seen her before, and although he's never described her to me, I know immediately that this is his wife, Wendy.

There's no reason why I shouldn't go over to them and there's no reason why Mick wouldn't want me to. It seems ridiculous, actually, that she and I haven't already met.

But I don't move.

As they walk past me, Mick nods, distant and courteous, and I know I've done the right thing. I also know I haven't done anything wrong, despite how I feel. We both love footy. We both love Glenthorn. It's a simple, ordinary friendship. Just like with Tara, Josh and the other cheersquadders . . . We're friends.

I watch Mick disappear into the dancing bodies and laughing faces that have begun to fill the room, his wife by his side, knowing that he will never introduce us. If that's what he wants, it's enough for me.

I return to my seat and sip my beer, draining the last dregs too quickly for my newly developed tastebuds to cope with, and am forced to stifle a cough. I look around for Red and see Bear watching me closely, a sympathetic smile on his lips. I dismiss him with a cold stare.

I can feel Tara glaring at me, judging and condemning every time I go near Mick. The familiar rush of blood roars in my ears and my chest burns as I turn away. I wish I'd never come. I wish this whole day had never happened. 'I want to go home,' I say to Tara.

'We just got here,' she says, annoyed.

Ignoring her protests, I slip off the stool and unsteadily weave my way through the thickening crowd, avoiding Red and Bear on my way out. I don't have to look back to know Tara's following me. We're near the exit before I feel her arm on me, tugging me back. 'Just wait a sec,' she says, and heads to the bar. I watch her buy another UDL and thread her way back to me. 'A traveller,' she smiles, as she guides us to the exit.

The cold night air hits my face as I stand at the entrance. The last of the cheersquadders have either managed to find a way in or have given up and gone home. A handful of new arrivals hover by the doorway, waiting to sign in.

Tara moves ahead, taking the steps in big leaps as though, having decided that we're leaving, she's suddenly determined to get home as fast as she can. Between long strides, she sips her UDL.

I'm about to follow her when I notice Mick's car across the street. His wife is helping him arrange his legs into the space in front of the passenger seat. Her brisk attentiveness and no-nonsense movements are more like a mother than a wife. But as he grimaces with pain, she touches his face, tilts her head towards him, and they look at each other for a long moment.

I feel like an intruder, but I can't look away. Mick doesn't notice me watching, too intent on the silent exchange he's sharing with his wife. But when she shuts his door and heads to the driver's side, she looks up and our eyes meet.

I stand perfectly still, the breeze lifting my hair and cooling my cheeks. After a long moment, she offers me a tight, noncommittal smile, then gets in the car and they drive away.

CHAPTER 17

POST-GAME ADDRESS

I turn over in the trundle bed in Tara's room, the soft mattress giving too easily under my shoulder. It feels like I'm sleeping on planks. I push my fist under my pillow, curl my legs under me and squeeze my eyes shut, determined to slow my racing mind. The room is as dark as a cave. The heavy drapes block any light from the street lamps outside, and the house is quiet and still.

Beside me, Tara's bed creaks and groans. I hear the padding of feet across the rug, towards me at first, and then away, towards the window.

I don't move. I don't want to face Tara right now. I haven't got the words anyway. I didn't speak the whole way home because a deep and terrible shame seemed to rob me of speech. Sadness and loss all over again, nameless and confusing because I have no idea what I've lost.

A slither of light cuts through the room. I turn over, grateful now for the absence of springs under me. Tara is staring at something outside her bedroom window. Her face looks eerie, almost ghostlike in the filtered light, her usually pale skin transparent. I see the glistening of tears on her cheeks before I hear the first sob. She presses her fist against her mouth, as though forcing the sounds back to where they came from.

I lie there, terrified she'll turn around, but unable to tear my eyes away. She is . . . *bereft*. That was the word Mrs McGuire used to describe how she felt in those first days after the accident. I didn't know that word until she'd used it, and yet I instantly understood what it meant. Despair. Emptiness. Grief.

Tara is grieving something too. I don't know what it is and I don't know how to ask her. But it's there before me, enormous and impossible, the depths of it emptying out of her in great, wrenching sobs.

'Are you okay?' I whisper.

Tara flinches as though she's been struck. Her head jerks up and her hands fly to her side, hiding the evidence of what they've been doing to silence her sadness. She stands like that, almost to attention, for the longest time.

My heart pounds in my chest. It's quite possible that I have officially destroyed the only friendship I have at

St Mary's. And it occurs to me that I don't want this. For all her cold and difficult ways, her distant and unforgiving manner, Tara Lester matters to me. I like her. She's my friend.

I consider my chances of waking up tomorrow and pretending I don't remember. Maybe if I don't say anything else and never mention it again, she can convince herself I was drunk or half asleep. That whatever this is – grief? – is still hers and hers alone.

'I hate her,' Tara hisses into the darkness.

I sit up, knocking my knee on the edge of the trundle in my rush. I assume she means her mum.

Tara turns towards me, her face lit by the streetlight through the crack in the drapes. I see her tear-streaked cheeks, pink nose and hard, moist eyes. Then she moves away from the window and the drapes fall together, enveloping us again in a blanket of darkness. And I think I know what Ginnie Perkins said to Tara that pissed her off, or I can imagine anyway.

'What about your dad?' I ask quietly, rubbing my knee discreetly. I'm both unsettled by Tara's admission and, strangely, warmed by it too. I don't know how long it's been since anyone has said anything as important as this to me. Thinking this, I'm seized with a momentary panic: What if I say the wrong thing? What if I mess this up? Dad says that sometimes you have to just play the ball that comes to you and let your instincts decide. And my

183

instincts are telling me right now that if I'm gentle and careful, Tara might begin to trust me.

'He's never here. He hates her as much as I do. It's better anyway, without him.'

I peer into the darkness, wishing I could see more, wishing I could watch Tara's face for all the signs I need to gauge how far to push this. 'You have sisters, though, don't you?'

Tara laughs, but it's a hard, grating sound. 'They moved out the first chance they could. Lissie's in Sydney and Olivia's in London, married with two little kids. There's twelve years' difference between Lissie and me.' Another bitter laugh. 'Mum was done with raising kids when I came along. Still is.'

Tara's mattress shifts against my back as she slips back under her doona, the creaking of the springs filling the room. 'It's good when they come back,' she says quietly. 'But after they go . . .'

I imagine the clatter and clamour of her sisters' return, noisy toddlers scampering through the wood-floored halls, filling this enormous house with the chaos of family life. Vibrant and unruly and alive. And then the silence. The sudden, heartbreaking stillness after they've gone. I know too well what that feels like. 'Is she always . . .?' How do I end that question? Drunk? Blotto? Off her head?

'It depends.' She turns to face me. 'What about your mum? Your family? You never mention them.'

The familiar weight of this moment threatens to crush me. What do I say? How can I say it? I can't – not all of it anyway. 'It's just Dad and me now. There was an accident . . .'

Tara's sharp intake of breath strengthens me somehow.

'It's just Dad and me now,' I say again.

'Your mum died?' she whispers with something like reverence.

I nod. 'Car accident. Two years ago.' The lump rises to my throat as though bidden, and I feel the hot sting of tears prick the back of my eyes. That's all I can manage now. For one night, that's enough. 'It's late,' I say.

After a long silence I hear Tara roll over. 'Yeah,' she says quietly. 'It is.'

CHAPTER 18

FULL FORWARD

'Huddo wins. No contest,' Dad says, pushing leaves of iceberg lettuce around the salad bowl, trying to get the French dressing to run evenly through it.

Josh offers an exaggerated eye roll in response, which Dad ignores.

I'm forcing down a Straz and tomato sauce sandwich, but the dough sticks in my throat. All I can think about is how much I want to get out of here. Dad's been watching me too closely, frowning at my long silences and crabby mood. He doesn't ask me what's wrong – that's not how things work in the Brown household. Though I couldn't tell him even if he did. My head is spinning with everything it has to hold – the way Mick looked at me at the social club, Tara's tear-streaked face, her mum's unsteady gaze, her absent father, and Mick's wife seeing right through me before she drove away – all these things I don't want to know or think about.

I know this much, though: the sooner I can get out from under Dad's prying eyes, the better. The only problem is that Josh is here and he's determined I make good on my promise to watch the Raiders.

'Come on, Mr Brown. Coleman was a superstar!' Josh counters. He's taking his sweet time over lunch. I shoot him my best 'Hurry up!' filthy, and nudge him under the table.

He blows me off with that wicked grin, deliberately slowing his chewing rate. I should know better – no one rushes Josh McGuire.

You'd think he'd be in a hurry too, now that I've finally agreed to watch him play. Dad even offered to pack our lunch. But Josh plonked himself down at our kitchen table like somebody's king. Sometimes I wonder what goes on in Josh McGuire's head. If anything.

'Coleman was spectacular to watch,' Dad says, refusing to let his favourite subject slip. 'That's why so many people say he's the best full forward in history.' I feel a small pang in my chest as I watch Dad, his face as animated as it gets nowadays. I used to be able to do that to him – make him light up. 'But Huddo did what no one else could – be ahead of the ball, like he knew where it was going before the ball did.'

Josh leans forward, his eyes dancing. They've had this conversation many times before, and I know Josh starts it deliberately to see Dad come alive like this. I feel my stomach slowly unclench itself, and I can taste my sandwich again.

'He was so far ahead of the ball – and his opponent – they didn't have a chance. Nobody did.' Dad spears a slice of Straz and makes another sandwich for us both. I've finished mine and have unexpectedly regained my appetite. I take the sandwich he offers me and slather it with tomato sauce.

'But Coleman could fly like no one else,' Josh argues.

'You're right,' Dad agrees. 'Huddo rarely took speccies.'

'Right, and a full forward needs to dominate overhead. That's how they win the ball – how they set up shots at goal.'

Dad shakes his head gravely. 'It's not that he *couldn't* take a big mark, Joshua. He just didn't *have* to.'

I grin at Josh, who grins at me. Maybe this wasn't such a bad idea after all.

'He knew what was going to happen before it did and would barely break a sweat. He could get into position and force his opponent *out* of position, while the ball seemed almost to hang in the air. And he'd mark it on his chest. You always want to do that if you can. Safest way to take the ball. Whether you like how it looks or not.'

'Still,' Josh persists, 'Coleman kicked so many goals. Took *so* many marks. He must have been incredible to watch!'

Dad sets down his sandwich, looks us both evenly in the eye and nods slowly. 'Coleman was spectacular, no doubt about it. But Hudson . . .?' Dad leans forward. 'Hudson made it look *easy*.'

I sit back and smile. I'm stuffed, but I feel better than I have all day.

I think about Mick, carefully replacing the memory of the night at the social club with the image of him on the football field – the moment he kicked the last of seven goals, right before we slaughtered the Gorillas. 'Mick Edwards is doing all right,' I say.

'Not in the same league,' Dad says, dismissively.

A part of me knows he's right, but not the part that controls my mouth. 'Give him time. He's got a way to go still.'

Josh lets out a dry laugh. 'Yeah, a long way. Like to *Antarctica*.'

I frown at him. He's supposed to be on my side. 'Give him a couple more years.'

'If his leg holds up. Be lucky to get through one,' Josh says, oblivious to my irritation.

'He kicked an almost-perfect game against the Gorillas,' I argue, my voice rising in frustration. 'Seven goals.'

Dad shakes his head, his brow furrowing. 'He could kick ten and he still wouldn't be a patch on Hudson.'

Josh is too caught up in teasing me to notice my shift in tone. 'You just like him 'cause you're mates,' Josh says, nodding at Dad as though he's in on the whole thing.

Dad's face freezes. Josh has no idea, chomping away on the crust of his sandwich like nothing's happened. Slowly, Dad returns to his chewing, carefully, deliberately. Twenty-one times. He swallows. 'How do you mean?' he says to Josh, as though I'm not there.

Josh offers a brittle laugh, finally noticing the mood. He does the only thing he can do in the face of Dad's question. He stalls. 'You know . . . her favourite player.'

Dad isn't buying it, and suddenly I don't care. 'At training,' I say. 'We hang out.'

'You *hang out*?'

'Yeah.' My voice is more confident than I feel. I jut my chin and level my gaze, but my fingers are trembling. I fold my hands in my lap so no one notices.

Dad stops eating. 'What does that mean, exactly?' He looks like a coiled spring, holding everything in as tightly as he can.

I shrug, forcing a lightness neither of us feels. What does that mean, exactly? When I'm with Mick it's so perfect and clear, but then I see how it looks in other people's eyes, see what they're thinking or hear what they're saying – Tara, Mick's wife and now Dad – and it changes in ways I don't understand. 'He's my friend, Dad. We talk at training and he gives me a lift to Stonnington sometimes.'

'He drives you . . . *In his car?*'

'Just to the station.' Like the fact it's only a short distance will make a difference.

'You're alone, when this happens?'

'Well, kind of. I mean . . . we're in *public*. He waits while I catch the train – when it's dark. To make sure I get on okay.'

'He's a grown man! What can he possibly want from you?'

He sounds like Tara. Why wouldn't Mick want to be my friend? It's so obvious to me what we have. Why can't anyone else see it? 'He's new,' I start, knowing it's more than this. 'And lonely . . .' My throat tightens and a lump like a fist restricts my breathing. 'Like me,' I rasp. Words I've been avoiding for two years, and now they're out there and can't be taken back.

'Jesus,' Dad whispers.

I've never heard Dad swear before. He's making it sound ugly and wrong. He's making it sound like Mick's face looked at the social club – like a secret, a lie. Something a man doesn't want his wife to see. The queasiness in my gut has returned. I get up, my whole body clenched in frustration and something that feels a lot like fear.

'He's my friend!' I yell, hot tears stinging my eyes. 'He understands me – better than you do, that's for sure!'

I suck in air, hold in my fury, and stare him down. I refuse to cry.

Josh has turned pale, his face trying to gesture apology, while Dad won't even meet my eyes.

'This is what you do at the football club? You *hang out* – alone – with sweaty footballers?'

I breathe deeper now, my lungs struggling for air. 'You make it sound horrible!' I choke, cringing at the whine in my voice. I clear my throat and fight back tears, but still my voice croaks and simpers. 'He's my friend, and the best thing that's happened all year!'

Josh stands up. 'Mr Brown? Are you okay?'

For a terrible second I think Dad might have a heart attack. His chest is heaving, his face granite.

I shake my head. 'Dad? Please, it's no big deal. Are you okay?'

He takes an excruciating minute to find his voice, and it's so soft when he speaks that I wonder if I've heard right. 'You're grounded,' he says, his eyes glazed over like a blind man's, his hands spread out between us, as though reaching for something that makes sense.

I stand there, stunned. I want to move, to get away, but a horrible paralysis pins me in place.

'No more football. No more Fernlee Park. No more *Mick Edwards*.' He spits out Mick's name like it's something foul.

'No! Please! I promise I won't let him drive me

anymore. Tara can come too. And there are others . . .'
But it's clear I've lost him. Dad's mind is made up and
there's no going back. 'Please,' I whisper, the hurt huge in
my throat, my voice weak and trembling.

'Wait outside, Joshua,' Dad says briskly, managing
to seem something nearer to reasonable. But his eyes
are cold.

I steal a glimpse of Josh. He can't look at me or at
my dad. 'Mr Brown . . .' he starts nervously. Josh is always
so confident but right now he looks like a child. 'Shelley
would never . . .'

Dad's gaze swivels hard onto Josh.

Never *what*? I want to scream at Josh. At Dad. *That's*
what they think of me?

Josh can't finish the sentence. He doesn't have to.
Somehow, to them, I've become a person who could
do this thing they can't even say.

'I'm not a kid anymore!' I cry.

Dad snorts in disgust or disbelief.

'I'm not a kid,' I say again, quieter now. Fighting the
panic in my chest, I turn away from him.

'Come back here, Michelle.' Dad's voice is like gravel.
'Come back *now*.'

I continue to walk, each step taking me further from
something that I'm not sure I can ever come back to.

I lie on my bed, counting the Falcons posters that line my walls, to soothe my racing heart. I look at the photos I've begun to collect around my mirror – Mick with his sheepish grin, outside the gym entrance; Mick and Chris Jury passing short kicks between each other in the grey twilight of a training session a few weeks ago; Mick with a footy thrust in front of him, his face a little weary with having to pose yet again for the camera.

I turn away, unable to look another moment. I reach up to take *My Brilliant Career* off the bookshelf and carefully, reverently, open it. I can't always face this story. But I'm desperate now and I can't think of a single other thing that will make me feel better, short of a trip to Fernlee Park – now forbidden and impossible. For the first time since I made that trek down Leafy Crescent, I'm not sure it would help anyway.

The first page is a handwritten inscription from Mum, with a picture of her when she was young sandwiched between the pages. She's staring straight at the camera. I trace her mouth with my finger, then her chin. Her beautiful dark eyes smile up at me and her rich black hair is curled into soft ringlets that look like they've come out of a hairdresser's salon, except they haven't. I don't know how I managed to miss out on Mum's beautiful curls or even her silky raven-black hair. Dad used to say I looked like her when I smiled but I don't see it.

I pull myself up from my bed and stand in front of the mirror. I draw back the black felt and force a smile at my reflection to see if I can uncover those dimples that used to mimic Mum's. I study the image, twisting and turning my head to catch the right angle, to find her. But it doesn't work. The face in the mirror is all Shelley.

Disappointed, I shove the mirror back in place and return to my book. I read the inscription for the thousandth time, still able to extract from it the small thrill it gave me that very first time.

To my darling Shelley,
  May this story of strength, love and hope inspire you like it did me when I was a girl.
  Always, your loving Mum.

She put two kisses and two hugs after her name and, underneath, in that perfect script, the date: 11 June, 1979. My tenth birthday.

I think long and hard about turning the page, taking a minute to consider the idea of the next page and whether I'm ready to see it. Breathing slowly, I take the thin paper between my fingers. One. Two. Three . . .

A harsh knock at the door startles me and I stop. I think I'm relieved. I look at the time: 1.45. It'll be Josh wanting to leave. 'Come in,' I croak.

Dad is standing there, his jaw set firm and hard.

I slam the book shut and push it under my doona, burying the evidence of my weakness. But not before Dad sees it. A flicker of something unidentifiable flashes in his eyes, and then it's gone. 'Josh is waiting.'

I lift my chin, preparing for battle. 'Tell him to go without me.'

'Go with your friend to the game.'

I shake my head, take a deep breath and force my gaze to meet his. Defiant.

'Now.' His eyes are two shiny stones.

I shake my head again. 'I'm not going,' I manage through gritted teeth. 'I'll tell Josh.' I get up, the strength returning to my legs with a rush, and push past Dad on my way to find Josh.

I feel his hand before I realise what's happening. He grabs my arm and pulls me towards him. 'You *are* going, and you're going now.' Anger is cut deep into the lines on his face. The heat of his fury radiates across the small space between us. 'Someone has to represent the family. You've made a promise – *I've* made a promise . . . Do the right thing for us all.'

'The family! *What* family?' My heart is in my throat. Blood pounds in my head – outrage and fury and that overwhelming feeling of loss. 'We haven't been a family since –'

'Stop!' he yells, a kind of terror in his eyes. I haven't seen that look for two years, and it shook me then too.

My chest heaves. My face burns. Panic rises in my chest. I twist out of his grip and push him away. 'You can't stop me!' I yell as he reaches for me again. This time his grip is so fierce that I can feel a bruise forming. 'If Mum was here, she'd understand!' I'm screaming now. I'm not even making sense, but I don't care. I haven't let loose like this since the funeral, since those first days – the beginning of the end. Not since Dad told me we were drawing a line. 'And Angus.'

Dad flinches.

'You act like they don't exist and you made me act like it too! You did this to us! *You* did!' I shout in his face, even as I know that I did it too. 'You.'

Dad's hand shoots out so fast I don't even see it, but some deep-seated instinct drives my hands to cover my face.

'No!'

I hear a smash, and tear my hands away to see my photo frame in pieces on the ground. Dad is clutching his hand, in obvious pain. We both stare at the broken glass – now in two pieces, almost perfect halves. One for each of the ones we've lost.

I fall back, away.

We stare at each other in horror at what he's done – and at what I've said. What we've become. Neither of us able to speak. There are no words, anyway, that can fill the void between us. I don't hear Josh enter the room.

'Shelley?' Josh asks, confusion and shock lining his features. 'Mr Brown?' He faces my father, but Dad can't take his eyes off the photo on the floor.

Dad slowly lifts his head to look at me. 'I would never hit you,' he says, but I'm not sure even he believes it. I stare at the photo again and barely hear him mumble an apology as he leaves.

Josh is beside me now, his hand on my hand, his warm eyes searching mine for an explanation. I can't speak, or move. All I know is Dad has left my room, left *me*, and I've never felt more completely alone in my life.

'You okay?'

I shake my head, no. Then nod, yes. Because I am and I'm not. I reach down to pick up the photo frame, careful not to cut myself on the broken glass. One shard is on the carpet beside the photo; the other still lodged in the frame, cutting a clean line through Mum's shoulder and . . .

'I miss them too,' Josh whispers.

. . . *Angus*. I finish the thought the same way it started – silently, letting the shape of his name sit there, taking a long minute to feel its edges, see its size.

Angus.

I realise then that I don't want Josh to say his name out loud. I can't face the sound of it from his lips. Not when I have refused to say it myself all this time. I want Josh to leave. I shake my head. 'No, please don't.'

And he stops. Of course he stops. He hates it just as much as I do. Josh steps forward to help me stand.

I push him away. 'I'm fine,' I tell him, touching my arm where my dad held me, feeling the heat from his grip. 'You'd better hurry, or you'll be late for your game.'

Josh hesitates, his eyes scanning my face.

'I'm okay. Really.'

'Come with me,' he says finally, still hovering over me like I might fall over.

'I can't. Not today.' I straighten to face him, eye to eye.

He nods but doesn't leave.

I twist my lips into something near to a smile. 'You can't let the Raiders down, Josh. They need you. I'll come to your hundred-and-fiftieth. There's no way I'd miss it.'

'Promise?'

I nod. 'Promise.'

Josh turns to leave, but stops at the door. 'I know it's not true,' he says, his hand twisting around the door knob. 'Your dad does too, you know.'

I laugh hollowly.

'But, Shell . . .?'

'What?' I ask guardedly. I don't want to hear. I don't want to know.

He takes a deep breath, like it's the hardest thing he's had to say, and frowns. 'I mean . . . what do you *think* it looks like?' he asks finally.

'To who?' I say flatly.

'To everyone? To your dad? The players?' His voice drops to barely above a whisper. 'To Edwards.'

I shake my head, exhausted. 'We're just friends.'

There's a long pause before Josh speaks again. 'Yeah. That's what you said.' And then he walks out, closing the door behind him. But the words hang in the room long after he leaves.

Pain spreads through my whole body. I can no longer fight the tears I've tried to hide these past two years. I don't even want to. So I let them run open and free down my face, the relief barely registering on my dull and damaged heart.

After a while, when the tears have dried and my legs are numb from standing still for so long, I retrieve *My Brilliant Career* from under the doona, set its heavy shape on my lap and slowly, deliberately, turn the pages. Through the first, the second, pausing briefly before I flip the third.

My fingers shake. I shut my eyes, open them, then shut them again. My hand is steadier now. I take the thin paper between my fingers and slowly open my eyes as I turn the page – and see it all. On the page, and in my head, travelling to that place and that time, even though my heart rages against it. Between the pages of this story is a photograph taken *that* day. That horrible day, only hours before everything went so terribly wrong. The photo should be an ordinary family snap – a happy, joyous birthday celebration. Nothing special or unusual, except for the time it was taken and what happened next. Extraordinary and unusual *after* the fact. I look at my family, all the pieces still intact, my world still whole, and remember the power of being a part of something else. The whole of my world stares back at me with the kind of abandon that Dad and I will never know again. I count them, one by one: My father. My mother. Me.

And Angus. My twin brother.

CHAPTER 19

THE INTERCHANGE

I've gotten used to the tension. The last few days have been made up almost entirely of broken conversations about lunchboxes, dirty laundry and bus schedules. At home, I've spent every chance I can in my bedroom, working on my Mighty Falcons scrapbook. But the details and the facts just don't have the urgency they once had. And with Mossy done for the year, there's a big gap where there's been nothing to add. But I keep working on it, hoping the shine will come back, hoping Mick's stats will help him do what he needs to do. In the meantime, Dad's been taking longer walks, sometimes disappearing after dark, which is a whole new weirdness, even for him. I don't ask him where he goes, and in turn, he doesn't ask me.

Josh hasn't called. But that's no surprise, given how he feels about Mick and Fernlee Park.

I've been hanging around training every day after school – even on Mondays, when the only people there are players who need to see the physio or who work at the club during the day. I'm not supposed to go there anymore but Dad relented on the matches. Maybe the idea of silent weekends is too much for him. Anyway, I gave it a couple of days before telling him I'm training for the athletics team after school. I pack my runners and P.E. uniform, sometimes going for a run before training starts just to cover my tracks, and so far he's swallowed it whole. Sometimes I really do go to the morning athletics training sessions so it doesn't feel like a total lie.

I should be relieved that he believes me, except I'm not. It's too easy. I'm not even trying. *He's* not even trying.

And that breaks my heart.

I've barely seen Mick these past two weeks. He's always rushing to the physio or disappearing into team meetings. I tell myself I don't mind, he needs to get his knee right. That's all that matters. So I'm surprised when he calls me into the gym before training today. No one else is around, which is odd for a Thursday. But it feels so good to have him talk to me again that for a minute I worry that I won't have anything to say.

'Don't you ever have homework?' Mick asks me as he drop kicks the ball straight at me.

I mark it cleanly and line up to return it. 'I do it before I get here.' I send a pearler down the guts of the gym, the perfect spiral. I don't tell him that I wagged the last two periods of school today. I haven't finished my History essay on the Falcons and didn't want to get in trouble for not handing it in.

'You've been practising,' he says. I blush furiously. I have been practising and I know I've improved, but I wasn't expecting him to notice.

'Handball it back,' I say to change the subject, 'or you'll hurt your other knee.' His left knee is still taped up but it's got good movement now and there's talk he'll be back next week. Just in time for the finals.

'You sound like my wife,' he laughs.

Silence settles and it doesn't feel natural or right. We just stare at each other like there's nowhere to escape. 'Well, she's right,' I blurt, hating how stupid I sound.

He handballs it back and it feels like she's here, standing between us.

I can't breathe. 'I'd better go,' I say, sending a wonky pass towards him, and head out of the gym before he can stop me.

For the first time since I started coming to Fernlee Park, I miss the start of training. I lose myself inside Coles for a while, then run into Tara in the car park, just as I'm debating whether to go home. I don't want to. But I'm not sure I can face Mick either.

'Red said you were at the club before.'

'Yeah. I had to pick up some stuff at Coles,' I lie.

Tara looks at me weirdly, but doesn't argue.

'You hungry?' I ask quickly. I really could do with some food.

Tara shrugs, and we head over to Greasy Joe's. Tara is taking ages to decide what she wants so I tell her I'll wait outside. As soon as the door shuts behind me, the Lovely Ladies show up. They must have gone home to change out of their school uniforms because each one looks like she's spent hours fluffing her hair and painting on make-up.

'Hey.' I smile at them, hoping this will be the extent of our conversation. Ever since the social club I've been feeling more awkward than usual when they talk to me. They hardly looked at me before, but now their eyes seem to eat me up, measuring me in ways I don't fully understand, then dismissing me before I can work out what they were looking for in the first place. I know the only reason they talk to me is because Mick and I are friends. I also know they don't like Tara. But how either of these facts shapes what they think of me is a mystery. 'You going to the social club?' I ask, filling the awkward silence.

'Hasn't opened yet,' Kimberly replies. 'Wait here for a bit?' she says to the others, who nod.

I rack my brain for something to say.

'Big night at the club after the North Yarra game,' Renee says, smirking.

'Yeah. It was fun,' I lie.

'Went on all night,' she adds.

'Good party, hey?' I ask, not sure I want to know. Red told me that after we left all three girls went to a party with some of the younger players. I think about what might happen at that party and about what Red said at the social club. I know Tara and Red think these girls sleep around. But how could they know, *really*? I mean, maybe the Lovely Ladies don't do that at all. Or maybe Kimberly does, and Renee, but not Lisa. She's smart and friendly – she wouldn't want anyone talking about her like that.

'Huge,' says Renee, looking to her friends for agreement.

But Lisa just shrugs. 'It was okay.'

Renee shakes her head. 'That's not what you said about Blackie the next day.'

'I didn't say anything,' Lisa says quietly.

I don't want to look at Lisa, but my silence is too obvious. I force a smile and focus on Renee and Kimberly.

'Jonesy was more than okay,' says Renee, elbowing Kimberly and laughing, trying to get a better response from her. But Kimberly doesn't answer; she just watches me, the hint of a smile on her lips.

I want to know what happened. Or I think I do. I know what it sounds like, what Renee wants me to think. But is that the truth? And if it is, why would they want everyone to know? People say things that aren't true all the time, so maybe that's what this is. We live lies, keep secrets, hide the truth. I'm living proof of that.

'Eddie's wife is pretty,' Kimberly says, studying the ends of her crimped hair as though she's talking to all of us, when we all know she's talking to me.

'For a wife,' Renee adds, laughing.

'Yeah,' I croak, turning away before they can see the tears that sting my eyes. I struggle to think of a way to end this. 'Where the hell is Tara?' I complain too sharply in the quiet night. 'She's taking forever.'

For a long second they stare at me uncertainly, then Lisa laughs. 'They're shockers in there. You wouldn't want to be dying of hunger.'

And even though it's obvious Lisa is trying to rescue me, Renee and Kimberly, incredibly, let it slide. I decide right then that I don't care what anyone says about them – they're fine by me. They start chatting about something that happened at school – a teacher whose skirt was caught in her undies after a visit to the toilet. Lisa does a theatrical imitation, while Renee and Kimberly giggle until their faces turn red. They look so different caught up in each other like this, laughter turning these women into girls. They are so utterly complete and confident together. Oblivious to anyone but each other. Like they belong wherever they are. I decide that they're not just from another world than mine, but a whole other universe.

I watch uncomfortably, offering a nervous chuckle. But soon I'm laughing too, for real this time, and it feels great.

We calm down, the giggles fading naturally when Tara finally appears and hands me a chunky lamb souvlaki. She gives us all a weird look, and an awkward silence falls.

'Hey,' she manages, a forced smile on her lips. 'They called your number.'

'Thanks,' I say, and we all look at each other.

'We should head,' Kimberly says, Renee agreeing with a quick nod.

'See you later,' I say.

'Yeah – Saturday probably. Oh, and don't worry about Mick,' Lisa says, her hand briefly touching my wrist. 'I'm sure he'll be fine.'

'They're saying he could be right for Saturday, but we'll know more soon,' I answer. I love that I know this stuff before they do. Even before the newspapers sometimes.

Renee frowns. 'Weren't you at the club before?'

'A while ago.' I look at my watch; it's been more than an hour since I left.

Lisa cocks her head, confused. 'You didn't stay for training?'

'No,' I say, panic rising in my chest. 'I had to . . .' I struggle to remember what I told Tara. 'Um, do stuff. What happened?'

Lisa's eyebrows shoot up in surprise. 'Eddie broke down . . . in the warm-up.'

'What? How? Is he okay?' My words run together, the questions losing all meaning. How have we been talking all this time without them mentioning this?

Renee blinks. 'Last I heard they took him to hospital.'

I want to shake them, to make them tell me what they mean. But I control the shrill edge in my voice and clear my throat, determined to stay calm. Or at least *sound* calm. 'But he was fine.'

Renee shrugs. 'I saw Jim-Bob at the station. He said they snuck him out the back in an ambulance.'

In an *ambulance*? 'But I just saw him! What did Jim-Bob say?'

Lisa smiles gently. 'I don't know exactly – just that they were warming up. He never made it out onto the oval.'

'Are you sure?' Mick was still inside when I left. I swing around wildly, checking their faces for any hint that they're messing with me.

Tara frowns at me. 'It's probably just his knee again.'

I stare at her in disbelief. '*Just* his knee! It's almost finals – he can't be injured *now*.' My voice cracks in my rising panic, but I'm too worried to be embarrassed.

'Geez, calm down,' Tara says.

'He'll be okay,' Lisa offers, her expression caught between compassion and confusion. She thinks I'm over-reacting. They all do. 'O'Reilly's doing well. Better for stability not to upset the team.'

I think I might throw up. This is *Mick*, not just anyone. 'Where did they take him?' I croak.

'How would we know?' Kimberly shrugs easily, her lacquered frizzed-up fringe not moving a millimetre, care of at least half a can of mousse. 'Let's go. It's freezing.' She walks off with Renee, who follows, the usual two steps behind.

Lisa hesitates. 'I don't know anything else but I'm sure he'll be fine,' she offers.

I manage a weak smile. 'Thanks.' The souvlaki is falling apart in my hands, the juice running down my wrist and under my sleeve.

'I'll see you later,' Lisa says, sending me another quick smile before rushing off to catch up with her friends.

Tara and I watch them head down Leafy Crescent towards the social club, their thin blouses and strappy heels ridiculous in the damp, wintry night – the giggling girls they were earlier vanishing in a cloud of Impulse and hair gel. I suddenly wish Kimberly and Renee would trip as they negotiate the broken footpath. Lisa turns back halfway between us and her friends and offers me a reassuring wave, reminding me why I've always separated her from the other two in my head.

I throw the souvlaki in the bin by the 'No Standing' sign. My hands, dripping with grease, stink of garlic and lamb juice. The smell turns my stomach; I just want to crumple on the footpath and curl up into a ball.

Tara hands me a serviette.

I wipe my hands and bin the rubbish. 'I have to go,' I tell Tara, half worried it's too late to use the usual excuses on Dad, and half not caring if he sees through it anyway. I don't have the energy to keep it up. That's the thing about secrets and lies – they might start off small and manageable but they grow bigger and heavier, no matter what you do. Even if you don't add to them, even if it's just a single decision to remain silent or to try to forget, time makes it worse anyway, so before you realise what's happening, it's so big and unspeakable that it's no longer in your control. You're not shaping it anymore – it's shaping you.

Me. It's shaping *me*. I'm a lie. A great big, enormous lie. My whole life. Dad's whole life. It's not even a choice anymore. It's just who we are.

I stand in the living room doorway, wishing I'd made it home in time to see the news. *M*A*S*H* is on TV, and Dad's asleep in his chair. I missed the last bus from the station and spent the long, dark walk home wondering how I can find out the latest on Mick.

The reek of garlic and onion from my stained shirt is overwhelming, and my bones ache with the cold.

I want to change out of my uniform and wash my hands in warm soapy water, as much to get the feeling back in my fingers from the icy air as to rid myself of the smell. But I have to find out about Mick first. I can't think about anything until I know. I have to wake Dad. I have to ask him what happened.

I scan his face in the flickering grey of the TV. He looks as relaxed as I've seen him, despite the almost ghostly shade his skin has taken on in the filtered light. The lines around his eyes have almost disappeared and the usually firm etch of his mouth is slack. Unworried.

I reach out to touch his shoulder, but my hand stops before I make contact. I can't wake him. I can't hate him, either. I want to – it would make life so much easier if I could just shut it off, like I've shut off much of my life from before. But it's not in me. I'm not strong enough or good enough or . . . angry enough. I withdraw my hand, tucking it under my blazer where it can do no harm. I don't want to rob him of this momentary calm. I wish I could be the one who gives him peace and not the one always driving it away.

Even as I wish this, I know it's too late. My mind wanders to that day, before the accident – my thirteenth birthday, *our* thirteenth birthday – and I remember my words. I remember the look on Dad's face, on Mrs McGuire's, how Dad followed me when he should have stayed behind. How loud those words sounded in the months after, even though he never once repeated them to me.

It's okay though. He doesn't need to; I hear them all the time – in his eyes, every time he looks at me. In my eyes, every time I look at myself.

I dump my bag, heavy with the homework I haven't done yet, and head to the bathroom, where I strip off my clothes and wash my face, neck and arms. But the smell is still there. I turn on the taps and let the hot water warm up, filling the bathroom with steam. I step into the shower and feel the powerful stream squeeze the tension out of me. I'll check the late news after my shower. I remember then that I have to finish my History essay on the Falcons before I go to school tomorrow. My heart sinks at the prospect of how much I have to do, and then I quietly thank God – or whoever's in charge of things on this earth – that I chose a subject I can get lost in, because it's going to be a long and sleepless night.

CHAPTER 20

OUT OF POSITION

I hurry to the train station and stop at the newsstand. Despite staying up for the late news, there was no mention of Mick on the Channel Seven broadcast. I buy a copy of *The Sun* but, incredibly, all I can find is a tiny paragraph two pages in from the back. There's not a lot of detail, but they say it was his knee again and that he was taken to a hospital in the city.

The train ride to school passes in a blur. It's only when Tara asks me if I'm going to training that I realise how distracted I've been all day. I honestly have no idea what we did in any of my classes.

'Not sure,' I answer quickly. There's a training session on Friday because we're playing Sydney on Sunday.

'When do you think you might know?' Tara asks dryly. The bell has finished ringing and we're packing up our stuff to go, so she has a point. I focus on the thick, four-ring binder that won't fit in my bag while I buy myself a minute to get my story straight. I don't know when I decided to lie but it comes out suddenly and naturally, like I'd planned it all along. 'Dad's arced up about it and wants me to cut back.' It's not really a lie. Dad *has* arced up. It's just that I'm not going home either. But I can't tell Tara this; I know what she'll say. I can feel her eyes boring a hole through the back of my head as I frown and huff at the ridiculous binder. I sigh, giving up. I look over at Tara, who's shaking her head in disgust. 'What?'

'You think you're special, don't you?' she says. 'You think you matter to him.'

'What are you talking about?' I turn away, the heat of her gaze cutting through me. I suddenly don't know what to do with my hands. I let go of the binder and try to make room around it. Yes, I know exactly what Tara is talking about – and why – because I *know* I matter to him, but that doesn't make it any less infuriating. I blush, because that's what I do exactly when I don't want to, and any chance I have of maintaining the look of innocence goes sailing out the window.

'He's married, you know. With *kids!*' Her eyes glitter like shiny gems. She looks like she might cry, which only confuses me, and suddenly my innocence is back where it should be – front and centre.

'So? It's not like that.' It's not. It's really not.

'You have no idea what you're doing,' she says. 'No idea at all.' Tara pushes past me with the kind of disgust she saves for Angels supporters – or worse, umpires.

'What?' I say, to the empty space left in her wake. '*What*?'

––––––––

Two tram rides and a half-k walk later, I'm hovering by the reception area of the small private hospital on Mary Street, trying to convince the nurse to let me in. After much negotiation she purses her lips, and calls Mick's room. She doesn't tell me what he said, but points me towards the lifts opposite the empty cafeteria, her lips still pressed into that tight line. 'Third floor, Room 312,' she says curtly.

As soon as I see Mick's face I know he's hurting. And it's not just about the knee.

'Hey.'

He smiles. 'You didn't have to come.'

He makes it sound like I'm doing him a favour. As if I *wouldn't* come. The only hard part was waiting for school to finish and getting away from Tara. 'So what's the deal?'

He shrugs and taps his leg, grimacing. 'They don't know. It should have been fine by now but it's not. We have to wait and see.'

I let the words sit in the room while I adjust to this turn of events. I want to say something, to offer reassurance, but I know I'll sound naive. He's in hospital and he's out of the team. Telling him he'll be okay won't cut it. When in doubt, change the subject. 'At least it's warm in here. Like the bloody Antarctic outside.'

'I'll have to take your word for it.'

Mum always said that if the weather's all you have to talk about, it's best to say nothing at all. Saying nothing right now is easier said than done. I drag the visitor's chair over to his bedside and plonk down, buying myself a few moments while I fiddle with my schoolbag, pulling the zip shut before making a show of deciding where I should put it. I push it back towards the wall where the chair was, turning away from Mick in case he sees through my cover. I straighten my skirt, brush the hair from my eyes, then pull it down over them again, and stand up, fixing my face into careful detachment. I sit down again.

Mick raises his eyebrows but doesn't say anything.

'So an ambulance, huh? Seems like a lot of drama for a leg. It's not *The Restless Years*, you know.' I'm doing an excellent job of feigning nonchalance, considering I tossed and turned all night, imagining all kinds of career-ending illnesses. I finished my essay with the telly on in the hope they'd break with some details after the late news. It was after midnight when I slid my essay into its

217

folder, finally done. But I stayed up until the channel had shut down, taking a full five minutes to realise the hissing static wasn't just bad reception. I finally dragged myself to bed at two o'clock, so tired I didn't even touch my scrapbook. 'Not like it's life or death, Mick.'

He smiles but it doesn't touch his eyes. There's more going on that he's not telling me.

'So . . . how long do they think you'll be out?'

He won't look at me now. He can't. 'We'll know more on Monday. I'm sure I'll be fine by then.' The dismissal in his voice takes my breath away. I dip my head, intended as agreement and understanding, but really I'm hiding the tears that sting my eyes. I make myself look up at him again, feeling the distance between us in a single glance. He's so cold now, so distant.

'I finished my History essay,' I say, just realising that I'm genuinely pleased with what I wrote. I was exhausted by the time I'd finished, but I woke up early this morning to check it over and handed it in during third period. Sister Brigid tsked-tsked because it was two days late, but let me off this one time because she liked my idea. She told me her cousin worked at Glenthorn, something to do with sales, and that he could have helped me if I'd asked. That was never going to happen, but it's the first time anyone at St Mary's has done anything really nice for me. The tears that threaten to spill burn hotter behind my eyes just thinking about it.

'Well, I hope you feel better soon,' I say, carefully avoiding Mick's gaze. I bend over to find my bag, stealing the moment to wipe my eyes. I'm a mess and I have no idea why. Or what's happening. I just know I can't let Mick see. I can't let anyone see.

'That was quick.' He smiles, but there's an edge of confusion in his voice.

I laugh. It's a brittle, uneven sound. It doesn't sound real. 'Yeah, well, I'm meant to go to athletics training tonight. There's time to make the last half if I leave now.' Another lie that comes out too easily. I pull my bag over my shoulder, straighten my skirt and yank my hair out from under the bag strap, then offer him the coolest smile I can manage. 'Hope you feel better soon,' I say, and turn to go. 'And say hi to your wife,' I add.

The room falls silent as though the sound has been turned off.

'Shelley?' Mick's voice is rough, quiet.

I stop and turn to face him, bracing for . . . I don't know what.

Not this. Not what I see. His face is gaunt, his eyes are unsteady. His hand shakes . . . He's frightened. He's not hiding it from me now and my heart breaks as I absorb this. I don't know if it's because he's hurting so much or because he trusts me to see it, but I know I'd walk over broken bottles for Mick Edwards right now. I'd do anything he asked.

219

'I have to come back,' he says. His voice catches and he clears his throat. 'I can't lose the season. It's my last shot.'

I nod. 'You'll be back for the big one. I know it.'

'Not at full forward.' His voice barely above a whisper.

'No, probably not,' I say before I can stop myself. Brendan O'Reilly has done well in Mick's absence – just like Lisa said he would – but that's not what Mick needs to hear right now. Sometimes I wish my football brain would shut up and let the other Shelley – the one here, standing before Mick Edwards, wishing she could heal ruined knees and soothe broken hearts – take over.

But all I've got – all we both have – is this Shelley. The stupid, naive, blushing one.

Mick's hand clenches and unclenches the blanket across his legs. He turns away to stare at the wall. I reach out to touch his hand. To hold it, like Mum used to when I was trying to be strong, back when the only thing I had to cry about was Gabriella Johnston not talking to me in Year 2, or the sting of gravel rash on my palms from my latest bike stack. I curl my fingers under his hand, feeling their warmth spread through me like something alive. I have no idea what to say. I want to tell him it's not all about full forward. That all he needs to do is get back into the side in time for the grand final, and that he can do that – that he *will* do that. As long as we win, he'll be okay. None of this will matter then. I want to say all this

220

to ease his mind, but after an impossible silence his whole face shifts and the moment has passed.

He forces a grim smile and shakes it off – my hand, the moment. He'd looked like he was about to say something more, but whatever it was doesn't come out. 'Thanks for coming,' he says instead. Polite again, and distant.

I can't help feeling like I've just lost something, though I have no idea what. I don't answer or even nod. It's too late. The tears squeeze out of my eyes, and I grab my bag and run out of his room. I know he'll think I'm immature and pathetic, but I can't watch this special thing fall apart too. I can't see properly as I run towards the tram, blinded by tears and humiliation. I just know that I need to get back to that place where he trusts me and needs me.

The place that feels like home.

CHAPTER 21

THE TALENT SCOUT

It's a surprisingly warm day for August, despite the breeze. The sun feels good on my arms and face. I stand in a splash of sunlight, using a paperbark gum tree as a windbreak while I watch the Raiders warm up. It's like time has stood still. I let myself pretend that no one I love is dead, that Tara doesn't hate me and that Mick didn't look at me in the hospital like I was some stupid little kid. Like I was nobody special.

Today, while the sun beats down, bright and cheerful, all that exists is the excitement of the game I love and the chance to see Josh make his dream come true. The Raiders are in the grand final, which is pretty exciting on its own. But bigger than this, it's Josh's hundred-and-fiftieth game – a club record he's managed sooner than anyone else because he played an extra year in the under 8s, as well as all those fill-in games in the higher grades. Everyone is pumped – parents have brought streamers and flags, while some of the younger kids from the junior grades have made a banner for the team to run through. The Raiders haven't won a premiership for years – not since we were little – and there's a rumour that some professional scouts are going to show up.

I didn't want to come; I'd thought long and hard about making up some excuse to stay home. The idea of seeing all those faces that I've grown up with, so familiar yet strange now, is bad enough. I haven't heard from Josh at all since that day at our house. A part of me is angry and hurt, though it's not like I've called him either. I have no idea what he's thinking. I just know that all the stuff that used to be easy between us is suddenly not easy at all. And that makes me sad.

So that's why I'm here – to get back to what we know: simple, uncomplicated football.

Seeing everyone hasn't been as terrible as I'd dreaded. I thought they'd act really weird about it, or weirder than they have. But I'm still here, still standing. And really, if I'm totally honest, I couldn't let Josh down. If the rumour about the scouts is true, Josh is why they're coming. Cameron Evans is slick and exciting when he's on song, but Josh is the real star of the team. Since the accident, anyway – since Angus.

I brush away that thought. For today, at least, I'm determined to direct all my energy into hoping Josh pulls a blinder.

As though reading my mind, Josh jogs over, still in his tracksuit and runners.

There's only fifteen minutes before the first bounce. I glance over at the club rooms, just in case Jacko is looking for him. 'Careful. They'll start without you,' I joke.

It's working. The footy, as always, does its magic. The way the grass smells, the chirp of the umpire's whistle signalling the final warning, the joking commentary on the sidelines while parents await the first bounce – all of it melds together into something so familiar to me, so good and warm and real, that I can almost pretend that none of the other stuff happened. I half expect to see Mum waving from the car or Angus haranguing me for stealing his lucky pair of Raiders socks, as though nothing has changed in two years and we're still a whole family.

Almost.

Josh smiles and looks away, kicking the dirt with his left foot. 'Just finishing the warm-up. Got a few minutes.'

'Avoid that wing,' I tell him, pointing to the far side where there's a huge patch of soft ground in the middle. He's got the prettiest blind turn I've seen on anyone this side of the pros, but he can't do it in the wet. Even at his cockiest, Josh knows this.

He's still avoiding my eyes, and it's making me nervous. He keeps stealing glimpses towards the clubhouse, but I can't make out what he's looking at. Or *for*. It's as if he's on guard, like he's waiting for something bad to happen.

I wonder briefly if his mum told him she'd asked me to come. She's here, of course. But having faced her that night, seeing her today doesn't worry me so much. She saw all there is to see.

'What's going on?' I ask finally.

'Nothing. Not really. I need a big one, today. You know, in case the scouts show up.'

'You'll be fine,' I tell him, meaning every word. Everyone says he's playing his best footy this year. 'Just keep off that wing and you'll be fine. Don't get fancy. It's the small stuff – the hard stuff – they look for.'

Josh's familiar grin is fighting through his discomfort. I can see it – the battle between his nerves and his cockiness.

'Hey. What are you doing here?' A high voice from out of nowhere slices through the tension, startling us both. I turn to see Ginnie Perkins standing behind me. She's smiling at Josh but talking to me. And she's not happy, despite the light tone of her question.

The feeling is mutual.

'I live here,' I reply before I have a chance to stop myself. I sound like a moron. 'I mean, I've been here for years.' I don't say that my whole family belonged here once, all of us entrenched in the side, from the bottom up. I don't say that I used to play for the Raiders either because, *technically*, I didn't. Besides, she'll only turn it into something embarrassing or pathetic. It sounds tragic, now that I think about it. Playing football for a junior team without ever being allowed to play in a real game is as pathetic as you can get.

'Josh is my friend,' I add, not even tempted to mention Angus, even though my supposed *friend* is standing there in total silence, gawking at Ginnie Perkins like she's Elle Macpherson. I stare hotly at Josh, wondering what the hell he's thinking.

'Hey,' he manages eventually, not helping my cause one tiny bit.

'Hey, Josh. Good luck today,' Ginnie says with disturbing familiarity, each word slicing through me. She's smiling at Josh like she knows him well, like he's someone special to her.

'Thanks.' He grins like an idiot. It's the voice that bothers me again – *his* voice this time. He knows her, and I think he *likes* her. They're sharing something right now, this moment, while I'm standing between them like some kid who's tagging along at her big brother's school dance.

'You know each other?' I ask, stating the bleeding obvious.

Josh tears his gaze from Ginnie long enough to send me a strange, almost pitying apology. 'We hang out at the station sometimes.'

They hang out together? How can I not know this! Why didn't he mention it?

226

And then I remember that morning I saw Josh at the station. He never told me why he was there, just that he'd had a half day of school. But I saw Ginnie, didn't I? With her clique heading towards him before my train left.

But none of this is the point. It doesn't matter when or how. The point – the sharp and painful point – is that he likes her. And she likes him.

'Cool,' I say, my heart a dead thing in my chest. 'See you after the game,' I manage, encompassing them both in an awkward wave that looks more like the universal signal for drowning, which is kind of right. And even though I'm mortified and hurting, I don't blush. Thank God, for once, I don't blush.

———

The first half of the game is excruciating. Josh does all right but not great, and while the Raiders are only nine points down, it's due more to the Mountvalley Comets' inaccuracy in front of goal than any real success on Glenvalley's part. The wet is slowing the game right down, forcing the players to rely on short kicks and handballs in a dull kick-for-kick arm wrestle that lacks skill and purpose. They need to break it up.

I manage to avoid Ginnie for the first half, although it takes enormous effort not to follow her into the clubhouse at half-time. I'd normally listen to Jacko's address – I love to try to out-think his game plan or identify changes in strategy. The thinking part of football is almost as much fun as the game itself, which makes my distance at half-time all the more frustrating. I watch Ginnie disappear into the dressing rooms as though she has a right to be there, even though she wouldn't know a drop kick from a torpedo and probably doesn't care if we win.

As I wander along the boundary, fighting the urge to check up on the team, they start yelling out at me, their deliberately light voices determined to pretend that nothing has changed since the old days. It seems that whatever Brown-family amnesty the Raiders' parents had silently agreed upon has been lifted by half-time.

'We should send you in to sort them out,' Cam Evans' father says to me, while everyone laughs with way too much enthusiasm.

'How's that right foot now, Shelley?' Richard Leckie's brother shouts. My very last kick for the Raiders was a shanker down the back line that ended in a free kick to the other side, along with the title for the lightning tournament. It was not my finest hour, and although it happened more than two years ago, apparently they haven't forgotten.

The thing is, they're ribbing me because that's what they do – what *we* do. Basically, they're trying to be nice. While I know that and even appreciate it, somehow I end up feeling more alone than ever. No one wants to ask about Dad or acknowledge the fact that I'm here alone when this was always *our* thing. Our family thing. And now Ginnie's here poisoning this place for me too. The whole point of putting Glenvalley High behind me was to move on, to draw that line so that the world Before did not clash with the world After. I've been trying to claw them apart with my fingernails these past months and now they've come crashing together.

I realise I don't want to be here another minute, and it hits me with a force that takes my breath away. I hunch over and clutch my stomach. Then, remembering my athletics training, I straighten up, put my hands on my head and breathe in, out, in, out, slowing the rhythm of my lungs, opening my airways wide. My head is spinning, blood rushes to my temples. In. Out. In. Out.

It works – the breathing, the momentary stillness. I'm okay.

'Shelley?'

I feel a hand on my back and turn to face Josh's dad, who is watching me closely. 'You all right?' Mr McGuire is in his Raiders' tracksuit, a dirty white towel around his neck, looking very official as the team's trainer. He's club president this year, too, and spends most of the match sprinting around the ground, tending to the boys. He stepped up when Dad stopped coming. I think he thought it was temporary, but has been stuck in both roles ever since.

I nod. I want to fill the awkward silence but nothing comes. A twisted smile is the best I can do.

Mr McGuire nods, understanding. 'We've missed you,' he says simply.

I could cry. I want to cry. I think about where I can go to escape this weight, the pressure against my ribcage, the hard stone in my throat. I can't go home. I can't stay here. I shake my head and look away.

Josh's dad places an arm around me. The warmth of this gesture and the familiarity of it is almost more than I can bear. 'Josh is so glad you came, Shell. It means a lot to him. To us. Thank you.'

Mr McGuire is not the most expressive of men but he has a way of making you feel good even when what he has to say is bad. He's the Human Resources Manager at Big Ten Hardware, in charge of hundreds of staff across the whole of Victoria. Mum used to joke that if he ever had to tell anyone they were sacked, there's a good chance they'd walk away feeling like they'd won the lottery. I don't quite feel like I've won anything, but the pressure on my chest is easing. 'I'm not sure I can stay,' I manage, ashamed at my weakness.

Mr McGuire nods. 'You do what you need to do, Shell. It's enough that you came at all.'

The weight has lifted now; I'm free to go. I smile gratefully at Mr McGuire. 'Tell Josh he needs to step up. It's now or never.'

'I'll do that,' he says. 'Tell your dad I said hi.' He looks at me carefully then and I realise he knows more about what's happening at home than I thought. I don't know why I didn't expect Josh to tell his parents. I'm mad at him for saying anything but also oddly relieved that

230

Mr McGuire spoke up. It feels a little less like I'm doing this alone.

'I will.'

Mr McGuire jogs off to the Raiders' bench, stopping to chat with some parents along the way.

I'm about to leave when I see the Comets' dressing-room door open and the team runnning back onto the field. A moment later, the Raiders trudge out. Josh is in the middle of the pack, a grim look on his face. He sees me and cocks his head. He knows I always listen to the half-time address. I shrug and look away, knowing that the moment has passed. I can't leave Josh's game, no matter how hard it is to stay.

I watch Josh jog by, determined to push the picture of his moronic gawking at Ginnie Perkins out of my head. 'Come on, Josh!' I urge. 'Go long – go hard.'

Josh nods in acknowledgement. It's his signal – our signal – that the fun's now over. This is when the real work begins.

I'll stick it out for Josh. It's his moment and it's right that I'm here for him. I scan the crowd for unfamiliar faces. I'm not sure what a professional scout looks like, but the arrival of two men in a shiny new Ford Fairlane has my attention. They're wearing normal weekend gear and don't look any different to the bulk of parents around the boundary, but the fact that there are two of them and that they came at half-time instead of the beginning of the match tells me they're not here to watch their kids.

I wave at Josh as he gathers the practice ball. Everyone is waiting for the umpires to come out so there are a few minutes before the match will resume. Josh looks up and I nod in the direction of the two new arrivals. He studies the men who are now walking around the boundary, talking quietly between themselves, their eyes scanning the players and the field.

Josh bounces the ball, spins it in his hand then bounces it again. When he smiles at me I know he'll blitz. And he does – he turns on a pearler. The Raiders win by fifteen points, stealing the game in time-on when they kick three in five minutes, forcing our hearts into our throats. When the siren sounds, the players roar, their bodies exhausted and spent but their spirits soaring. The scouts disappear soon after that, their Ford Fairlane nosing its way out of the crowded car park before the inevitable post-match traffic jam.

Mrs McGuire comes out from the canteen and waves at me before she rushes up to hug Josh in front of the entire team. He looks mortified but doesn't pull away. He couldn't if he wanted to. His teammates are crushing him to her, to each other, the bruising joy forcing her to laughingly extract herself. Mr McGuire and Jacko slap each other on the back, stepping back then pushing forward, part of it one moment, not wanting to intrude the next, but unable to hold back in the end.

Ginnie hovers just outside the circle, a bemused smile on her face; her perfect blonde hair and white, white

232

teeth stark against the mud and grime of the sweaty boys who are dancing around like mad things. I see Josh escape from the middle. He looks up, scans the crowd, searching for . . . Ginnie. My heart sinks. He sees her, grins and waves, before he's once again lost in the chaos of his teammates' delight. I try to ignore the ache in my chest, the bitter taste in my mouth. The way he looked at her, looked *for* her . . .

I press back my shoulders and pull my coat more tightly around me, determined not to let it get to me. This is Josh's day. It's not about me, or even Ginnie. I haven't been here for him when I should have been. But I'm here today, and I can do this much.

I take a deep breath and smile, joining in the celebrations with the other Raiders fans, moving away if any of them stay with me for too long, or seem likely to ask me how I am. The umpires call the teams together and declare Josh Best on Ground. He accepts the award humbly, his grin hidden beneath the layers of dirt and his awareness of the losing team slumped on the ground, struggling to even look up.

Finally, Josh's eyes find mine. We look at each other for a long time; the only gaze I have been able to meet all day. And I know that Josh is the only one who feels a lot of what I'm feeling and understands what it took for me to come here. I smile, genuinely happy for him, knowing Angus would have been too. But Josh's smile is a little lopsided now, like he's trying to rein it in. Maybe he's thinking about Angus too, missing him just like I am. I want to tell him not to. I want to tell him to celebrate wildly, *freely*, without worrying about who isn't here. But the words stick in my throat. The best I can do is offer the brightest, shiniest smile I can muster. I guess it works because Josh grins back wider, clearer. Truer.

Feeling a lightness I don't expect, I wink at him exactly how he'd wink at me – a huge cheeky, carefree gesture, so unlike me that I feel quite dizzy with my boldness. Josh throws back his head and laughs, and I feel such a rush of delight that it takes all my energy not to grab him in an enormous hug, just like his mum did. But not like his mum, either.

As the players jog around the muddy oval, arms entwined, ribbing and mocking each other, whooping and hollering in bursts as though feeling their joy in waves, I hang back and smile. This is what it feels like. In a couple of weeks, I'll get to experience this with Mick and the boys, multiplied by a hundred.

I leave the McGuires at the ground despite their offer of a lift, determined to walk alone. I want to take my time. Let the beginnings of excitement grow in my gut in preparation for my moment next Saturday. I want to fan it and build on it, knowing I'll need to draw on that warmth to get through the long and difficult silence that waits for me at home.

ONE DAY IN
SEPTEMBER

CHAPTER 22

QUALIFYING

Mick got out of hospital the week after I visited but he's been so busy with physio at the pool and at the clinic that I haven't seen much of him. It's not like he's mad with me or anything. It's just that when he sees me now, the way he smiles, polite and cool . . . I could be any of the other kids. I know it's because he's worried about the grand final. I know it'll go back to normal soon. I just have to be patient.

I check the members' area before the game to see if he's there, squinting through the cyclone fence that separates us. You have to have a special pass to get into this section. Geoff from training sometimes gives me a spare one, but as the end of the season gets closer, all those extra privileges are harder to come by. It's the first quarter in the early game, so there's not a huge crowd yet. I spot Mick's head poking out above the other players who fill the stand. They're all dressed neatly, the injured and dropped players watching the reserves match like they care, when you can see they just wish they were playing. Some of the players' wives and girlfriends have come, and in the back row I recognise the Lovely Ladies slotted between some under 19s, more interested in each other and the player they're next to than the game. Mick's alone, though. I've never seen his wife at a match. She hasn't once come to watch him play with the Falcons. I wonder if she used to in WA.

When Mick sees me he gets out of his seat and threads his way past the injured list, his smile wide and open. 'I'll be fit, Shell,' he says, pulling me towards him in a rough hug the moment he comes through the gates. 'You were right.'

I almost step back, so surprised by the feel of his warm, strong arms around me, and I can't seem to make eye contact. I'd told myself that it was just a matter of time before we'd be back to normal, but maybe I didn't believe it after all. He releases me from the hug too quickly, but grabs the iron railing of the stairwell, his hand just touching mine. I study the iron railing where I'm clinging on for dear life. I don't move even the tiniest bit, just in case it scares him off. We're partly blocking the entrance to the members' area but there's no way I'm going anywhere. If Mick's hand is going to leave mine, he'll be the one to move it.

I look up finally, braving a glimpse of his beaming face, trusting myself not to weep with relief that we're okay; that we are untouchable, like I've believed all along.

He nods at the oval, his hand falling away naturally. 'Good start, hey?'

We're up by twenty points – a nice lead for the first quarter. I drag my gaze away from him, half convinced he won't be there when I look back. And nod.

'I feel good, Shell,' he says, and it's like all the tension inside me has gone.

I grin back stupidly. 'You look it,' I say. I'm too delighted by his hug to feel any shame.

He winks and tells me he'll see me later, returning to his spot among the other injured hopefuls. I float back to the cheersquad, finding my way to Tara. 'We're gonna win,' I announce to Tara the second I get back to my seat.

'Don't!' she warns too late, screwing up her face. I've broken one of her rules. But Tara is either too nervous to make a big deal out of it or she's getting used to me, because she lets me prattle on about Mick and his knee long after she'd usually tell me to shut up.

When Danny and Bear climb across the seats to slum it with us in the fourth row for the rest of the reserves match, I could swear Tara's face is going to crack with all the grinning.

––––––––––

When the final siren blows, the Falcons are a hard-fought eight points up against the Warriors. I hug Tara so hard I think she'll suffocate.

'We did it! We're in the grand final!' Tara gushes, jumping in place in the tiny space between rows. I try not to overreact to Tara's joy, but she looks so different, her face flushed and glowing, her eyes wide with excitement . . . I want to tell her how good she looks, how *happy*. But we're quickly caught up in the joy of the crowd around us, and I'm pretty sure that would have been a mistake anyway.

Bear and Danny are high-fiving and David is down the front with his arms up, getting us all ready to start a chant. This is the game we needed to win – not just because it gives us an advantage to have a week's rest before the grand final, or even because beating the Warriors in the semi is a huge confidence boost, but because it gives Mick time to get his knee right. Premierships are what it's all about, no matter what players say about taking it one week at a time. There's only one game that matters. Only one day that counts. And the Falcons have secured a place in that game, proving my faith in a single, delicious afternoon.

As the rest of the cheersquad launches into the 'Are we good? Are we good?' chant, I notice Mick move out to congratulate his teammates on the ground, his clean Glenthorn polo shirt looking out of place against the filthy woollen jumpers of the other players. He looks so happy, so pumped. We all are. My heart soars at the idea of what comes next. I study the faces around me, all rapt and lost in the sheer joy of success. Nothing else matters right now – for them, for Tara, for me. We're in this together, and all the crap that's dragged us down is forgotten. I knew we'd make it. Just like I told her. I remind her of this as we hug awkwardly one more time, the result in and untouchable. 'Told you so,' I grin.

'Yeah,' she smiles, a funny, twisted smile that I don't quite understand. 'You did.'

'You coming?' I ask, as the crowd begins the slow exit from the chaotic Valley Park car park. It's the worst of all the grounds. You take your life in your hands just finding the bus stop.

We catch the shuttle back to Glenvalley Station, losing the rest of the cheersquad in our hurry to make the replay. From there we walk through the meandering parkland to my house, rehashing the game, the highlights, the lowlights all the way there. We argue about who's going to play where, who's going to miss out and what Stretch will say before the match. She doesn't mention Mick and I don't rabbit on about him playing full forward.

When we arrive at my house, I don't feel the uncertainty I'd expected about Tara being here. I'd originally struggled to picture Tara and my dad under the same roof and, although I don't remember making a decision either way, I think I subconsciously kept putting it off, thinking that the longer I kept my home life apart from St Mary's, the better my chances at holding it all together. But Tara is so different from the St Mary's girls, so cut off and remote that, really, it wouldn't have made any difference if she'd been here before.

Dad offers a nod and a 'hi' when we come in from the game, the TV already tuned in for the replay.

'Hi, Mr Brown,' Tara says politely. 'Great game today. You should have come.'

I don't know what I expected from her when she met Dad, but it wasn't this. The surliness and grim courtesy have vanished. She seems just like a normal kid.

'Next time, maybe,' Dad says.

'What's for dinner?' I ask, changing the subject.

'Pizza,' Dad says, smiling at Tara. 'Do you like pizza, Tara?'

'Yes, Mr Brown. I love it!'

I can't ignore the pang in my chest. Pizza is still very much a novelty in our house. Fish and chips on a Friday is fine, not flash or special. But pizza is a birthday thing. A special event. But here he is, offering it up on a normal Saturday night just because I have a friend over. Maybe this matters to him more than he'd let on.

'Awesome!' I cry, way too enthusiastically. He's trying. Maybe it's just because of Tara, but I don't care. I'll take what I can get right now.

Tara shoots me a weird look but lets it pass.

'Why don't you two get sorted before dinner?' Dad suggests.

I show Tara to my room. 'I'll set up your bed,' I say, before heading into the spare room. Dad stores our stretcher bed under the single bed against the wall. I hesitate only briefly when I lift up the bedspread, the familiar tiger-emblazoned bedsheets still in place as if Angus is about to slip in between them at any moment. It's the only thing Dad hasn't changed. I don't know when we stopped calling it Angus's room.

I drag the stretcher to my room and open the squeaky hinges while Tara studies my Glenthorn memorabilia approvingly. I unfold the bed and give Tara a clean set of sheets. I return to the spare room to straighten the bedspread when I see an old metal Arnotts biscuit tin protruding from under the bed. The stretcher must have knocked it free on the way out.

I remember the tin. Mum used to keep her sewing odds and ends in it. Buttons and thread, scraps of cloth and other bits and pieces that needed to be altered or mended. I stand there for a long minute deciding what to do. It's hidden there, out of the way. Deliberately out of the way. I glance over my shoulder. I can hear Dad moving around in the kitchen and Tara is still busy in the next room. I shut the door behind me and sit on the bed, setting the tin on my lap. The edge is rusted, the corners rough from age or dampness. The lid doesn't loosen easily, but after a solid tug and a neatly split fingernail, I manage to pry it loose.

Inside are photographs – lots of them, of all different shapes and sizes, from different eras and with different textures and shapes. Small square black-and-white photos with a shiny surface and grainy faces; larger, round-cornered colour ones; and older sepia-style photographs that look like they were taken by a professional. Most of them, though, are more recent. The only pictures I knew we still had that were taken before the accident are the ones in my room – the one of the whole family on the beach and the photos in my mum's book. I never knew what Dad did with these ones, and I never asked. Part of me couldn't bear to see them anyway. The other part of me couldn't bear to see Dad look at them.

But here they are.

I take a handful out and splay them on the bed beside me. The first ones are black-and-white images of Mum and Dad when they were young – all those bold 1950s clothes – the hats, the sunglasses, the tiny belted waists and tight busty sweaters. There are also photos from their wedding day – Mum looking stunning in ivory silk, her rich, luscious hair curling gently around her olive skin. She looks like a movie star. Dad stands tall and straight, barrel chest thrust out, chin high and strong, so proud and in love. He's staring adoringly at my mum as though there is nothing else in the world more beautiful – more important – than this woman standing beside him. It's intimate, the way he's looking at her. No one else exists.

I wonder what that would feel like. To have someone look at you like that.

The photos change as the years shift from the 50s and 60s to more recent ones. Some of them seem to have been taken on the same day as my photo – Angus and me at the beach, Mum and me on a cliff's edge looking out over London Bridge in Sorrento, Dad with his back to the ocean, the waves lapping at his feet. There's also a shot of Mum, Angus and me outside Luna Park. It's just the three of us – Dad is taking the photo – and yet we look so complete, as though the four of us are so strong and united that he doesn't even have to be there to be included. We're smiling at him, grinning hugely, having just come out of the Giggle Palace or the Big Dipper – I can't remember which.

That's a *family*.

The door to the spare room opens and I startle, knocking the tin off my lap. I stoop to cover up the evidence, worried it's Dad, already seeing the horror on

245

his face in my mind's eye, at the same time hating that I feel like a trespasser in my own house.

Tara stands in the doorway, curious but reluctant to come in. 'What are you doing?' She sees the photos and instinctively bends down to try to help me clear them off the floor.

I push her hand away. 'I'll do it,' I say brusquely, glancing over her shoulder to make sure Dad doesn't come in.

She sees this and rises to shut the door. Then she bobs down on the floor again and, ignoring my objections, helps me return the photos to their box.

I seal it shut, feeling something heavy and dark shift inside me. I don't want to put the tin back, hidden away, out of sight. I have no idea if Dad would check or if he even remembers the tin's here under the bed. I want to slowly and indulgently sift through them all, one by one, to recapture this part of my life – our life – that has been stolen away. That I gave away. I drew a line too. And here it is in front of me.

'Let's go. Dad'll want to get the pizza.' I tuck the tin under my arm, pulling my jacket loose to cover it.

'Okay,' she says simply, eyeing the Arnotts tin. I know she wants to ask about it, about the photos, but our silent agreement on all things private prevents her from speaking, and for this I'm extremely grateful.

In my room, I slip the tin under a pile of clothes in my

246

wardrobe, placing some shoes and clothes in front of it so that, even if Dad happened to open my wardrobe, he'd have to actually go hunting in order to find it. Dad is a lot of things – difficult, distant, uncomfortable, intensely private – but he's not a snoop.

I shut my bedroom door behind us, ignoring Tara's ever-watchful gaze, and we go to find Dad to ask him if it's time for pizza.

———

Tara is extremely polite to Dad throughout our whole meal of Hawaiian and Capricciosa pizza. *Excessively* polite. I wonder if she's doing this for me, or because the St Mary's girl inside her still beats on despite her nearly pathological hatred for teachers and their rules.

The other thing I notice is that, although Tara and Dad have so much in common – their love of football, their shyness, their quiet certainty about anything that doesn't involve feelings and emotion – you wouldn't know it to look at them right now. Instead, their difficult silences become more obvious. Mum always said that the things you really dislike in other people are often the things you dislike about yourself. Maybe that's what's happening here.

After dinner we watch the replay with Dad, then tell him we want to watch the end of *Hey, Hey it's Saturday* in my room. By the time we're ready for bed, the show's almost over. I turn down the volume so that it's barely audible, then we both slide into our beds.

'Your dad's really nice,' Tara says suddenly.

'Um, yeah. He's okay.' I wonder if she's being sarcastic, and wait to see if there's more to come.

'Your mum was really pretty.'

I'm used to the lump that forms in my throat at the mere mention of Mum, but hearing Tara say something so unexpected and generous strikes me almost physically. 'Yeah,' I manage to whisper, after a while. I'm not sure she hears me because there's another long silence.

'What was it like?' she says, as the *Hey, Hey* credits roll up the screen.

'What was what like?' I stretch my feet out under the sheets, pressing them against the 'hospital corners' Dad insists I use when I make my bed, trying to loosen the edges.

'When she died,' Tara says simply.

The words sit in the room, loud and sharp in the quiet dark. They have a shape and form, a presence that towers over us both, given life by Tara. There's no answer to that question. 'I don't like to think about it,' I say, and it's possibly the truest thing I've said in two years.

'Who was the kid?' Her voice is so soft and gentle I almost answer. Almost confess.

'What?' I punch my pillow, pretending to shape it for my head, even though it was perfectly fine the way it was.

248

I make a show of pressing it flat, smoothing it out, twisting my shoulders one way then the other, to get comfortable. There's no way I'll sleep tonight.

'In the photos . . . there's a kid. Ten or eleven maybe? With you and your mum.'

I think of the photo and the broken frame in my drawer. I've bought a new frame to replace it, but every time I look at the shattered glass and those sunny, smiling faces in the photo, it just reminds me of my argument with Dad. And I chicken out.

'He looks the same age as you,' she continues, those eagle eyes narrow and fast on me.

I could say it now. Just come right out and say that he's my brother, Angus. My twin. The piece of me that's missing. The other half of Dad's and my grief. The person everyone around here is looking for and half expecting to see whenever we walk into a room. Even now, after two years, not really believing he's gone. I could tell her that I miss him every day, just like I miss Mum. That I still expect him to bang on my door in the morning to make me kick the footy, or race him to the car, or wrestle with him over what we're watching on TV.

My lips move to shape the words. I train my mind on saying it just right – the right order, the right tone – dreading the pity I'll see when I do, but knowing there's really no way out of this unless . . . I lie. 'Nobody,' I say, the words coming from outside my body, in complete betrayal of what's in my heart. 'Just a family friend. Don't even know him anymore.'

'He's cute. Is that Josh – the guy you talk about?' she asks, watching me closely. I stare at the TV, my focus so concentrated that my eyes sting. I do something that's half a shake of the head and half a nod, hoping it's vague enough to mean nothing but clear enough to shut her up. 'What time do you have to go tomorrow?' I ask, the edge in my voice carrying all the warning Tara needs. I cross the room and turn off the TV, slipping back into bed without looking at her.

There's a quiet sigh. I can hear her shrug, if such a thing can be heard. 'Any time. There's no rush.'

CHAPTER 23

A WEEK'S REST

The following week drags on impossibly. Even the next weekend's footy does nothing to ease the suspense. Glenthorn isn't playing, so I have to contend with watching the Warriors win the preliminary final. At least we now have an opponent for the big day, so that's settled something.

By the time the Monday of grand final week arrives, it feels like we've been caught in a time warp. All I want is for Saturday to come, but instead I'm faced with a whole new week of suffering the excruciating experience of St Mary's girls chatting about their dream man, their dream car, their dream date . . . Even their dream clothes. I watch them in awe. It's like they don't know what's happening outside. Don't they feel it? All the excitement and tension? Sometimes I think I live in a different world to them, one that only Josh and Tara – and Mick – operate in. Except, thanks to Josh and Ginnie, these two worlds have collided and there's nothing I can do to wind it back. If there was any doubt of this, Ginnie Perkins kills it before recess in a double period of English Lit.

Ginnie's been on holidays with her family – Surfers or Noosa, or somewhere sunny and expensive, her rich tan glowing against the rest of the girls' wintry pale skin. It's her first day back, and I haven't missed her one tiny bit. The minute I sit down, Ginnie saunters over to my desk and smirks, reminding me why I hate her so much.

'I know a secret,' she hisses, not pausing for even a second before taking her seat across the room in a perfect hit-and-run.

I have no idea what she's talking about but the possibilities are both endless and terrible. As I open my exercise book to review our homework, dread settles heavily in the pit of my stomach. Literature with Miss Whitecross is a complicated experience for me normally. I love the books we're studying – *The Great Gatsby*, *Memoirs of a Survivor*, *A Difficult Young Man* ... I don't even hate *The Watcher on the Cast-Iron Balcony*, even though everyone else does. But for reasons either alphabetical or coincidental – the process of selection seems to change but the result doesn't – I generally end up in Ginnie's group, which always ends in everyone doing what Ginnie wants to do the way Ginnie wants to do it. This is frustrating enough without the secret Ginnie thinks she knows hanging over me.

As usual, Miss Whitecross divides us into groups and, as usual, I end up with Ginnie. But also, unusually, Tara is in my group too. Just seeing these two sitting so close to each other bothers me, knowing their history, and how Tara feels about her. Throw in Ginnie's triumphant declaration earlier, and I know the day can't end well.

We're supposed to choose one of the books we've studied, and answer a related question. I'm leaning towards discussing the symbolism of the green light in *The Great Gatsby*, but I know Ginnie will want to do *A Difficult Young Man* because she's already pronounced Dominic Langton a 'major spunk'.

True to form, Ginnie chooses Martin Boyd, and the question is a tricky one – to explore the idea of 'geographical schizophrenia' in *A Difficult Young Man*. But at least Ginnie's read the novel, which I'm not sure applies to the alternatives. And Tara hasn't read any of them. The process will be the same anyway: Ginnie will take over the discussion, I'll pick up the crumbs and the rest of the group will defer to Ginnie with puppy-like adoration (Caroline Hall, Debbie Assange and Justine Deckland) or disinterest (Anna Barnes and probably Tara, because she doesn't care enough to argue).

We work through the exercise, jot down points of discussion and Ginnie typically appoints herself as public speaker, which is fine by me. Ginnie does her bit, as do all the other group representatives, and the class is going more smoothly than I'd expected. I begin to relax, just in time for the usual wind-down of the double period. Miss Whitecross likes to take this time to explore some of the issues that came up. It's my favourite part of the class because everyone gets involved, and even Ginnie steps down from her pedestal long enough to seem like a normal person.

A Difficult Young Man has captured everyone's interest. Dominic does sound like a spunk, I have to admit, and the Langton family are about as strange and fascinating as any I've encountered, so I don't mind when the conversation moves towards this novel, directed largely by Ginnie.

'I think Boyd's obsession with his family, his brother in particular, is kind of weird,' Ginnie says, and looks at me.

I'm not sure if she's asking me a question or addressing the class, but everyone seems to think I'm supposed to respond, so I do. 'There's some autobiography there, isn't there?' I say. 'I guess when your family is as complex as theirs – and as big – it makes sense that a writer would want to write about it.'

Ginnie's smirk is horrible. I mean, truly horrible. 'You'd know all about that, Shelley. Wouldn't you?'

I study the novel, staring at the pages in the hope that I can avoid answering, but the class is eyeing me curiously when I look up. 'I don't know what you mean,' I croak, barely above a whisper. But I know exactly what she means.

'I want you to focus on the story, Ginnie,' Miss Whitecross interjects, sensing that something is going on. 'What about this family makes it so worthy of a novel?'

Ginnie turns to Miss Whitecross, that smile now magically innocent. Ironically, it seems more hateful than the knowing smirk. 'It's just that with Shelley having a twin brother, she's in a unique position to explain the brother relationship.' Ginnie is beaming now – the heat of it radiates across the room, zeroing in on me.

'What?' Tara turns to me, ignoring the entire class, as though we're the only people in the room.

Words die in my throat.

'I don't see how –' Miss Whitecross tries again.

'*What* twin brother?' Tara shouts.

'Girls!' Miss Whitecross rises from her desk, but no one's listening to her or paying any attention at all. They're all looking at me and Ginnie. And Tara.

'She hasn't told you?' Ginnie says to Tara, those great big eyes as innocent as a shark's. She turns to me then. 'I'm sorry,' she says, smiling, 'I didn't know.'

I want to kill her. In that sudden, hateful moment, I want to kill her.

'Everyone, quieten down. I'm surprised at you, Ginnie.' Miss Whitecross looks at Ginnie, the tiny frameless glasses perched on the tip of her nose, killing any hope she'll be taken seriously.

Ginnie does a reasonable impression of looking ashamed. 'I didn't mean to, Miss,' she says, offering another apologetic smile.

'No,' I say, my voice sounding cold and hard and foreign. 'I don't have a brother. Not anymore. My brother, Angus, is dead,' I finish, turning to Ginnie with a level gaze.

Miss Whitecross gasps. 'I'm sorry, Shelley. There's no excuse for this. Ginnie, apologise right now!'

But I'm not listening. I have eyes only for Ginnie Perkins. I watch my words settle on her, keeping my gaze as steady as a surgeon's knife. She flinches, as though she's been struck. She didn't think I'd answer. Or maybe she didn't know. For a tiny moment I'm enormous beside her. She meant to hurt me and wanted my reaction. I decide right then that I won't give her the satisfaction. I tilt my head, stand as tall as my stature will let me and wait for her to speak. If this moment is going to end, she'll have to end it.

'I'm sorry,' Ginnie says flatly.

I study her, my gaze unflinching. Her eyes flicker, her mouth twitches. She pulls at her hair, twisting it nervously. I think she means it. Or regrets it, anyway. I nod, just barely.

Tara is watching us both, hurt and anger plainly written on her face. 'What is she talking about?' she asks, her voice barely above a whisper.

'Shelley?' Miss Whitecross is beside me now.

'I'm fine,' I say.

Miss Whitecross looks uncertainly about the room. 'Move on, everyone. That's quite enough.'

The bell rings, and after a shocked silence, the class gradually returns to its usual end-of-period chaos.

Miss Whitecross checks with me again, then nods and returns to her desk to gather her things.

I look at Tara, who hasn't moved. She's waiting for . . . I don't know what. An apology maybe? An admission? She isn't going to let it go. I slowly close my books and pile them carefully on top of my desk, stalling for time. I can feel Tara's impatience grow, her eyes burning into me with the kind of fury I imagine exists in Hell.

The thing is, I don't care. Or I care less that Tara knows and more that Ginnie does, because the only way she would have found out is through Josh. My Josh. And I can't believe he'd betray me – *us* – me, Dad, Mum, and most of all, Angus – like that.

'He died with my mum,' I say to Tara. 'Two years ago,' I add, as though the distance between this moment and that might offer an explanation or soften the fact. I should know – I *do* know – that time has done nothing at all.

Tara is staring at me like she's never seen me before. Like I'm a total stranger. One she doesn't like very much. 'Was that him . . . in the photos?'

I nod.

Tara clutches her textbook to her chest as though preparing to fend off attack. 'You lied about your brother?' she whispers, not even angry now. She is . . . *bereft*. There it is again, that word.

'We don't talk about it.'

'You told Ginnie Perkins.' Tara spits out her name.

'I didn't tell her,' I say, but can't bring myself to say out loud what I know happened. It's hard enough to realise your oldest and best friend has betrayed you, without having to declare it to the world.

Tara shakes her head. 'Whatever.' And then she turns her back on me, taking the fragile thing we'd built between us with her.

I have no one to blame but myself.

And Josh.

CHAPTER 24

THE COUNTDOWN

I wonder how other people do it. When it feels like the world is falling apart and nothing makes sense anymore, what helps them get through the day? This happens to everyone at some point, surely, so they have to do *something* to cope. They must have some kind of hobby or distraction. Something that allows them to forget and just breathe – in, out, in, out – even when all they want to do is curl up on the floor and sleep forever.

When I was little, I used to write stories. I'd take out some paper, think about something good or nice and build a world around it. Like fairytales but without the evil witch or the cunning fox. They were probably pretty boring when I think about it. No suspense, no danger, no drama, because only good things happened. It was always about the same little girl who played and laughed in her tiny world, went on amazing adventures, and lived happily ever after. But then one day the stories turned monstrous, their gentle outlines and flimsy plots twisted and contorted into the shape of a mangled car, with a whole family trapped inside – or the part of it that made it a family. One dad and one half of a set of twins were left outside, staring through the shattered windows, watching their lives disintegrate before them.

Football was all I had. Football always lured me in, held me close, a reliable barrier against the emptiness and silence outside. Play first, watch later. The Raiders then, Fernlee Park now. There was never a decision, just the delicious feeling of falling in love and forgetting myself – *losing* myself – in a whole other place. I get the same feeling when I see the Mayblooms Stand towering over Fernlee Park now that I did whenever I began a new story.

And that's how I know, no matter how Dad looks at me, or who Josh tells my secrets to, or whether Tara trusts me again, there is no way they'll bring me down. Not now. Not when the Falcons are in the grand final and the world is caught up in this magical week. It feels like everyone is talking about the game.

So rather than let the things I've lost hurt me, I escape to Fernlee Park every chance I can, to hang out with Mick or talk to the trainers, the other players, even the rest of the cheersquad – anyone and anything that wears the brown-and-gold and loves the way the Sherrin bounces. The way it feels in your hands. How it stands out red and shiny against a wintry sky.

When the club is quiet and no one's around, I wander along Fernlee Park Road to soak up the atmosphere. Glenthorn is positively buzzing. Shopfronts are decorated with brown and gold crepe paper, cars drive by with Glenthorn scarves streaming from their windows, and even the streetlights are strung with 'Go Falcons!' flags. It's as though the whole of Glenthorn – the whole of my world right now – is on our side. On *my* side. They want what I want, just like I want it, and it's all I can do to keep my feet on the ground and continue walking, when really, it feels like I could fly.

By the time Thursday night training comes around I'm ready to burst. The whole club has come alive. Tara and I have avoided each other since Miss Whitecross's class. But I can't let it follow us to Fernlee Park. There's a huge crowd at training when I get there – more than a thousand people, maybe two thousand. They're even making you pay to get in, like it's an actual game and not just a token training run. I don't have to pay because kids get in free if they're wearing Glenthorn colours. The bloke on the gate is one of the club volunteers, and he recognises me as soon as I approach the entrance.

'Hey, Shelley,' he says, smiling.

'Big one tonight,' I say, nodding at the enormous crowd, unable to shake the feeling that none of this can be real. I feel possessive of this place as I watch the masses take up residence in all my favourite spots. I want to stand where I usually stand and do the things I usually do – the routine calms me, particularly now as the mounting pressure of Saturday squeezes me tight. And yet, seeing all these people wanting to share my world for a night warms me too. Being one among the thousands watching the team train is almost as exciting as watching a real game. My heart throbs wildly in my chest. I can't imagine what the players are feeling if this is how *I* feel.

I buy a barbecued sausage from beneath the Mayblooms Stand and make my way towards the cheersquad, which has taken up residence over by the past players' room. The cinder block building is barely visible beneath the swathes of brown and gold crepe and the piles of Glenthorn floggers amassed in front of it.

The cheersquad has nothing to do tonight except watch training because we finished making the banner a week ago. David got the main picture designed by an artist. It really looks amazing. There's a painting on one side the size of a house, with a picture of Killer Compton and a Falcon devouring a Warrior. It's huge. On the other side is the beginning of 'The Man from Snowy River', which continues on banners that will be hung all the way around the ground, the words changed to support the Mighty Falcons. It's a big secret that only a handful of cheersquadders know.

I hear the cheersquad all the way across the stand. Despite the noise of the crowd and the occasional roar of the Yarra Valley train, Bono's voice pierces through the din, blasting out of Danny's boom box propped on a table outside the past players' room. I stand at the boundary, between Red and Bear, and wait for the players to run out onto the ground. Tara is further along the fence, her eyes trained on the oval.

I head over to take my place beside her. We both stare at the oval, waiting for a reason to be distracted. The silence presses down on us both, tense and impenetrable.

If I don't break it, no one will. 'Hey,' I say, quietly.

After the tiniest pause, Tara nods. 'Hi.'

That she is even talking to me – a single word, yes, but it's a start – gives me the courage I need to push forward. 'I'm so nervous I can't sleep.'

Tara nods her agreement, and I feel more confident that I can make it right.

'I'm sorry about . . . everything.'

Tara shrugs. 'Whatever.'

I turn to face her, finally, but she doesn't move. 'I didn't tell Ginnie,' I say. 'She found out.'

'I don't care about her.'

'No, I know.'

Tara faces me squarely now, her hands shoved into the pocket of her duffle coat, the shiny faces of the Glenthorn players smiling up at me from her badges, mocking the tension between us. 'Just don't lie to me. Okay?'

I think about all the lies she tells her mother, the silences that save her from telling me anything about her own life. And then I remember her mum's vacant gaze, her workaholic dad and his pretty assistant, and her absent sisters. 'Okay,' I say. 'No more lies.'

The noise level picks up a couple of notches as some of the team officials emerge from the gym. Expectation ripples across the crowd. Someone has begun to pound the metallic signs that string the boundary – a slow, rhythmic beat a lot like the one that follows Dennis Lillee when he bowls. It picks up speed, gets louder and more urgent, crescendoing into a thunderous roar.

My heart feels like it might explode, and I want to share it with Tara. I want to marvel out loud at this beautiful thing. 'I love how this feels,' I gush, knowing I haven't said it quite right, but hoping Tara is with me enough to understand anyway.

She doesn't answer. The silence between us is engulfed in the roar of the expectant crowd. 'I hope Eddie makes it,' Tara says eventually, her voice so low I have to lean in to hear her properly. 'I hope he can play.'

'Thanks,' I say, because I know she says this for me, not for Mick or Glenthorn. Wanting Mick to play is one thing but saying it out loud, right to my face – that's a peace offering. 'We'll know in a couple of hours.'

Tara sucks in air. 'Yeah.'

We both look over as the clacking of cleats on the race interrupts us. The players jog onto the track, wearing their best training jumpers, all clean and neat with their numbers in place. Usually they wear all kinds of stuff to training, mostly brown and gold, but never their playing numbers.

I peer into the playing group, trying to pick out individuals. Killer Compton and Chris Jury lead the way, while Brendan O'Reilly brings up the rear. I can't see Mick. He must be getting treatment inside.

Lights flood the oval suddenly and I notice news cameras from two different networks sticking out from the crowded boundary fence. I recognise the team from *World of Sport* and the new bloke at Channel 10 who looks about sixteen. They're all hovering around the cameras, clapping their hands and stamping their shiny shoes to keep the blood flowing. Puffs of steam escape their mouths, lit briefly by the powerful camera lights.

A lump forms in my throat, hard as a knuckle.

'They won't stay out long,' Tara says.

'No?'

'It's for the cameras, the crowd. This isn't real training. They'll just play around a bit, get the crowd pumped, then go inside for the team meeting.'

The knuckle-sized lump has grown to a grapefruit.

'Where's Mick?' I say out loud, half to myself, half to Tara.

'There,' she says. I look at the ground to see Mick jog out past the cameras towards the players, now in a huddle in the centre of the ground. The players break apart and Mick heads towards the goals. Stretch shouts something to Mick, who looks over, nods, then heads deeper into the pocket.

The music is blaring even louder than before. I watch the players kick the ball back and forth, the thud of the ball against the ground or their chests, their feet stomping, divots of mud spraying, the heat of their bodies glowing under the floodlights. 'New Years Day' kicks in, and almost immediately, Gavin Black breaks from position and heads towards the boundary, right up to me.

I wait, breathless. 'Hey, Blackie,' I say, as coolly as I can manage. The entire crowd is watching us now – or that's what it feels like.

'Turn up the music, Shelley. I love this song! Turn it up!' He's grinning like a mad thing, steam rising from his body.

'Okay,' I reply, wishing I could come up with something funny or smart to say. He's so handsome up close. 'I'll tell them.'

He runs off, knowing that whatever he asks, I'll deliver.

I sprint over to Danny and Bear outside the past players' room. 'Blackie said to turn it up,' I say.

Danny smiles, like I've just told him he's been selected in the side, and immediately turns the volume up so loud that the Warriors could probably hear it at Flemington Hill. We start singing at the top of our voices, and although he's on the other side of the ground by now, I swear I can hear Blackie joining in.

As soon as the song ends, Danny switches the tape. The opening notes of the club song blast across Fernlee Park, grabbing everyone's attention, and soon the entire crowd is singing along, drowning out the boom box completely. Unable to resist, Tara comes over and joins in beside Danny. Midway through the chorus, he swings his arm loosely around her, and although she's grinning widely, she also looks a tiny bit terrified. Which seems perfectly reasonable to me.

The players are back in the huddle as we sing. Danny has multiple copies of the song on the same tape, so it starts again only seconds after it finishes. I watch Stretch addressing the players, slowly, seriously, probably trying to calm their nerves. I imagine his patient drawl, the careful, unflinching way he delivers his address. I wish I could listen.

As the club song breaks through the night for the third time, some of the players turn around to face their adoring fans. The younger players look confused and almost scared. The older guys don't even look up at the crowd, but slowly make their way back towards the race, heads down, their minds already targeting Saturday.

I see Mick standing alone in the pocket, a pile of footballs by his feet. He's not going in yet. He's not ready. I can't see his face but I can guess what he's thinking. He'll know in a matter of minutes whether he's going to be selected to play, whether he's going to be given a chance to save the career he so desperately needs.

He kicks a batch of balls deep and long into the crowd, most of them sailing comfortably through the goalposts, a couple shaving the edge, all of them met with a roar by the remaining audience. He looks so tall and mighty as he stands alone in the middle of the oval, the whole world as we know it centred around him. He kicks a massive torpedo into the crowd, so deep this time that it lands in the stand above the press box. The crowd explodes when a little kid triumphantly holds the ball above his head as he's lifted onto his dad's shoulders.

'What's he doing?' Tara asks, as though reading my mind. 'How long is he going to stand there – doing nothing?'

I know what he's doing. He's stalling. He's holding out as long as he can because the moment he crosses the gym threshold and enters the players' room, the answer to his question will be as irreversible – as *absolute* – as life and death. As simple as win or lose. Win, he lines up at full forward on Saturday. Lose, Brendan O'Reilly keeps his place and Mick is forced to watch the game from the sidelines; all that work in rehab and therapy wasted, his hopes for a new contract fading to nothing.

Finally, Mick straightens up and jogs slowly towards the players' race.

I lean over the boundary fence, alongside the hundreds of other kids doing exactly the same thing. I want to tell him he's not alone, that I know Stretch is going to select him and that Saturday will be the greatest day of his life.

'Good luck, Eddie!' Voices around me join together to wish him well.

'You're a champion, mate!'

'Knock 'em dead!'

What can I say that hasn't already been said? 'Good luck, Mick,' I say, my voice drowned out by the sea of voices.

With his head down and his eyes on the ground, Mick jogs up the race and, without a word to anyone, disappears into the gym.

———————

Tara and I shiver in the rain, huddled under her Falcons umbrella. It's barely big enough to shelter her, let alone both of us. Large drops of rainwater gather on the spiky ends before dripping down my right shoulder. I shake them off as they land, but can't do much about the wet patch forming on my blazer.

'I'm going home,' Tara says after yet another car drives out of the Fernlee Park car park without a single player having emerged. It's dark and getting darker. The rain drives steadily and doesn't look like it's going to let up any time soon. 'You coming?'

'No, I'll wait,' I say lightly. I was hoping we'd have heard the team announcement by now – I don't want to be alone, just in case . . . I don't let my head finish that thought.

'See you tomorrow.' Tara shrugs, taking her bag and the only shelter I have with her. In hindsight, her small inadequate umbrella is looking pretty good as it disappears into the dark street. I press myself against the damp bricks, hiding beneath the narrow eaves, but the water drips relentlessly and there's nowhere left to hide. It feels like the whole club has emptied out and I'm nervous about being the only one left. *Is it possible,* I wonder, *that the players all went out another way?*

As though hearing my thoughts, the first of the regular senior players emerge. It's two hours later than usual and they look like they've had a long and difficult day. Some of the players nod at me or tell me I should get out of the rain. I've got my schoolbag above my head now and it's doing a reasonable job, but I shudder to think what my maths folder looks like, or the soft-cover copy of *Modern Australian History*.

After another twenty minutes or so, Mick emerges. He looks shocked to see me and glances around the almost-deserted car park as though checking out who else might be there.

'How'd you go?' I say, unable to wait another second. I thought I'd know the instant I saw him, but his expression is unreadable and he seems more confused by my presence than anything else.

'You're soaked,' he says, his voice flat. He steers me and my drenched schoolbag towards his car.

'Shake off a bit first,' he says when I'm about to open the passenger-side door.

I brush the excess water off my bag and blazer, the droplets freezing against my numb fingers. Then I get inside and sink into the warm seat. It feels so good to be inside his Holden that I almost start to cry. There is so much I don't understand right now – things I can't seem to fix or change or even face. The one thing I've held onto – that's kept me sane – is the grand final. And all he's worried about is whether I make his car wet. 'Well?' I say, daring him to say a word about the crack in my voice.

He studies me, and for a second I think he's about to touch me. His hand rests on the headrest behind me, so close to my cheek that if I moved, even the tiniest bit, we'd make contact. 'You're soaked,' he says again, making that clucking sound parents make, before starting the engine and twisting around to make sure the path is clear. He backs the Holden out and steers it through the car park, his eyes focused straight ahead.

We're a block from Stonnington Station before he speaks again. 'Yeah,' he says, as though I've only just asked the question. 'I made it.'

But he's not exhilarated like he should be. Like I am. 'But that's great! That's it! It's all you need,' I gush, relieved.

'Of course it is,' he says quietly.

'What then?' I lean forward, trying to get him to look at me.

'Shelley . . .' he begins. He's using that voice adults use when they think we know what they want to say, like they've said it a hundred times before.

'I don't understand. You're in. We're in. And we're going to win.'

Mick looks at me carefully, turning back to the road too soon for me to work out what he's thinking. Or maybe I'll never work that out. Maybe there's never enough time to look at someone long enough to understand them. 'You must be freezing,' he says again, and I know that's all I'm going to get out of him.

He pulls up to the train station, and I wish it was further away. Whatever is going on, I need to know now. I don't care that it's late and that Dad will know where I've been. I don't care that I'm cold and wet and a long way from home. I just need to know that it's going to be okay. 'Tell me,' I plead in the dark silence.

Mick sighs long and hard. He leans back in his seat, letting his hands fall by the side of the steering wheel. If I move my right hand to rest beside my leg, the backs of our hands would be touching. I look at my hand and his, picturing that moment, knowing it won't happen.

'It's now or never, Shell,' he says quietly, his voice faint and uneven.

'It's the *grand final*. Of course it's now or never.'

'I mean, for me.'

'What do you mean?' I'm shivering again, but I don't think it's from the cold.

He turns to look at me, finally letting me see his face properly, or as properly as I can under the faint glow of the station lamps. 'You should go, it's late.'

It feels like I'm losing something, like it's all disappearing before my eyes. 'You're going to blitz on Saturday, Mick,' I say, my voice strained with the beginnings of panic. 'It'll be a whole new start. Everything good that you want to happen will happen. I know it. I can feel it.' I ignore how empty those words sound, how wrong I've been about this in the past. This is it. It has to be.

Mick chuckles. 'You never give up, do you?'

'No,' I say simply, because I don't. I can't. 'It's all about to happen for you – for us.'

Mick looks at me oddly then and I realise my mistake. 'I mean for the *Falcons*. You're the best full forward in the competition. Everyone knows that. Everyone.' And I lean in towards him and kiss him lightly on the cheek.

Mick stares at me in shock but doesn't pull away. He stays there, his face near mine.

I don't know what's happening. My lungs feel tight and I can barely see. I have no idea what I want him to do next, what I want to happen. Except it feels like he is really seeing me, *all* of me, and I've never felt more important in my whole life.

'Shelley.' He says my name like a caress. He touches my face with his long, strong fingers, holding my chin in their tips. We don't move for a long time.

A train toots in the distance and it startles us both out of the moment.

He sucks in air, his breath ragged. 'You'd better go,' he whispers, before touching his lips to my cheek. Then he sits back, gently pushing me away. But he smiles to soften it, and I know it's okay. 'You'll miss your train.'

I can't speak or object. All I can do is grab my bag and slam the door behind me. I run from the car, through the cold, hard rain, arriving at the platform just in time to see the headlights of my train approach from Yarra Station. I don't look back. I can't stand the idea of hearing him take back what he did. Right now, all I feel is magic and light. Like I'm flying. Like I'm free.

As I step onto the train, my blazer no longer feels damp and uncomfortable, and my feet tread lighter than they ever have. Suddenly I don't care if the whole of St Mary's is onboard, ready to judge and condemn. They can't hurt me. They don't matter.

No one can touch me now.

CHAPTER 25

BEST ON GROUND

Dad doesn't say anything when I walk in and he doesn't argue or complain when he sees how sodden I am. 'Have a shower,' he says, not asking for an explanation. 'You'll freeze like that.'

'Missed the bus. I stayed back to help Tara with her book review,' I say into the silence, his back already turned away, the TV doing an excellent job of providing the distraction we both count on. His eyes are trained on a brief recap of the swimming from the Friendship Games that nobody seems to care about except for Dad. 'She's pretty hopeless at English,' I add lamely.

Dad drags his gaze from the screen and eyes me tiredly. 'Next time, call from the station.'

He knows I'm lying. He knows but doesn't care. 'I will,' I say, telling myself that this will make the whole weekend much easier to get away with.

When I get in the shower, I stand there for so long that my fingers shrivel to prunes. I don't get out until the hot water runs cold.

When I finally get to bed, the sheets warmed by my electric blanket, I feel completely drained of energy. Drained of everything. Despite the confusion of thoughts clouding my mind, I won't have any problems sleeping. One more day of school and then I'll know.

If it's all been worth it.

———————

'We need to get our stuff from the warehouse first,' Tara reminds me, as we head out the school gates, past the six-foot fence. Tara told me it was only three-feet high when she first came to St Mary's, but the nuns were always shooing the St Ignatius boys away from the front gate. She came back to school in Year 8 after the summer holidays to see the fence had been raised to twice its previous height. 'Next it'll be razor wire,' she'd joked. That's probably why Dad was so keen on me coming here.

The party-supplies warehouse is a few blocks from school. We've already bought coloured hairspray and theatre make-up in gold and brown, but we still have to get balloons and crepe paper for the mini floggers. We walk the first block, keen to put distance between school and the weekend, then we break into a jog for the next kilometre. Like everyone, I love Fridays, but the day before the grand final is magic. I start laughing for no reason and Tara joins in. It feels like summer, even though it's barely twenty degrees in the sun.

We buy the last bits and pieces we need for our costumes then catch the tram back to Tara's house. We've almost finished the floggers and have laid out our costumes neatly when her bedroom door opens. A dark-haired, thickly built man stands in the doorway. He looks younger than my dad, although on closer inspection, I realise it's his hair that makes the difference. It isn't grey, while Dad's is. But his eyes have that same crinkled unevenness at the edges, and the five o'clock shadow on his chin is speckled with grey. I wonder if he dyes his hair to keep it that smooth brown colour. It doesn't look real, and doesn't match his whiskers at all.

Tara's face lights up. 'Daddy!' she says, leaping at her father with an animation and excitement I've never seen before. She suddenly looks like a little girl, the worldliness all gone.

'Tara,' he says, without any of his daughter's animation. He nods curtly at me, but doesn't ask my name.

'How long are you back?' Tara asks, her fingers still twisted in her father's. For the moment, I don't exist.

'I'm not. The car's waiting outside. Next week, though. We'll have a special lunch.' It's a kind of apology, one that seems to come easily.

Tara's face does something remarkable then. First, it collapses in despair, which turns into something resembling rage, with a glimmer of grief, and then her features reshape themselves into her usual cool detachment. These shifts happen so abruptly, so intensely, that it's almost comical.

Her hand drops from her father's and dangles awkwardly beside her thigh. I look at her dad and realise he didn't see any of it. He's already halfway out the door, glancing down the corridor or into another room. 'Where's your mother?' he asks, turning back to face his daughter.

'I don't know,' Tara answers, any hint of her earlier joy obliterated. Whatever she's feeling, she doesn't want him to see.

My heart wrenches as I watch her performance and recognise it as something painfully, unbearably *familiar*. We have never been more alike, Tara and me, than at this moment.

'Typical,' he says lightly. But there's a slight sneer on his lips.

Tara flinches, just barely, but doesn't move.

I want to stand between them to protect Tara.

'Tell her I was here, will you?' he says, then manages his first real smile. 'Or don't and see if she notices.'

Tara matches his smile, although hers doesn't have the cruel twist to it that her father's has. 'You'd have to empty the liquor cabinet for that to happen,' Tara says unexpectedly, her voice dry and grating.

Mr Lester looks up sharply as though ready to rebuke his daughter.

She stands there defiant, and yet brittle, too.

A car horn toots outside and the moment passes as he checks his watch. 'I have to go,' he says. 'Are you okay? Do you have money?' He doesn't wait for Tara to answer. He's already pulled out his wallet and is rifling through it, extracting some twenties and fifties and holding them out to her.

For a long second, Tara doesn't move.

He cocks his head, waiting, impatience etched into the line of his mouth. He isn't going to move closer or meet her halfway. I think of Tara's coat and my surprise that her father would sew on all those bits and pieces. The idea is suddenly ridiculous.

Finally, Tara steps forward and takes the money. She doesn't look at him. The delight at his arrival has been replaced with something I can't quite name.

He leans in to kiss her brusquely on the cheek, and I think about Mick's light, easy kiss the night before. They are nothing alike, and yet . . .

'See you next week, honey,' he says, without a trace of emotion, and shuts the door behind him.

Tara returns to our tasks like nothing has happened, laying out our props, straightening our costumes and getting everything ready for our early departure. But where before there was a nervous energy in the activity, now her movements are slow and deliberate. Every action seems to take an enormous effort on her part. And yet she doesn't skip a beat or ask for help. She doesn't even look at me.

There is a long moment of perfect stillness when we hear the front door bang shut, as though time has frozen and no one else exists outside this room, and then Tara steps across to the window beside me. Her dad's car is shiny and silver – sporty, like something a famous footballer would drive. In the passenger seat is a young woman with dead-straight blonde hair and lips so red I can see the swollen shape of them in profile before she turns towards us. She's very pretty and *young*.

I know better than to look at Tara. We both remain fixated on the vision of this handsome couple disappearing in their shiny car. After a difficult silence, Tara steps away from the window, freeing me to do the same. Without once looking up at me, she whispers flatly, 'That's his assistant.'

Neither of us believes her.

Tara returns to our arrangements, continuing to collect her things, her back as straight as a rod, her head stiffly turned away from the door and away from me.

When she tries to close her backpack, bits of flogger and scarf protruding in all their brown-and-gold glory, I notice her hands shaking so hard that she can't manoeuvre the zip. I don't speak as she fumbles with the metal tag – I don't dare. Instead, I reach in to draw the contents of the bag in tighter for her, pulling the tracks together so she can slide the zip shut. The metallic *zing!* of the teeth connecting on their tracks cuts through the silence as clearly and as finally as a slamming door, the teeth gleaming like a brand-new sports car.

CHAPTER .26

ONE DAY IN SEPTEMBER

Tara is already awake when I open my eyes. Her hair is all mussed-up, her face even paler than its usual pasty white, and her eyes have neat, dark circles under them, stark against the strange blue of her irises. I don't have to ask her if she slept well.

'Morning!' I say, forcing a brightness I don't feel.

'Don't even talk about it,' she says.

Okay. 'How about breakfast?' I suggest, ignoring the double-backflip-with-pike my stomach is doing at the idea of food.

'I mean, not at all,' she says, as though I haven't spoken.

'What?'

'You'll jinx us.'

She's talking about the game. I can't mention the game – at all. It's going to be a long day.

'Silence is golden,' Tara adds, without even a hint of laughter.

During the finals, she's taken her superstitions to a whole other level. The rules are simple enough. I am not to mention winning or losing or the opposition team. All conversation is restricted to the ground where we're playing, the plan to get there and the chance of rain. More detailed discussions of the weather are okay but not encouraged, while possible food choices at half-time are the best option. That's until we get there. Once the players run out onto the ground, the rules change and we – *I* – am free to measure and gauge, criticise and applaud whatever I want to. I just can't declare us winners, no matter the margin, until after the final siren. That's the new amendment, in honour of our finals success: even if we're one hundred points up and there are only a handful of fit players left on the opposing side, no victory cries until the final siren sounds. Given how well we've travelled this year under her rules, I'm happy to go with it, just in case.

Mrs Lester is setting the table for breakfast. It's the first time I've seen her since the afternoon we met and I'm relieved to see that she seems sober. She must have come in some time during the night. Tara and I had picked up some Chinese take-away from around the corner and eaten our dinner alone.

'Hello, dear,' she says to me like we're old friends.

'Hi, Mrs Lester. Thanks for inviting me over.'

She waves this away, a chunky diamond ring flashing in the morning light. 'No problem. Tara doesn't ask her friends around much,' Mrs Lester says. 'It's good to finally meet you, Shelley.'

I look at Tara, wondering if I should correct her mother. But there's no need, Tara's on it. 'She came over weeks ago – remember? *After the Redbacks game?*'

Mrs Lester raises an eyebrow at her daughter. '*Tone*, Tara,' she says. 'Well, Shelley, I hope you enjoy the game.'

'We'll be late tonight,' Tara says, munching on a piece of Vegemite toast. 'Don't wait up.'

I manage half a slice before the salty tang is too much for my dry mouth. I gulp down some orange juice, then try again, with more success.

Two slices of Vegemite toast and half a litre of orange juice later, we're ready to go.

The two-block walk to the train station is uncomfortably warm. It's going to be a gorgeous day – hot for this time of year. I'm wearing gold pants several sizes too big that are held up with Dad's gold suspenders, Glenthorn socks, a brown shirt with a gold spray-painted collar sticking out over my Glenthorn jumper, capped off with Glenthorn beanie, brown jacket (with player badges and name tags, and a huge number

5 on its back) and brown-and-gold spray-painted tennis shoes that, I suddenly discover, are probably a little on the small side. Fifteen minutes later, the train being late and the station seats all taken, I decide they're a *lot* on the small side.

Tara is wearing brown pants in a better, more Glenthorn kind of brown than my shirt. I'd wanted to buy them but she'd spotted them first at the Silverdale Salvos. She has a gold skivvy under her Falcons jumper and scarf. On her feet she's got Dunlop Volleys that didn't look all that old before she spray-painted them in brown and gold stripes. The outfit is finished off with her duffle coat, covered with every sewable or pinnable piece of memorabilia available in brown and gold. To top it off, our faces are painted and our hair sprayed gold.

We catch the 7.12 from Silverdale and sit among the private-school kids, who are all on their way to Saturday sport. I notice a bunch of Celtic boys in their tracksuits, around the same age as Josh, and I wonder what he's up to now that the junior footy season is over.

I haven't spoken to him since the Ginnie incident, although he's called a few times. He's probably worked out I'm angry with him by now. But that's his problem, not mine. I can't forgive him for telling Ginnie about Angus. He, of all people, should understand that. But I can't worry about that now. Today is *not* about Josh

McGuire. Today is about Glenthorn and football and Mick. Or, really, today is about *me*.

Finally, today, I get to win.

———————

The MCG almost glows in the light of the bright, sunny day. The light towers glint in the sun and the busy traffic noise fills the air. The mood is electric. The only people around this early are the ground officials, some club people, the police and both cheersquads, but everyone driving past toots their horns or yells out the window, marking the day hours before the real fun begins.

Tara and I head towards the footbridge. Under one end the entire Glenthorn cheersquad has gathered, a good fifty metres from where the Warriors fans mill about. We each have portable barbecues set up, alongside eskies of soft drink and champagne, and huge green garbage bags. I wonder if their flogger bags are similarly loaded with the illegal 'snow' that we've packed into ours, alongside the brown-and-gold floggers and streamers. We spent a good part of last week ripping up old phone books into small squares and loading them into the bottom of these bags.

Most of the cheersquad is huddled around the barbecue, trying to keep their costumes and paraphernalia out of view from prying Warriors' eyes. The moment we arrive we're greeted by Jim-Bob, Danny and Bear, who are covered head-to-toe in brown and gold. Even the Lovely Ladies have dressed up. Unlike Tara's and my collection of hand-me-downs and op-shop rejects, the Ladies are wearing expensive-looking short brown skirts, tight gold tops, stockings and high heels. Their hair is sprayed gold like ours, but Tara and I look like derros while they look like cheerleaders. Their long hair is crimped and they have matching topknots, all brushed smooth and neat. Red is serving sausages and I can hear Sharon and Jim-Bob debating the condition of the ground and the effect it will have on the game, while their kids play kick-to-kick at the other end of the bridge.

'It's perfect for the forwards,' Sharon says.

'Yeah,' Jim-Bob agrees, eyeing me knowingly. 'Perfect for Eddie to kick a tonne.'

'Let's just hope he doesn't stuff up,' Sharon says, voicing my fears, the squawk of her tobacco-ruined voice particularly rough after the bottle of Great Western she's been sucking on. She passes it to Jim-Bob and then to Tara, who helps herself.

It's *really* going to be a long day.

We finish our second breakfast, then help tidy up the mess. Tara is already a little unsteady on her feet. She laughs loudly when she trips on a forgotten flogger. Danny catches her by the elbow, but he isn't doing much better. They both collapse in a giggling heap on the hard patchy grass.

'You're not drinking?' Bear asks me, when I wave off another warm bottle of Great Western that's doing the rounds of the last remaining cheersquadders. Most of the committee people have disappeared to set up inside the ground, so it's just a few stragglers picking up the leftovers.

'I need to concentrate,' I say.

He stares at me blankly, like he thinks I might be joking.

I force a broken laugh to make up for my weirdness. 'Later. After we win,' I say, remembering to make sure Tara isn't in hearing distance. I have a moment of panic when I try to decide if I've mozzed us by saying that out loud, but decide with the blind certainty of all superstitious people that it's only a problem if Tara hears me say it.

When the area is cleared and the last couple of bags are taken into the stands, Tara and I are free to find our seats. Fifth row this time, three rows behind Danny and Bear, who have plum seats I'd die for. But at least we're in front of the Lovely Ladies. Tara has managed to smuggle a bottle of Spumante in under her coat, and although it's barely eleven, she's drunk half of it by the time we sit down.

It's hot. The weather report predicted a top temperature in the high twenties, but it's already hotter than that. I start to unravel my layers, wishing I'd chosen a T-shirt to decorate rather than this stiff cotton shirt.

'Go North!' I yell as the North Yarra reserves run onto the ground for the last quarter. They're playing the Warriors in the curtain raiser, and we don't want the Warriors to get a sniff of victory, even in the reserves. Dad always says it's what's in your head that wins grand finals. Not necessarily the better team but the one that believes it is, and keeps its head in the process. I don't agree. I believe passion wins grand finals – what's in your heart. Simply, who wants it the most.

The game is close and the crowd is pumped. Everyone is getting into it and the champagne is flowing through the cheersquad like the game is already won. The problem is, the real game hasn't even started yet.

'Aren't you worried you'll get too drunk to watch?' I say to Tara, who is draining the last dregs of the Spumante in between shouting abuse at the Warriors reserves.

'I'll be fine,' she says, frowning at me. But she's sweating and her brown-and-gold make-up is beginning to melt in the heat. She wipes her mouth with the back of her hand, smearing her war stripes across her left cheek.

'Uh huh.' It's not like I can stop her. At least that's the last of her stash.

'Go North!' she shouts, the words running together so that it sounds more like 'Gar-nawth!'.

'Yeah,' I say, rolling my eyes. '*Gar-nawth.*'

Despite our efforts, and even with the Glenthorn Cheersquad on their side, North loses in a close match.

My heart constricts as the siren goes. The Warriors fans have gone berserk watching their second side snatch victory in those last minutes. They're so pumped up I'm scared the senior players will feel it when they run onto the ground. The Warriors' Cheersquad is insufferable – shouting all kinds of abuse at us while cheering for their victorious reserves team.

This is not good. Winning is contagious.

Eventually, the reserves are herded up the race and the ground is cleared of all the streamers and snow that – as it turns out – the Warriors cheersquad also managed to smuggle in. And then we wait for what seems like the longest time while the banner is brought out, photographers are directed to key positions and the news cameras pan the crowd for interesting faces. They sit on the cheersquad for a moment, moving from war-painted kids to gold-hatted adults, settling on the Lovely Ladies for an unnaturally long time, if you ask me.

Then it starts. The Falcons burst onto the field, breaking through the enormous banner that screams 'This is Glenthorn's Year!' as thousands of brown and gold balloons are released. The seat beneath me shudders from the weight of the moment. The weight of the noise. I'm screaming but I can't hear my own voice over the chaotic din. Everyone's gone mad and it feels fantastic. My head rushes with the power of that scream, blending with the hundred thousand voices that rise with it, letting go completely, not caring who can see or hear, not caring who I am or what I do. For those seconds, I'm all-powerful.

Then the Warriors run out and I watch them circle the ground warily, keeping their distance from their opponents, until they have to come together for the national anthem. In the seconds before the first notes of the band sound, the crowd falls silent, as though commanded. It feels like the whole of Melbourne has stopped moving and is waiting, breathless. Those seconds before the grand final starts are probably the quietest in this city. There is nothing else like it.

The crowd rises at the emcee's request. All the faces around me, some painted in brown and gold, others bare but rapt and glowing with something I can't identify . . . Pride, maybe? Devotion? 'Advance Australia Fair' kicks in, and my heart swells and pounds. Listening to more than 100,000 people in the greatest stadium on earth sing the anthem – or most of it anyway, since nobody knows the second verse – is awesome. And the whole stadium shakes when the band plays 'Waltzing Matilda'.

The players take their positions on the field. The umpire raises the Sherrin up high and the roar from the crowd is the loudest sound I've ever heard. It's so deep and all-consuming that it seems to swallow everything whole. Well beyond not hearing my own voice, I can't hear my own *thoughts*.

The umpire bounces the ball, the crowd ratchets it up a notch higher again, and just like every year, the players start a blue. It's like a small explosion has been triggered; the noise of the crowd and the burst of activity on the field all combine in a frenzied mess of voices and whistles and screams. I usually hate seeing men fight. But on the footy field, watching the players push and shove – especially on big occasions like this – it's incredibly exciting. I can't get enough.

I scan the field for Mick, but he's way down in full forward, still stretching and jogging on the spot. Nervous. I can see it from here.

'Go for it, Rocky!' Jim-Bob screams.

'Get off him, ya thug!' Sharon yells at Paul Weston, who's sitting on top of Blackie.

'Somebody get in and help him!' Tara shouts.

By the time the umpires have calmed the players down, the crowd is on its feet and we're dying, more than ever, to see some football. The game starts again and Brendan O'Reilly runs towards the ball with the passion of ten men. He is solidly met by Daniel Ladd and is left in a heap on the ground, bloodied and dazed, but still holding onto the ball.

'Too high, ump!' I yell, nudging Tara for a response. But Tara ignores me, her eyes riveted to the game. Her face is white as a sheet, and I wonder if she's sick. 'You okay?'

She doesn't even look at me. She shakes her head and says quietly, 'This doesn't feel right.'

'We'll be fine. It's barely started.'

The look she gives me would make the demon girl from *The Evil Dead* cry. I wonder if it's the alcohol that's messing with her. At least she's stopped drinking for the moment.

I decide it's best to leave Tara alone for now. Red is in the row behind us so I spend the rest of the quarter directing my comments at her.

David leads us in his typically bizarre chants:

'Warriors smell terrible!' *(Clap-clap-clap.)*

'Go home, you pretty boys!' *(Clap-clap-clap-clap-clap.)*

At quarter-time Glenthorn is two goals up but we're only slightly ahead of the Warriors in the play. It feels like we haven't really let loose yet. Danny climbs over the seats towards us and I move over to make room between Tara and me, but he continues past us with a wave, and squeezes in between Kimberly and Lisa at the back.

'I'm getting something to eat,' Tara says, and without waiting to see if I want anything, climbs over the benches and disappears into the crowd. I don't know what she's thinking – she'll never make it back before the next quarter. Then Red disappears to the toilet, and I find myself watching Kimberly and Danny flirt, dread growing in the pit of my stomach.

Tara comes back before the break ends, despite my prediction, but she's got a can of beer with her.

'You're going to be off your head before the game ends. You won't be able to focus,' I say, sounding a lot like someone's mother.

Tara takes a long, deliberate sip of the VB and smiles, the foam glistening on her lips. 'Yeah right,' she says, and turns away.

The players scatter and everyone takes their place for the second quarter. I'm glad we're ahead, but we have a long way to go. Mick started at full forward but he's been moved to the forward flank. Killer is playing there instead. Neither Mick nor Killer is doing anything special, but Mick often starts slowly, so there's time. He needs to do something in the second quarter or . . . No, there is no 'or'. He just has to.

In the second quarter, the Falcons pick up. By half-time we've just about doubled the Warriors' score. By the end of the third quarter, we have a twenty-three-point lead which, in a grand final, is about as good as you can hope for without it being a total blow-out.

The sun is out in full spring force by the time the last quarter starts. I peel down to the bottom layer of my costume. I have the sleeves rolled up to try to let some cool air in under the cotton shirt, but I refuse to take it off because I don't have any Glenthorn colours underneath. My face is starting to burn and the morning's breakfast is rolling around in my stomach.

Tara scoffs the rest of Jim-Bob's champagne and moves onto Bear's cask riesling. Even the smell is enough to drive me to take deep, slow breaths to stop myself revisiting breakfast. I steal a look up at the Lovely Ladies to see Danny and Kimberly laughing like old friends. Tara has not looked back once but there's no way she hasn't seen them. Everyone else has.

Two minutes into the final quarter, Mick heads down the ground to full forward, and I watch Jury run off the ground and wrap himself up in a gold robe. 'Tara! Tara! Look!' I yell, unable to stop the shriek in my voice. 'This is it! Mick's going to seal it for us.'

Tara looks at me like she's seeing me for the first time. I don't like what I see there, me reflected in her face like that. I look away, turning my focus back to the footy. I need to keep my mind on the match, make sure it all goes to plan.

The pressure is definitely on the Warriors – we're twenty-one points up – but you wouldn't know it by the way they're playing. We look tired and, frighteningly, the Warriors don't. And then, as though something has ended, or perhaps it's just about to begin, the play shifts, and I'm watching the Warriors control the ball. It starts with a goal by Paul Weston and takes off from there. A snatch here, a tackle there, and before my eyes the mighty brown-and-gold is looking lost and overwhelmed.

In six minutes the Warriors have closed the gap by three goals, then they score again and are, for the first time all day, equal to our score. The cheersquad is quiet. Stunned. The cask of riesling that was being passed around has now stalled in Tara's hands.

'Come on, Glenthorn!' David screams, and the rest of the cheersquad rouses.

The players look exhausted, but there are no more than ten minutes left in the match and we desperately need a goal.

Eventually, Blackie gets possession for the Falcons and sends a healthy pass towards Brendan O'Reilly, who takes an easy mark dead in front of goal. I watch Mick drop back as soon as O'Reilly lands and, although the Irishman isn't much more than forty metres out and something near a sure thing, Mick is jogging on the spot, preparing for a short kick. He's about thirty metres from me and the sun is bright, but I'm convinced I can see his expression – the concentrated frown, the narrow eyes focused on the ball and his opponent, and I feel a strange sadness go through me, a mixture of longing and loneliness. And then it's gone and it's all I can do to concentrate on breathing.

O'Reilly's kick is high and long and looks like going all the way through, except suddenly there are two brown-and-gold arms reaching for it, touching it, stopping it, and what was sure to be a clear six-point goal, is suddenly, unbelievably, a touched behind. One point, not six.

And now the Warriors get possession of the ball.

Everyone just stands there for a minute like they aren't sure what they saw, then one Warriors player gives Mick, the owner of the brown-and-gold arms, an ironic clap and goes to lead his teammates back to position for the kick out.

For a long second, Mick looks like he's going to shrug it off. He stands there in silence, immobile, until another Warriors player passes by, nudging Mick with his elbow, pointing at the scoreboard with a wide, taunting grin.

Don't do it, Mick. But he can't hear me and I see his arm rise even before his opponent does. I see it in his eyes, in the shift of his body, and then there's the crack of fist on cheek and the thud of the Warrior hitting the deck.

Players flock to the crumpled heap on the ground. For a second I think there's going to be an all-in brawl but Mick stands alone, his teammates running back to position when they see what's going to happen. The whistle blows. The umpire shouts. The crowd cries out in horror. The Warriors fans boo and then cheer as the umpire awards them a kick down the ground, setting up the play right in front of their goals.

Mick stays where he is, his face crumpled in anguish. His whole body is closed in on itself, and I think he might curl up on the ground and cry. But he doesn't move. He just stands absolutely still, staring at the goals like they're about to give him another chance. And then O'Reilly comes by him, says something in his ear and they both run to pick up their opponent.

The Warriors kick a goal. Then another. And within three minutes they're eleven points up. Mick is dragged off the ground, and the Warriors go on from there. One more goal and it's time-on, five minutes and they're four goals up. There's nothing we can do. Not me. Not the players. Certainly not Mick, a gold-robed, solitary figure on the bench. The sound of the final siren tears through me like a canon.

It's over. The Warriors have won.

I sit down. Shock and disappointment are thick in the air. The cheersquad is no longer chanting or cheering. No one speaks. Then Sharon starts to shriek as though she's been stabbed, and the people around me slowly come to life. 'I can't believe it!'

'What just happened?'

'What the hell was Eddie thinking?'

I feel responsible, guilty. A couple of the cheersquad kids shoot me a disbelieving look as though to say, 'And you *like* him?' Behind us, Red is sobbing.

Tara doesn't move, but her face is white and stiff like a mask, the smeared war paint like dried blood across her cheeks. 'Fucking sandgroper,' she says finally. She doesn't look at me. She just sits there clutching the empty bladder from Bear's cask of riesling and stares at the devastated Glenthorn players, some of them tucked into a ball on the ground, others wandering dazedly or staring at the heavens, lost. Mick is off to the side, refusing to join the group.

After what seems like an hour, Tara turns to me. 'It's all about fucking ego.' And even though I know she's talking about Mick, I suspect she's talking about me too and, as unfair as that seems, I can't think of a single thing to say in my defence.

CHAPTER 27

THE INJURY LIST

I watch the ceremony, numb and disbelieving. Everyone drinks and drinks to take away the pain, but I'm so sick with disappointment that even the smell of champagne turns my stomach. I watch Paul Weston hold up the cup with their coach, Magic Jones, and I notice Mick sitting alone on the ground, his head and legs tucked in like he's trying not to take up space, the Glenthorn robe wrapped tightly around him even though it's thirty degrees. He doesn't move even when Stretch Davis taps his shoulder and waits beside him. Every part of me aches to watch this.

Midway through the third rendition of the Warriors' victory song, Tara stands up. 'I'm going home,' she says.

'I thought we were going to stay until the end of the ceremony?' It seems right, as much as it hurts.

'Do what you like. I'm leaving.' But she doesn't leave. She just stands there, waiting.

'I have to check on Mick.'

She stares at me in disbelief and then those hard eyes turn to stone, as though I've let her down, just as she knew I would.

'I'll meet you at Fernlee Park,' I say, offering a compromise. 'I won't be long.'

Tara looks away and shrugs. 'Yeah, whatever.' I watch her fade into the crowd of Glenthorn fans, escaping the horror of the Warriors' victory speeches. And that song.

I needn't have bothered worrying about Mick. The Glenthorn dressing rooms are closed to visitors. Even the media aren't allowed in. At the door, Geoff's face is as stern and bitter as I've seen it, and he looks right past me, like he doesn't know who I am. There's no way I'm getting in.

I wait for the train to Fernlee Park and run into a few of the other cheersquad regulars. Red is miraculously silent when she sees me, while Bear and Danny are arguing about what might have happened *if only*. I don't hang around to listen. I don't want to relive it before I have to.

As I get on the train, I can hear Sharon shrieking all the way down Platform 9, so I hide behind a group of

Warriors supporters, keeping my eyes down to avoid any victory taunting.

At Fernlee Park Station, I see Kimberly and Renee enter the toilets. I decide to change here rather than risk not getting into the social club dressed like I am. The Ladies have already shed their cheerleader costumes and are wearing tight jeans and midriff tops, their make-up thick and their hair brushed out. Although their clothes are similar, the effect is different for each of them. Kimberly looks like a movie star, or a TV star anyway, while Renee would have no trouble finding work on Fitzroy Street.

'Bad luck, hey?' Renee doesn't look up from the mirror when I walk in. Her lipstick is smudged near the corner of her mouth and she's trying to rub it off.

'Yeah,' I say, the pain still hovering somewhere nearby. It hasn't hit me yet, and though I know it's coming, I sure as hell am not going to reveal it to these two.

'Should be a few broken hearts at the social club, I reckon,' Renee continues, turning to look at me. 'Eddie probably not the least of them.'

I shrug, wetting a paper towel to wipe my face clean, faking cool. I retreat to the toilet cubicle to change. I don't even want to look at them, or anyone really, let alone chat.

'Yeah, I reckon Eddie's the best bet for tonight,' Renee continues, her voice sailing smoothly over the top of the toilet door.

Kimberly mutters something I can't hear, then adds, 'Not for me. He's history at the club anyway. Ask anyone.'

I yank my jeans on hard and pull my T-shirt roughly over my chest, grabbing my bag without looking back. I can barely open the stall door fast enough. 'You're just bandwagon supporters!' I yell, like there isn't a greater insult. 'It wasn't Mick's fault! We lost by *twenty-eight points*! Or are you too stupid to understand that?'

Renee and Kimberly stare at me. 'What's up your bum?' Renee asks.

'Why's everyone blaming Mick?' I rage.

'Because he stuffed up,' Renee answers, shrugging. 'And we lost. But hey, it's just a game.' And she turns back to the mirror, while Kimberly keeps watching me, like there's something she doesn't understand but wants to.

'What's up with you and Eddie? I mean, are you together?' She's asking the question like she doesn't think it's possible.

I don't know if I'm more offended by the question or the fact that she thinks it could never happen. I'm offended by both, I decide. 'You know he's married, right? With a wife?' I say. As if there's anyone else he'd be married to. 'We're just friends,' I add weakly. 'I don't want to hear any more shit about him leaving,' I say, this time without any hint of uncertainty. 'He'll be at Glenthorn until the day he retires. He's meant to be. It's his home.'

Then I storm out of the toilet block, only later realising I've left my Glenthorn scarf behind.

But it doesn't matter. I can't go back.

———————

The social club is packed and the queue outside winds all the way down Leafy Crescent. I can't find Mick or anyone else to sign me in, and Tara hasn't shown up. I take my place in line, amazed at all the unfamiliar faces that have decided to show up at the club to commiserate our loss. I wonder how many more people would be here if we'd won.

My head feels thick and heavy and I can't get past the ache in my ribs, like someone has wedged something hard and sharp in there and left it behind to rot.

When Tara finally appears, I still haven't spotted Mick and my head is pounding all the way to my feet. She must have gone home like we'd planned, because her face is free of war paint.

'You're late,' I say, not giving her a chance to speak.

She shoves into the line in front of me, ignoring the other members who tell her to go to the end. She's drunk and oblivious. Suddenly that seems to be the only way to get through this – for me too.

'Did you bring anything to drink?' I ask.

She eyes me warily, then dives into her backpack and

hands me an Island Cooler. 'I've got one more each – you can pay me back inside.'

I open the bottle, taste the sweet bubbly wine and decide that it tastes way better than beer. I take a long swallow, and then another, the cold bubbles burning my dry throat. 'Thanks,' I say.

The line begins to move and I scan the crowd for a familiar face. Mick must already be inside.

'Where are the Ladies?' Tara asks. We move another step closer to the front door.

'Kim and Renee were at the station,' I say, not adding that I'd basically told them to get lost. 'We might need to ask Lisa. Or someone else,' I add, hoping Tara doesn't press it. I glance across the street and notice Mick's car pulling into the car park. I wait for him to cross the road before I call out. 'Mick!'

He's already being mobbed by a sea of brown and gold, most of them kids, some of them telling him off for giving away the penalty, others trying to make him feel better. He doesn't look up, not for them or for me.

'Mick! Can you help us?' I race towards him, hoping Tara is sober enough to hold our place in the queue. 'Can you sign us in?' I ask, standing between him and the steps to the social club. 'Mick?' I ask again, finally getting him to look up. He sees me, I know he does. But he doesn't stop or answer, he just walks steadily through the milling crowd, towards the social club doors, past

305

the queue, past me, taking the steps in long strides and disappearing inside.

I stare after him, stunned.

'Shelley!' I can hear Tara calling me but I can't move. I don't want to see the satisfaction on Tara's face.

Lisa appears beside me and takes my arm. 'I'll get you two in if I can cut in line with you,' she says, already leading me back to Tara, knowing I'll say yes.

I'm still reeling when we approach the bar. The music is loud – probably to drown out our thoughts – and the crowd is drunk and roaring. There is a desperate intensity to it; a nasty edge that makes me nervous. Everyone's lost in those minutes where it all went wrong. Reliving it, over and over. No concern for tomorrow, or hopefulness about next time. They can't get past today. No one can. And every angry conversation ends at the point where Mick spoiled O'Reilly's shot and gave away a goal.

'He might as well have kicked the bloody thing for them himself,' one drunken voice slurs.

'Fucking has-been.'

Tara and I drink together for a while, not mentioning the game or talking much about anything. Lisa drifts in and out, forcing her way through the crowd long enough to order a drink beside us, exchange a word or two, then leave. It's only now that I realise how Bear hovers wherever Lisa is and how obvious it is that he likes her.

Meanwhile, I've moved from Island Coolers to mixed drinks. Tara orders us both a Fluffy Duck and then a Blue Lagoon, and then something with a name I can't pronounce or remember but is the colour of a burnt-orange sunset. I have two of these. Or three. Then I stop counting.

Things begin to blur rapidly. The music blares songs I hate and songs I love, all mixing and shifting into something I suspect I'll never forget, blending with this feeling of anxiety, loss and anger, forever connected to the pain. Time stands still, and then the DJ cuts in and the Glenthorn theme song fills the noisy club. A tired but determined chorus of voices rise, defiant in their refusal to remain quiet and, it seems, stay in tune. Someone shouts out that the players are coming, and the doors to the players' room open. Everyone's attention turns towards them as they emerge from the darkened room. They're drunk already. Or maybe it's me and not them. Either way, I can't see Mick and no one's asking where he is.

Some of the players mingle with the crowd, offering apologies and accepting condolences, while others hang back, mute and sullen. Everyone looks lost and angry. But also profoundly *hurt*.

'I need air,' Tara rasps in my ear.

I'm about to follow her out to make sure she's okay, but then I see Mick and my feet are riveted to the spot. The doors to the players' room have been propped open and, through the gloomy light, I can see him leaning against the bar, standing alone, ignoring every offer by the other players for company and consolation.

I hesitate. Tara is already lost in the crowd. I almost follow her as I know I should, but then Mick looks at me – right at me – and there's nowhere else for me to go but to him.

The bouncer stops me at the door. 'You need an invitation,' he says, but he isn't rough or rude. He seems almost apologetic.

I smile and nod, turning away to look for Tara.

'Let her in.' I look back to see Mick talking to the bouncer, who nods and lets me through.

I'm nervous. I want to tell Mick I know what everyone is saying but that he shouldn't listen, it isn't true and that the pain will stop soon enough. Or not stop exactly, but shift and change, become something less powerful, something blunter and more even. More *predictable*. That's what I want to say, but I can tell he's in no mood to listen. So I go with the old favourite. 'I'm sorry, Mick,' I say, wishing there were other words, an alternative to 'sorry' that actually means something.

'About what, Shell?' He sounds tired, like he isn't really listening. He studies his drink – something murky brown.

'It's not your fault, you know.'

'So everyone keeps telling me.'

'Well, they're right. No one's blaming you,' I lie, convinced that after the pain has faded and more time has passed, the memory of Mick's mistake will fade and people will realise it's about the team, not just Mick. In the end, it's always about the team. 'It'll get better.' At least this much I know.

He turns on me then, his face so angry that, for a split second and for only the second time in my life, I feel physically threatened. 'You might think you know everything, Shell, but you don't.'

'I don't mean –'

'What? You don't mean *what*?'

'Nothing. I don't know what I mean.'

'Of course you don't. You're just a kid who thinks she knows everything. But you don't. Not about this, anyway. You know full well that even if they're not saying it to me, they're saying it to themselves – to the world. And they're right. Of course it's my fault. It's *entirely* my fault. And that's why I'm standing here on my own and why I won't be back next year. Not here, anyway.'

'What?'

'I'm talking to other clubs. If they'll have me.'

'You can't leave Glenthorn! It's too early to worry about this stuff. It's just happened. It's still new. Don't think about next year yet. It's too early.'

309

'Actually, it's too late. I've made up my mind. There's nothing to say.'

'How can you leave?' The idea is so ridiculous to me, so *unnatural*. This is where he belongs. Where we all belong. This is . . . *home*. Doesn't he know that? 'They won't let you go,' I add, desperate to believe it.

'You're kidding, right? What do you think will happen? We'll all shake hands and put our heads down again for next year? Shrug it off and move on like nothing's happened? We lost! That's why we play – to win. And if we don't win, we've failed. It's that simple. Black and white. Probably the only thing in life that is.' He looks at me closely, like he's measuring me. 'I mean, that's why people love it. It's so easy to divide the game into good and bad. Win or lose. Right? Well, we lost. We lost the only sure thing we've known. We have to pay for that. *Someone* has to pay for that. And I'm putting up my hand before someone else does it for me.'

His eyes are so red I can hardly see his pupils. The lights are bright and flashing. The room keeps turning like we're in a whirlpool. I can't feel my feet and my blood is sludge in my veins. I'm so upset I can't speak. I don't know what I'd say anyway.

He looks at me, half disbelieving, half guilty. 'Did you really think nothing would change?'

I try to shake my head, no. No. Things *always* change. All the time. Especially the good things – things that make me happy. I learnt that two years ago. But

I can't say it out loud. That will make it so completely true and irreversible that I wouldn't know how to wake up tomorrow. 'What about me?' I say instead, my voice small and weak.

Mick gapes. 'You? What about you? This isn't your life. It's *my* life. For you, it's a game. For me, it's what I do. It's *everything*.'

'It's my life too,' I whisper.

'Your life?' Mick holds out his hands before me in a kind of surrender. 'Your life hasn't even started yet.'

No. I guess it hasn't. Or it did start and then it stopped. But he doesn't know this. Not any of it. This is the moment I should tell him. This is the right place to say that my mother and twin brother were killed in a car accident. That I was meant to be in the car with them – we all were – but I'd cracked it with Dad, in front of Mrs McGuire. It was right before Angus's game, a twilight tournament that I'd normally play. Dad had just told me he wouldn't support Jacko's appeal against the tribunal. That I was to be done with footy, full stop.

It was our thirteenth birthday, which was supposed to be a celebration, but for me it was the beginning of the end. It wasn't planned like that, I knew even as I ranted at Dad, but I didn't care about anything right then. The humiliation, the frustration. They kept telling me I was different suddenly when I felt exactly the same inside. Like my body was weaker somehow, less than it was, all because

I was becoming a woman. But I had to keep going – forced to watch Angus's games because that's what families do.

I remember Mrs McGuire's face, the gentle understanding, the kindness and the concern. I hate that she'd heard me that day. 'Why did I have to be a twin?' I'd screamed at Dad, Mum safely tucked away in the canteen, taking her turn on duty. The only witnesses were Dad and Mrs McGuire. And Angus, of course. Angus, who bore the brunt of it because he didn't want me to play. Josh had stuck up for me, but Angus never did. I wouldn't have to be there if I wasn't a twin, I'd reasoned. So it was Angus's fault I was hurting. I blamed it all on Angus. 'I wish you never existed!' I'd screamed at him in the seconds before I stormed off. '*I wish you were dead!*'

And then I ran, until my lungs hammered in my chest and my legs were mush. Dad had left Angus's game to come after me, catching up to me when I finally slowed down. We didn't speak the whole way home. It's the closest I think I've ever felt with him. He knew what I needed and truly understood.

And when we got home we talked. And I cried. And he said he'd see what he could do, but that rules were rules and there was usually a good reason for them. He didn't ask if I'd go back to catch the end of Angus's game. He just stayed with me until I was okay.

It was the only Raiders match he ever missed. I think about that a lot.

When the game should have ended, Dad and I waited for Mum and Angus to come home.

And waited.

The eerie twilight descended and Dad shifted from quiet patience to concern. We headed back to the ground, on foot again, walking faster this time. We didn't get very far. We stopped when we saw the car, or what was left of it, crumpled around a light pole, a truck twisted on its side a little further ahead. Ambulances, police cars, chaos. They tried to divert us, to turn us around, until Dad said the words that changed our lives forever. The words that marked the beginning of the end. 'That's my family.' His voice was flat and dead, the life seeming to have leaked from him the same way it was leaking from my brother. My mother was already gone by then.

This is what I should tell Mick, and yet I don't. 'It *is* my life,' I say quietly, beginning to cry. Silently at first, and then not so silently.

Mick looks confused and ashamed. 'Pull yourself together, Shell,' he says.

I can't, though. There's no more of me left. Even the bits that remain are too small and insubstantial to matter. I'm just this mess of odds and ends, bits and pieces with no shape, no form. No glue.

I don't know how long he lets me cry before he takes me roughly in his arms, pressing me against his chest, telling me it'll be okay. That all of it will be okay. He's talking like a stranger, like someone who doesn't know me. I have the sudden, scary feeling that if I ever see him again it will be on the TV or in the papers, watching his life go on with another club, with other people, watching it from a distance just like everyone else.

I stop crying and push him away. 'You have no idea,' I say, and leave him standing by the bar. I push the doors to the players' room open with an awkward bang, knowing that once they're shut I won't be able to go back in. And I don't care.

The temperature has dropped when I step outside. Forty or fifty fans have gathered on the footpath and the road outside, still dressed in their footy colours, most of them adults and teenagers, most of them drunk or drinking. The strains of the Glenthorn theme song are wobbly but persistent, punctuated by tired choruses of 'Carn the Falcons!' and 'Next year, fellas!' aimed at the sky.

I work my way through the crowd and cross the street, heading towards the rear of the stadium. The tall chain-link gates are open. I hear some familiar cheers echoing through the night as I take the stadium stairs.

'Shelley!' I recognise Jim-Bob's voice coming from the Mayblooms Stand, although I can't see anything. The whole stadium is pitch black, but the noise and laughter suggests there's a large group holed up there.

'Jim-Bob?'

'Press box,' he calls back.

I peer through the dark, my eyes taking ages to adjust as I stumble up the stairs. The cool air seems to have shaken me up or loosened the drunkenness inside of me. Suddenly things aren't as clear as they were, and it's got nothing to do with the darkness. I stand up straighter, trying to clear my head. I can see enough to make out the cheersquad. They've lit a fire in the stands – a small one but it's enough to guide me the rest of the way.

'Have you seen Tara?' I ask Jim-Bob, when I can finally make out his features in the fire's glow.

'No.'

'Anyone?' I ask the group. I only know about half of the people there. Bear is slouched in the corner, squeezed into a front-row bench. Bits of him hang over the edges and when I call out his name he can barely turn to answer.

'Hey,' I say, squatting down beside him. I rub his head, a gentle noogie. He smiles vacantly at me. 'Seen Tara?' I ask.

He starts laughing, stupidly, and I wonder if all he's taken tonight is alcohol.

'Bear?'

He shakes his head, laughing deliriously, dangerously close to smacking his forehead on the iron railing in front of him. He leans against the railing, his whole body

315

shuddering for a full minute before he looks up blearily and says my name.

I touch his shoulder. 'Take care, okay?' I stand again and survey the mess of drunk and noisy teenagers. Legs and arms are entwined in a tangle of shared empathy. Everyone is hurting.

I turn to go but the world seems to tilt crazily to the left, and I feel the back of the bench crack against my hip, as though it's risen up to strike me. I find myself lying on the cold cement, my head pounding and spinning at once. I squint into the black, the light from the fire robbing me of my night vision for the seconds it takes for my eyes to adjust. I pull myself up again, touching the graze just above my hip, the wet blood sobering me. I remember my mission and decide that Danny is my best option. Even if she seemed annoyed with him at the game, Tara is drunk. Everyone's drunk. Anything is possible.

I call out for Danny, hoping he's more coherent than his friends. Someone tells me he's down on the oval, so I gingerly make my way down the stairs towards the flat below. The steps seem to shift beneath my feet as I pick my way over broken bottles and plastic recyclables. There are discarded Glenthorn scarves, a shoe, someone's beanie and even a jumper twisted around one of the benches. I stop to pull it free, hoping I can return it to its owner. I see the big number 5 on its back, see Mick's signature scrawled across it in black texta and decide whoever dumped this here doesn't deserve to get it back. I leave it down between the seats where I found it. I feel sick and dizzy. I need to find Tara.

Out on the oval, I find a group of cheersquadders I don't know well. I recognise Sharon and David, but the other faces are not familiar enough for me to pick them in the darkness. 'I'm looking for Tara,' I say.

Sharon hasn't seen her, neither has David, but Red appears from nowhere beside me, her shiny orange curls almost glowing in the uneven light.

'You all right?' Unlike everyone else, Red is sober. Apparently she doesn't drink, not even when we lose grand finals that we're supposed to win.

'Have you seen Tara?' I suck in air, trying to get the spinning to stop. Deep long breaths, in through the nose and out through the mouth. I see another group near the fence and head towards the boundary, Red following closely behind.

'A while ago.' I've never been convinced Red likes Tara. In fact, I'm pretty sure she doesn't. But at least she's helping me. 'She was pretty drunk and pissed off about something.'

In the dark, I've only just begun to recognise the shape of two bodies twisted up together at the base of the press-box tower. Danny and Kimberly. They've got their clothes on but they're so tightly wound around each other that it almost doesn't matter. Any hope that today's flirtation was in my head has gone. My heart races, imagining what Tara felt when she saw them. Because I know suddenly that she did. She would have been looking for them to make sure.

'Where'd she go?' I'm trying to maintain focus, and the image of Tara freaking out is going a long way to helping, but it strikes in fits and starts. Red is multiplying before my eyes, like those cut-out paper dolls we used to make in primary school. I shake my head, which doesn't help at all.

'There's a party down the road. A lot of the players are there.'

I swallow. I don't know if I should leave Fernlee Park. How would I find the party anyway? 'Do you know where?'

Red shrugs. 'Of course.'

I wonder then why she hasn't gone herself. 'I need to find her. Come with me?'

Red shrugs again, which I take as a yes, and we make our way out of the stadium. It's a slow process. She occasionally places a steadying hand on my arm, guiding me with short directions. I feel like a child being led by her parent, but I don't mind. I'm pretty sure I wouldn't have made it by myself.

We head down Leafy Crescent, turning onto a side street about fifty metres before Fernlee Park Road. Red doesn't have to point out which house it is. The lights are on – all of them. People have spilled out onto the footpath, the front yard, the other side of the street. Like outside the social club, everyone has brown and gold somewhere on them, though they're mostly young men. I recognise some under 19s, some reserves players, as well as a lot of boys I think I've seen on the Fernlee Park Road tram. These are the boys who get off the tram at Riverglen Road and disappear into those enormous mansions with dates carved into them, or head down those pretty tree-lined streets.

Red walks a bit behind me now, as though using me for cover. I maintain the position, in a kind of shepherding strategy. I now know why she needs me. She wouldn't have come in alone – no one would have let her. She's nowhere near cool enough, or even normal enough, to make the grade, and she's pinning her hopes on me.

One of the boys nods as I walk in, recognising me and allowing me entry in a single gesture. He shoots Red a questioning look but shrugs and returns his focus to the pretty brunette who's half propped on the letterbox, half slumped against him. The girl looks at him adoringly, her lips shiny with pink gloss, pursed and ready for his.

I look away, an ache the size of WA in my chest.

Inside, there's more of the same. There are a couple of senior players here, though none who made today's team. They're drunk and miserable in a different way to

319

their teammates, the missed opportunity made worse somehow because of the extra unanswerable questions that fill their heads. If only they'd been selected . . . If only they'd been given a chance . . .

Someone hands me a drink, which I accept and drink slowly. I can't see Tara anywhere, but I'm sure she's here. Or if she isn't, she will be. I drink more and watch the lights and the floor continue to spin, let it swallow me up because anything is better than standing still. Red has disappeared and I've found a comfortable place in a corner of the living room. I rest against the wall, hoping Tara gets here soon, feeling a lot like I might fall asleep if I don't move, at the same time lulled by the delicious idea of sleep.

One of the under 19s players, Scott Wiltshire, grabs me by the hand and leads me to the bar. 'I need someone to help me behind the bar,' he smiles, not letting go of my hand until a full minute after I take my position beside him. He goes to Celtic and is a year ahead of me, though I don't think we've ever exchanged more than a 'hello' before tonight. He's always seemed very shy to me, not cocky like his friends. I wonder how drunk he must be to approach me like this. How drunk I must be to let him.

My whole body is awake now, although my brain is a good five seconds behind my actions. Like watching a slow-motion replay, I'm seeing things happen to me before I feel them. As though there's two of me, but only one is real. I pour drinks and top up my own, while Scott encourages me, laughing. His hand keeps touching mine, his body pressing against me whenever we squeeze past each other in the cramped space behind the bar. After a while he stops apologising and doesn't even bother to move away when we make what had earlier masqueraded as accidental contact. He stays tight against me, his body strong and unmoving. I don't move either.

He turns me around and looks at me. There's a long silence that seems impossible to fill. I think he's going to kiss me when he leans forward, but instead his lips brush my ear. 'I always thought you and Eddie –'

I shake my head quickly – 'No!' – cutting him off, and nearly cracking heads in the process.

Scott smiles, then lets me go.

We continue to feed the thirsty partygoers, getting into a smooth rhythm. It feels good to have something to do, to keep my head and my hands busy. And Scott is helping me forget. I become an expert at pulling beer from the keg and learn to flip a champagne cork from a bottle in one movement. At one point, I recognise Renee in the corner of the living room, her top exposing one shoulder, caught between two players from another club. I want to go to her, to see if she's okay, but then she laughs suddenly and there seems no point. An hour later, hardly anyone left is still awake. There are bodies everywhere, sleeping or just resting, half-conscious or not conscious at all.

Scott turns to me, holding me close. 'Hey,' he says. He leans in to kiss me, his body firm and unyielding. I don't resist, I don't even move. I feel nothing because it isn't happening to me. It's happening outside of me, to someone else.

And then a hand grips my arm, strong and firm and masculine, but it's not Scott's. It's as familiar to me as my own. I've watched that hand mark, punch, juggle a footy a thousand times before, never sick of marvelling at it, always impressed by its power and skill. And now it's on my elbow, pulling me away from this boy, the possessiveness as intoxicating as the Yellowglen and UDLs.

'Sorry, mate,' Scott says, backing off and shaking his head. 'She said you weren't together.'

Mick's jaw is a hard line of anger. His eyes glint with fury. I think it's aimed at Scott and for a moment I'm tempted to stand between them, but when Mick looks my way I realise it's aimed at me. He drags me out from behind the bar and through the house, not stopping until we're outside on the street.

'What the hell are you doing?' he says through gritted teeth, swinging me around.

'Hey, are you okay?' Scott calls out from the front door.

'She's fine,' Mick says, without letting go, his eyes pinning me in place.

After a brief hesitation, Scott returns inside, slamming

322

his hand against the doorjamb on the way, either in frustration or resignation. Whatever concern he has for me ends at the word of his senior teammate.

My mouth quivers, my lips part and tears fall. And fall. And fall.

'Jesus.' Mick steps away, releasing me like he's been burnt, but his eyes never leave my face. 'Jesus.'

I shake my head, ashamed and confused. 'I didn't want that . . .'

'What did you think would happen? What do you think they want from you?'

I blink numbly. How can I answer that when I don't even know what I want from them? What I want for myself?

Mick softens, his voice dropping. 'What did you think would happen?' he asks again, gently this time.

I want to tell him I don't care about that – about them. *This* is what matters. This thing right here. I want to beg him not to leave. To say that he's my family, my life, the only thing in my world that is consistently good. But I can't stop crying to form the words.

Mick slumps then, resigned, and he places his arm around me like a father sheltering a child, protective and determined but also awkward. I let him hold me while the tears flow. We stand like that for ages, neither moving, the dark silence shielding us from the world outside. We could be the only people left on earth and that would be fine by me.

Eventually, my tears stop and I'm all emptied out. I wipe my face, straighten my clothes and try to put some space between that child who couldn't stop crying and the girl I want to be. I move towards the front of the house and sit on the cold ground by the letterbox. My bones ache. My whole body feels empty and hollow. Whatever was inside me, holding me up, keeping me strong, is spent.

Mick sits beside me, his long legs stretching out in front of him. He moves his bad knee up and down, a habit that allows him to find a comfortable position so it doesn't ache. He flinches and straightens it, then flexes it again. We both watch this ritual in silence, the words piling up in the dark night between us.

'Please don't leave, Mick,' I whisper finally. That's all I need to say, and I'm glad I've said it.

'I have to,' he says simply.

I place my hand on his leg and watch my fingers shake, my whole body weak but determined. I kiss him on the cheek, then gently on his lips. He doesn't move, his body rigid with uncertainty. I press against him, press into him.

I know they're my lips, my breasts, my hand, but they feel like they belong to someone else. I'm looking down at this girl, who looks like me, doing this thing that I could never do. I'm not here. That's not me. And yet, my hands travel across his chest and my mouth caresses his face. His silence is impossible to read but he doesn't push me away, so I continue. This girl continues.

I'm not here. *I'm not here.*

'Jesus,' he says again, and then he's kissing me back, hard and firm. He pushes me down against the cold cement, his whole body encloses itself around me, holding me still. His hands travel inside my clothes as he kisses my face, my neck. His fingers start to pull open my top, his lips find my bra, my breasts, the icy air cutting through the layers like a knife, the graze on my hip burning.

I want to move. I want to stop him. This is not what I want, it's not how I feel. But I can't move. Or I don't because this is Mick and he's holding me close and maybe, *maybe* this means he won't leave. I force myself to stay still, to not push him away even though that's all my body wants to do. I try to control it, my tired, blurry mind caught between will and impulse, not surrendering to either, eventually betraying me completely when I start to shake.

Great waves of shock or maybe cold rip through me, beyond my control. My entire body is gripped by it. I can't stop. My hands quiver, my chest shudders, the tears I thought had emptied out of me spring to my eyes. Mick presses harder, his hands digging in, the footpath cutting into my back. He's hurting me and he won't stop. I struggle, finally, trying to say no, but just like me, he's no longer there.

Except suddenly I am and I want it to stop. 'No!' I manage to say, dragging my mouth out from under his, my skin bruised and raw, my lips burning in the cold night.

Mick takes a long second before, with a muttered curse, he pulls away, his eyes closed, his chest rising in short sharp breaths. He opens his eyes and sees that it's me. Sees what he's done. His face is ashen with horror. 'Jesus,' he whispers, no longer able to look at me.

I roll away from him, my stomach roiling as the world spins around me. I shakily draw breath, trying to stop the dizziness.

Mick looks like he's going to be sick. I feel both horrified and guilty, and have no idea who's done the wrong thing here, except I know absolutely that it's wrong. Any way you turn it. I pull up my legs, tugging my blouse straight. There's nothing I can do to take any of this back. Worse than this, there's nothing Mick can do either.

'I told Angus I wished he was dead.' The words stand over me, tall as a mountain. 'It's the last thing I said to him.'

Mick is shaking his head, confusion clouding his already uneven gaze. 'Who's Angus?'

But there's no time to answer, even if I could. I don't hear Tara's footsteps or her ragged, laboured breath before I feel her kick me. 'He's married, you slut!' she screams. 'He's married!'

Mick shouts something but I don't hear what.

'You slut!' Tara's words echo shrilly in the quiet night,

despite her drunken slur. She's standing over us both, her legs wide apart as though to hold her steady, her chest heaving with the effort. 'He's married,' she says again, quieter now, pain etched on her face.

Mick carefully pulls himself up and stands between us both. 'Hey. Nothing happened. Okay?' Fear widens his eyes. And shame too. I'm not sure what hurts most.

Tara looks right past Mick, her accusing glare saved for me. She shakes her head, disgust raw on her face, and throws the butt of her cigarette at us before turning away to leave.

'Nothing happened!' he shouts after her, and I know he's worried she'll tell someone. That this is what bothers him most.

I sit there perfectly still for a long time. I can hear Mick crouch back down beside me but I don't want to look at him. And there are simply no words to fill this silence.

'I'm sorry.' It's a small voice for a big man. The words, though, are useless. We're all sorry. It doesn't change a thing.

I drag myself off the ground, brushing the dirt and scum off my clothes, longing for a hot shower and my PJs. I want my dad. I want my mum. I want to go home.

'I'll take you home.' He takes my hand but I shake him off, my heart surging with a fury I can't control. Humiliation, disappointment, anger and hurt – all conspiring to destroy every last thing that matters to me. My pace quickens with every step until I'm running as fast as I can down the dark street. I run and run until I stop outside the social club, gasping for air, my heart hammering in my chest. I collapse against the wall, letting the great wrenching sobs take over, wracking through my wasted body until there's nothing left inside me except the toxic mixture of beer and spirits that now makes an unwelcome return as I stagger into the garden and throw up.

I recognise Mick's car by the sound its engine makes when it pulls up at the curb beside me. I must have fallen asleep.

'Get in.'

I can't move properly. Everything hurts, and I'm cold all the way to my bones. I drag myself up from the damp grass and let Mick steer me towards the car. The car smells like liniment and sweat. And beer. My stomach retches in the close air and the road swims before my eyes. Mick doesn't look at me as he drives. And I don't want to look at him either. Then I remember. 'We need to find Tara.'

'She's fine. I got her a cab and sent her home.'

Relieved, I sink into the warm car seat, the rumble of the engine and the rhythmic bump of the wheels on the tramline threatening to lull me to sleep. I shake myself and sit up.

Twenty minutes later, the familiar dark street looms. 'Just here,' I say, hoarsely, suddenly wishing I could say something to undo it all. It's over. I don't know what happened or what's happening now, but it feels like a line was drawn, and I've crossed it without meaning to. We both have. I turn to get out of the car but Mick reaches out to me, his hand gentle on my arm, his eyes wet and bleary.

'I'm sorry,' he says again. 'I shouldn't have –'

I shake my head. 'I don't care.' The tightness in my chest has turned into something harder. He wants me to forgive him but I can't even look at him. To look at him would be to look at myself. I was there too, after all.

We get out of the car only to see Dad on our front lawn, standing in the soft grey light, and then he's running towards me and my heart constricts in my chest. 'Dad? What . . . ?'

I stand by and watch as Dad hurls himself at Mick like a maniac, thrusting Mick against his car.

'Whoa. Whoa,' Mick says, holding his hands up in surrender.

'Dad! Please!'

Dad's face is twisted unnaturally, his eyes wild with anger, and something that looks like terror. For a moment I think he might have been crying.

I force myself between them. 'I'm okay, Dad. See? I'm okay.'

Dad steps back, almost falling as though a physical force has pushed him. 'What are you doing with my daughter?' he growls through gritted teeth. His face is ashen and gleaming with sweat, despite the cool air.

Mick looks away and shakes his head. 'I'm sorry.'

Dad looks ready to hurl himself at Mick again but I manage somehow to stay him. 'Dad! Nothing happened. He just drove me home. I'm sorry I'm so late.'

Scepticism crosses Dad's face. But when someone says something you desperately want to believe, when they tell you what you need to hear, then sometimes logic and truth don't matter. 'Where's Tara?' Dad says finally, clearly worried.

'She should be home,' I say, looking at Mick for assurance. 'Mick put her in a taxi.'

'Her mother's been calling – she's not there,' Dad says, the fact of Mick's involvement doing nothing to take the edge out of his voice. 'Where is she?' he shouts at Mick.

Mick won't look at me. The silence is suffocating.

'Mick?' I say.

Dad and I are both staring at Mick. It takes an age before he shakes his head slowly. I suddenly realise he's still drunk and I shudder then, realising how lucky I am we got home safely.

'She was at the taxi rank . . .' he says finally, lifting his shoulders in a kind of shrug.

'What?' My voice is just above a whisper. 'You didn't put her in a cab?'

'I'm sure she's fine,' he says, concern clear in his features, belying his words. He regrets it. But I can't ignore that initial shrug – the distancing between his actions and responsibility. I see it then, in that gesture. That's what we are to him, to the other players – to the whole club. We're nothing more than shadowy figures filling an empty space. The people they meet on the way to somewhere else. They move on while we remain in place, the dull backdrop to their stunning lives. Tara. Red. Jim-Bob. The Lovely Ladies.

And me.

I turn to Dad. 'We have to go back.'

Mick opens the car door for me, ready to fix the unfixable.

'No,' I say, pushing the door shut. I'm getting used to this word. It's not as difficult to say as I once believed.

'I should come,' Mick says.

'No, you shouldn't.' Nothing can make me change my mind. 'Dad? Please?'

Dad nods. 'I'll call her mother.'

Dad watches the Fernlee Park chaos with horrified awe. There are tired, drunken revellers still singing the Glenthorn theme song, with other distant, disembodied voices rising to join in an eerie kind of wail. Bits of clothing and rubbish are scattered throughout the stadium, along with broken glass and discarded plastic bottles. The stench of alcohol and vomit is overwhelming. My stomach does something acrobatic in the small space left to contain it.

I head to the press box because there's nowhere else to go. It's the only place I haven't looked and, I realise too late, the first place I should have. Dad follows silently behind me, his steps heavy. We climb the steps gingerly, the pre-dawn light doing little to brighten the dark edges of this secluded corner. I force the stiff door open to reveal Tara asleep on the ground. Dad and I rush to her – and I immediately see that her colour isn't right, even under what's left of her smeared make-up. She's so pale, even for her, and her arm is twisted unnaturally under her body.

'Tara!' I bend beside her, trying to wake her. Dad kneels on the other side of Tara, his face almost as pale as hers. He's been here before and it's killing him having to be here again. It's killing me too. Tara doesn't wake, and panic grips me tightly. I don't know what to do.

'Dad?' I cry, but he doesn't respond. 'Daddy!' I step back, my legs wobbling beneath me, my knees locking up in fear or shock. I'd scream but I've lost my voice.

Dad startles, as though suddenly awake. He pushes me out of the way and leans over Tara. I watch him check her breathing, turning her over and clearing her mouth. He goes through the steps of CPR, which I didn't even know he knew.

'She's breathing,' he says finally, relief thickening his voice. 'She's breathing.' But she still isn't awake. 'Call an ambulance, love,' he says.

I stare at him in terror, unable to move. His face softens, his whole body curls in towards me. 'Go call an ambulance,' he says gently. 'She'll be okay.'

The kindness in his voice, the love and understanding, shakes me from the paralysing fog. And I run out of there, straight towards the lone security guard at the social club, who disappears inside to call Triple 0. When the ambulance shows up, I guide the officers to where Dad is standing watch over Tara. When he looks at me, his eyes are tired and emotional but also strangely alive. For the first time in a long time, he looks genuinely alive.

I see then what it is I've given him – a child who he can save.

CHAPTER 28

COUNTING THE COST

Once Mrs Lester shows up, Dad and I have nothing else to do. The doctors in Emergency won't talk to us. Mrs Lester, though shocked and upset, is the most attentive I've seen her.

'Tara's going to be fine,' Mrs Lester assures us after she's spoken to the doctors. 'She needs to sleep it off and get some liquids back into her, but she'll be okay.'

When we leave, Mrs Lester grips my hands and smiles, her gaze even and her hands steady. 'Thank you,' she says, 'for taking care of Tara.'

'No,' I say, letting her hold me when really I want to push her away. 'I didn't . . .' She has to know that part of this is my fault. I'm supposed to be Tara's friend and yet I left her there, drunk and hopeless. And angry. All because of my obsession with Mick Edwards. 'I should have stayed with her,' I say. 'I . . .' But Mrs Lester smiles at me and pulls me into an awkward kind of hug. I don't argue, I just whisper that I'm sorry and, amazingly, I don't cry a single tear.

'Thank you for being there when I couldn't,' Mrs Lester says to Dad, who nods, all businesslike. I know she's talking about tonight, but I feel like she means something bigger than this. I hope she does, anyway.

———

I don't speak in the car on the way home. I've never felt so tired. I slump against the car door and press my head against the window, the seatbelt pulled roughly across me. Dad drives in silence. It's Sunday morning. Too early for church traffic. It feels like we're the only people awake.

I stare at the shadows as they cut swathes across the back of the front seat of the station wagon. My mouth tastes vile, my tongue thick and claggy in my mouth. It's possible I might be sick again. I pull myself up from where I was lying, pain like glass cutting through my skull.

'Almost there,' Dad says into the rear-view mirror, without meeting my eye.

I nod and swallow. I have no idea what awaits when we pull up to the house, but I can take it. I will face it. Finally. As we pull up, I notice that Mick has gone. Of course he would leave, I tell myself, ashamed that I care enough to check.

Inside, Dad leads us wordlessly into the kitchen, as though this neutral space is the only one where we can trust ourselves and each other. He immediately heads to the sink and places the dirty coffee mug and teaspoon into the dishwasher, shutting the door with a solid thud, removing the evidence of his restful vigil.

I watch him shift before me in our bare, brown-and-white kitchen. It's Dad again. The same man he was before we went to find Tara, the same tired, hard and difficult man. And that's okay, I decide. This man . . . The one who raised me. The one waiting for me to speak, his hands spaced evenly on the island bench between us, fingers spread, his weight pressing against them. This man is my dad, and that's okay.

'That could have been you.' It comes out little more than a whisper.

I wait for him to look at me but his eyes remain on the bench in front of him. 'Dad?'

A deep rumbling sigh escapes him, from the depths of somewhere dark and private. A heartbreaking sound.

'Please? We need to talk.'

He shakes his head slowly, sadly. The weight of it seems to drag him down. 'I can't look at you,' he says simply. He slumps forward and crosses his arms, resting his head against them, as though the effort to hold himself is too great.

'You have to.'

He doesn't move and I wonder if he's fallen asleep.

'I'm here.'

'Later,' he says tiredly, managing to lift his face long enough to answer, then returns to the benchtop as though gravity is a force too enormous to fight.

'No,' I say, surprising myself. I'm not sure I've ever refused him so completely before.

He faces me then, lifts his grey head high enough to study me. 'Don't start.'

'We can't ignore it anymore.'

'Not now.'

'Yes now.'

'Shelley, you need to go to bed.'

I shake my head, the tears welling. I slam my hand on the island bench. 'No!'

My dad stands up, defeat curving his shoulders. 'Please. I can't do this now. Go to bed. Sleep on it.'

'No.'

'Shelley!' His voice rises more in disbelief than anger.

'No! No! No!' I shout, crying. My hand stings where it caught the edge of the bench, and my head is aching with all it has to hold, including the hangover that threatens to evict the contents of my stomach.

He stares at me, confused.

'I miss them,' I say. 'Okay? I miss Mum and I miss Angus and I want to know that that's all right.'

'What does that have to do with anything?' He stands tall now, as though the very mention of Mum and Angus is enough reason to fight.

'It's everything!' I shout. 'It's all there is!' But even I know that's not true, not entirely. There's more here for us – there has to be. Yet, surely, that's where we have to start?

'You think I don't miss them too?' he says, incredulous.

'It's like they don't exist!' I wail. 'Like they died twice! The first time in the car and then, again, when we came home. You made them disappear! You took them away!' Great wracking sobs consume me. I take a long ragged breath, forcing my voice to calm and my heart to slow. 'And now I want them back,' I say finally.

'You think this is any easier for me?' Dad whispers.

I can feel the pain in my chest at the idea of his suffering. I feel like I always do – like I always *did*. But I can't just let my pain go in the face of this guilt. Not this time. I back away, refusing to give up.

I rush to my room, taking less than a minute to find the one thing he can't deny or argue, the one thing he can't ignore. I hold out the Arnotts biscuit tin, placing it between us like an offering, a precious, fragile thing.

I watch his face, lit by the early morning gloom, as it moves from tired confusion to awful recognition.

'Where did you get this?' His voice is hard like gravel.

'Where you put it.' I tilt my chin in defiance. My whole body tingles and my head feels light. And then Dad's face shifts. The frozen horror transforms in increments, the edge of his mouth, the look in his eyes, shifting visibly from closed to open, as though a door has been unlocked. The softness I saw when he'd placed his jacket to pillow Tara's neck reappears, but where before he seemed stronger for it, now he appears a little bit broken.

I suspect he already was. We both are.

I reach out to place my hand on his, crossing the chasm between us in the form of a brown Laminex bench. I move around the bench and touch his shoulder, draping my arm across his back. I realise I've grown since I last did this. I could barely stretch my arm across the width of him two years ago.

His back slackens and he leans against the bench as wracking sobs escape from him. For a long minute I don't move. I don't want to shift my hand from his back or draw attention to the fact that he is distressed and I am witnessing it. I understand that this is the most honest thing that has ever happened between us and that, if I blink or baulk, it will be gone and never mentioned again. So I wait until the sounds fade and the tears stop, then I take Dad's hand and lead him to the kitchen chair. For a moment he resists, but then he eases himself onto the brown vinyl cushion. I hold the tin out to him again.

There is the barest tremble in his hands, his face still pale but his gaze steady and unyielding. I feel the cool sides of the tin slip through my fingers. He sits it on his knee and slides the battered lid off. He picks up the top photograph, holds it high to the weak sunlight that falls in thin pools across the kitchen floor. He studies the picture as though deciphering a foreign language, searching it for subliminal messages or secret codes. He places the photo on the table, then chooses another, and another, placing them beside one another. Row upon row collects over the next minutes. When the tin is empty, he focuses on the spread before him, fully immersed in the task, considering each row solemnly. He starts moving the photos around, grouping them, not according to chronology or subject, from what I can see, but in line with some obscure or secret reasoning. I watch all of this wordlessly from my seat beside him. And by the end, forty or more photographs are laid out in nine groups of varying number and combination.

Finally, he looks up, the colour drained from his face. He looks exhausted. Yet the slump has left his shoulders, his back has returned to its usual straight posture, his chin is high and strong in its ordinary certainty.

'Dad? I'm sorry,' I say finally, the weight of it enormous and suffocating.

He cocks his head, confused. 'Sorry?'

'For what I said . . . to Angus.'

Dad frowns, trying to understand. And I realise he doesn't know. 'Tell me. Please. What are you talking about?'

'Before the accident –'

'No,' he says, cutting me off.

'I have to.'

He studies me in silence, weighing it all up. And then he nods.

'I told Angus I wished he was dead. That I wasn't a twin. But I didn't mean it. I wish he was here now. All the time, I keep wishing he was here.'

Dad breathes hard. Something like a sob catches in his throat. He nods again, tears running down his face. 'I know that, Shelley. I know that.' He sucks in hard. 'Angus knows it too,' he whispers. He stands tall then, composing himself physically. 'You need some sleep,' he says, moving away from the table.

'Dad?' I ask, not sure what I want to say exactly. Is he okay? Are we okay? I want to know if I can fix this, if there's anything left that isn't broken. But I can't seem to put a voice to those words. Too much has happened.

He manages a tired smile that doesn't reach his eyes, but I'm so grateful for this gesture that I almost start to cry. 'It's a lot, Shell,' he says, his hand sweeping over the photos sprawled out on the table. 'It's just a lot,' he says again. He means, let's take it one week at a time.

And for now, that will have to do.

CHAPTER 29

THE END-OF-SEASON TRIP

The ground is racing beneath my feet. My arms pump to the drubbing of my heart. I'm flying again. Alone for the moment and faster than ever. The pounding suddenly becomes louder and then there's an echo – another pair of racing feet, the thumping rhythm drawing closer to me.

I steal a glimpse over my shoulder. Josh has made up ground. I push harder and faster, the wind whipping my breath from me, blood throbbing in my ears. I pull away, further than before, and cross the line two metres ahead. Hands on my head, I bend over, exhausted. All I want to do is curl up on the ground and wait for my breath to resume a normal pace, but years of training won't let me. I stand tall, opening my lungs to their full capacity, hands high, gripping each other at the base of my skull, opening my airways just that tiny bit wider. And breathe.

Josh's face is red. He really pushed himself and it shows.

I grin at him, delighted to beat him for real.

'I held back,' he gasps, matching my stance almost exactly.

'Ha!' I chortle. 'Like you'd tell me if you didn't.'

A wicked smile crosses Josh's face. 'Best of three?'

I laugh and shake my head. I can still beat him – just – but there's no way I can do it twice. I'm okay with that, too. Knowing the things I can do and the things I can't. Dad says you have to take the ball that comes your way and make it work for you. 'Not on your life, Josh,' I grin. 'Not on your life.'

We wander over to the long grass and plonk down by the chain-link fence. He wants to say something, to apologise. After the Ginnie incident I began avoiding him, ignoring his calls and visits. He quickly worked out something was going on. She must have told him. They're not friends anymore, which is fine by me.

The thing is, Josh didn't say a word to Ginnie. He knew what it meant for me to start again. To walk into St Mary's, horrible as it was, and be complete. A singular, complete person. Not the half that's left behind, not the surviving Brown girl or the twin with the dead brother. Just me. Just Shelley Anne Brown. For a while there, I managed it too.

But I shouldn't have kept Angus a secret. Somehow I have to live with this – I have to keep him in my life, even as I make it entirely my own. I don't know how I'll do that yet, but at least I don't have to do it alone.

So I showed up at Josh's house this morning, enjoying the shock and quiet apology I saw in his eyes when Mrs McGuire let me in.

'Someone at the club probably said something,' Josh says, breaking into my thoughts.

'I know.'

'But she's a cow for saying all that.'

'I know.' I don't want to talk. I just want to lie here and let the breeze cool my hot cheeks, feel the soft grass against my skin and listen to my heart beating.

And Josh's. My head is close to his chest, barely touching, so that I can feel his heart pounding. And even though we've been resting here for some minutes now, it doesn't seem to be slowing down at all.

I smile to myself secretly. I did that. I'm doing it still. I'm making someone's heart beat faster, and it doesn't hurt at all.

———

Two weeks after the grand final, I visit Tara at her home to see how she's doing. She looks good, or much better than she did on grand final night, despite the plaster cast on her elbow and the disorder of her room. She broke her arm when she fell in the press box. No one knows when or how, but it can't have been long before we got there because she'd been spotted only half an hour earlier back at the party, according to Red, who's the only reliable witness.

Tara's room is stacked with neat boxes, ready for their move. Mr and Mrs Lester are getting a divorce. They're selling the house so Mrs Lester can move back to where her parents live in the country and she's taking Tara with her. Tara doesn't know what school she's going to yet, or if they'll stay near her grandparents. She says she doesn't care. Either way, she's happy to leave St Mary's.

Dad told me that Mrs Lester is getting help – with Tara, and with her problem. I hope she meant what she said at the hospital, and that seeing Tara so sick scared her enough to make sure it never happens again.

I know it has for me.

'What about your dad?' I hand Tara the last of her albums, full of pictures of Glenthorn players – whole generations of men who have pulled on a Glenthorn jumper are wedged between the pages of Tara's thick albums.

She takes a long time to answer. 'He used to buy me a present every time he went away.' She pushes one of the large boxes against the wall, stacking a smaller one on top of it, and smiles thinly. 'I got a lot of presents.'

'If it's okay with your mum, we can meet up over the holidays. You can stay with Dad and me. And, of course, when the footy season starts, at the games . . .'

Tara nods. We both know this won't happen. Or it might, every now and then, but it won't be the same. She'll start a new life because she has to and I'll make this one work better because I have to. That's what we do. *Pick ourselves up, brush ourselves off and get back to position.*

I'm not sure I ever want to set foot at Fernlee Park again, but I don't say that out loud – that's the kind of thing you can't take back once it's said. 'Angus . . .' I say quietly. It's still shocking to hear his name spoken out loud. To say it myself. But it gets a tiny bit easier every time I do. 'My brother Angus was eleven minutes older than me.'

Tara stops packing and faces me.

'We used to play footy together, Angus, Josh and me. For the Raiders for a while and just for fun.'

Tara seems afraid to move.

'I miss him,' I say. 'I miss them both. My mum and Angus. How we used to be, you know? I thought that if I didn't talk about them, I could start again. Dad and I both thought that. I didn't really expect him to make them disappear the way he did – to take all the pictures and the memories and to lock them away – but after a while, I got used to it. And it did seem easier, somehow, to just start again.'

'Draw a line between last week and next,' Tara says quietly.

I smile. 'Yeah.' I look up at the tower of boxes and around at the chaos of her room – at all the bits and pieces that form a life. I run my hand along one of the albums, the smooth cover lined with a fine layer of dust. I rub my fingers together.

'Do you think you can?' she asks. 'I mean, really?'

'No, not really,' I say, thinking it through carefully. 'You can't draw a line in time. It doesn't work like that, like something you can organise or stack in towers. It's more like . . .' I hunt around for something that makes sense. Something that shifts and slips through space. 'Like *sand*.' That's not quite right but it's the best I can do. 'All the tiny bits move when you separate them, but grains escape and blow about, and soon you can't see the line anymore anyway.'

'My mum's stopped drinking,' Tara says. 'I don't know if she'll last . . .' She holds out her hands, turning them up like she wants me to fill them.

'It's something,' I say, and she nods.

I'm not sure we'll ever understand what it all means, or what's going to happen. All we can do is make the best of what we know, and just keep going.

There's a knock on the door and Mrs Lester pops her head in. 'Your dad's here, Shelley.' Mrs Lester looks younger today. And . . . hopeful.

347

After she closes the door I smile apologetically at Tara. 'It's Josh's presentation night. I promised I'd go. He's convinced he'll win – cocky bastard.'

'Yeah.'

The silence hangs between us, neither knowing what to say next.

'I'd better go,' I say.

Tara nods, and manages a tight smile.

'I'll see you later.' I turn to leave, but she stops me at the door.

'Yeah?'

In her arms is her glorious duffle coat. I stare at it, not knowing what to do next. 'It doesn't fit me properly anymore,' she says, and pushes it towards me.

'Are you kidding?' It seemed to fit her perfectly on grand final day, barely three weeks ago.

'No. It's yours.'

I shake my head. 'You can get another year or two out of this. You're not that much taller than me.' I laugh, nervously. I'm touched by this, even though I can't accept it. I can't imagine what this costs Tara – to give me her coat, to risk my rejection. I realise too late that I shouldn't have protested.

Tara presses it against me. 'Take it.'

I stare down at the coat in my arms, overwhelmed. 'Thanks,' I say, my voice made small by such an enormous gift.

Dad and Mrs Lester are chatting in the living room as though they've known each other forever, except when I get closer I notice that Dad has his hands shoved deep in his pockets like he doesn't know what to do with them. I don't think he's all that comfortable inside this mansion, just like me when I first came here. Now that I know its secrets, though, I'm not quite so intimidated.

We say goodbye to Mrs Lester and Tara, Mrs Lester raising an eyebrow at Tara's duffle coat, which I'm already wearing. 'Nice coat,' she says, her eyes swinging back to her daughter.

'I've outgrown it,' Tara says with a shrug. The defensiveness isn't there anymore and the contempt seems to have gone, or at least to have softened. I look at them standing side by side – not touching, but leaning towards each other, as though at any moment they just might. It's a new week. A new season. Anything is possible.

I watch the Glenvalley streets streak past us through the car window. The gaps and wide, empty roads don't seem as suffocating as they used to. I wind down the window, push my face out into the cold rush of air and breathe deeply. It feels good.

We pull into the twilit car park at the Glenvalley Raiders' home ground and park behind the clubrooms.

Dad slams the car door hard when he gets out – too hard. Then he opens it and slams it again, as though it didn't work quite right the first time. He's nervous. This is the first time he's been back since Angus was playing for the Raiders. Since Mum and Angus died. He's seen the people, the players, the officials and other parents – at the funeral, on the street, at school functions – but not here at the club. I slip my hand into his, thinking that I can't remember the last time I held his hand for no reason. Then I realise that it's for all kinds of reasons. His fingers stiffen at my touch. For a second, my heart squeezing impossibly tighter, I think he's going to pull away. But he doesn't. Instead, his hand closes around mine.

The club is packed. It's been going for a while already. The queue for the pies is short, most of the kids and adults having already eaten theirs. The beer queue, however, remains consistently long.

Mr McGuire calls everyone's attention and tells us to take our seats. Hard plastic chairs are lined up in the middle of the room, though there aren't enough for everyone, and most of the boys are sent to stand at the back, forming a noisy cluster of jeers and laughter.

Dad and I take a seat in the back, just in front of Josh, who, as always, is in the middle of the chaos, the centre of attention.

'Hey, Shell,' he calls out to me as I take my seat, only to

be met with more taunts and jeers from his teammates. He laughs it off, completely sure of his place in this world. I wish I could buy some of that confidence, or even borrow it now and then.

We settle in and listen to the various speeches and introductions, the wrap-up of the season and the plans for next year. Then they move on to the team awards, age group by age group, all the way up to Josh's team. Jacko reads out each player's name, handing them their medal for having won the premiership.

The noise level lifts in anticipation of the under 16s Best and Fairest Award, the last of the junior grade awards tonight. Mr McGuire nods at Dad, and then holds up the trophy. 'We've made a change in the Glenvalley Raiders' Best and Fairest Award. From this year on, in honour of the contribution of a much-loved and sorely missed player, the award will be known as the "Angus Brown Award for the Most Valuable Player".'

I hear the words clearly enough, but it takes a long minute for the meaning to register. I look at Dad in confusion, wondering how this could have happened without us knowing, and panicking that Dad will freak out. But Dad turns stiffly towards me and manages a tight smile.

He knew. I feel a sudden, powerful rush of love for my dad. Do they know how much this cost him? The trophy is a symbol of all the things that Angus won't have – the brilliance of youth and the potential for an amazing future. I tuck my arm through Dad's, determined for him to know what this means for us.

When Dad looks at me, I see something lovely and unexpected – a deep and absorbing pride. And my heart soars a little that he might soon be able to remember Angus without that crippling pain that nearly destroyed everything else.

Jacko takes over, assuming his role as coach and team leader. 'The inaugural winner of the Angus Brown trophy is . . . Cameron Evans.'

I'm still absorbing the idea of the Angus Brown Award before I realise that Josh didn't win. I turn around to find him at the back, cheerfully pumping Cameron Evans' hand with his usual gusto, no trace of disappointment or shock in his expression. He sends me that infuriating wink-grin thing he does, his delight at my surprise all the more infuriating. He knew he wouldn't win – that was just the plan to get me to come.

My cheeks burn and I struggle with the possibility that it's not because I'm embarrassed he's fooled me but because I'm flattered and strangely pleased. It's starting to feel like we've entered a whole other dimension – a place where Josh McGuire is less annoying than cute, where grief is not the unmentionable ghost in the Brown house, where footy can be the thing we share but not all that we have. If the Angels start winning next year, I'll know for sure we've entered a parallel universe.

Later, after the last of the awards are announced, I hang back and watch Dad talking to Mrs McGuire by the bar, each with a half-drunk almost-flat beer in their hands. They've been talking for ages.

Josh comes up, doing a very uncool strutting action that probably looked funny in his head but ended up looking idiotic and uncoordinated in practice.

'Smooth, Josh,' I say, smirking. I want to ask about the Most Valuable Player award but don't know how to raise it without reminding him he didn't win.

'It was Mum's idea,' he said, as though reading my mind. 'She spoke to your dad first,' Josh adds quickly.

Except Mrs McGuire told me earlier that it was Josh's idea and I know she'd never lie. I want to hug him. He's irritating and as cocky as all get-out, but I want to hug him with all my heart. It takes a good measure of willpower not to give in. 'Thanks,' I say, ignoring his protests.

'Thank my mum.'

'Yeah, whatever.' He's so pleased with himself but I'm sure it's not just about the Angus Brown trophy. 'Go on, then. Tell me what's going on. You look like you're about to burst.'

Josh nods smugly, that ridiculous grin both infuriating and – it's so hard to admit – gorgeous. It's there, though, plain enough. I've been ignoring the idea for as long as possible, but have decided that ignoring my feelings and the things that matter – the things that make me *me* –

doesn't work. In fact, it seems to have made a lot of things worse. Admitting it to myself, however, is a very different thing to admitting it to anyone else, especially the person it's aimed at. But footy is safe. Or real footy is – the actual game anyway. It's the extra stuff around it that gets messy.

'You should have won. Cam Evans is a hog.'

Josh laughs. 'Thanks for the support, but you only saw one game.'

'I've been listening,' I say, defensively, realising my absence mattered to him more than I thought. 'I'm not the only one who thinks you were robbed. Besides, he's always been Jacko's pet.'

Josh shakes his head, enjoying this conversation way more than he should. Why isn't he disappointed? Why isn't he angry? He knows I'm right. 'Yeah, well, I've got bigger fish to fry, Shell.'

I raise my eyebrows.

'Got some news,' he says, deliberately dragging it out.

'I can see that. Go on then.'

Josh looks around, then he grabs my hand and leads me outside. Night has set in and the temperature has dropped several degrees. He takes me to the dark corner of the car park, near Dad's car. We're just outside the glow of the club lights, as private as this clubhouse could ever be. Some of the younger kids are playing kick-to-kick on the dark oval, oblivious to the fact they can't see, their voices breaking the still night in between the hearty thump of a football.

My fingers are still tingling when he lets go. Nothing that happened on grand final night feels even a bit like this. My feet are cold from the damp ground, the breeze is steady on this cool spring night, and Tara's duffle coat is hanging uselessly on the back of my chair inside the clubhouse. But I feel a warmth rise through my whole body, starting at my toes and ending somewhere around my furiously blushing cheeks. 'Have you been drinking?' I blurt out, even though it's the furthest thing from my mind.

He frowns and shakes his head. 'No. What? No.'

'You're acting weird, Josh.' So am I. But maybe if I focus the attention on him, he won't notice. Despite the chilly air, two damp patches of sweat are forming under my arms. I hope to God my deodorant holds up.

'Shelley . . .' He stops.

I'm staring at his mouth. I have to force my lips shut so I don't kiss him right then.

He sees this and he knows. I'm quietly dying here and he knows exactly why.

'So what's the surprise?' My voice is way too loud for two people standing only inches apart.

'Just a minute,' he chides, like I'm an impatient kid. I bristle at his arrogance but that turns to water when Josh leans in to me, his voice dropping to a whisper. 'First I have to ask you something.'

My pulse throbs in my ears so hard I can't hear my own thoughts.

Josh pushes his hand through his hair, his floppy fringe settling right back where it was before. But in that gesture, I glimpse the freckle by his hairline, the one Angus used as an excuse to call him 'Spot'. My fingers itch to touch it, to brush his hair back so I can see it more clearly. His eyes are so intense, boring into me like a laser beam.

'What?' Amazingly, my voice doesn't catch. I sound angry.

He steps back, as though suddenly aware of how close we are, how intense the moment is, and I worry that he's misunderstood. He laughs nervously, looks over his shoulder again. 'You're not going to make this easy for me, are you?' he says, a glimmer of amusement in his eyes, but I think I see uncertainty too.

I want to. I think I want to.

'Okay, I'm just going to say it.'

I wait.

'The Eastern Panthers have invited me to train with the under 19s.'

'Oh.' Disappointment sits like a rock in my stomach. I try to find saliva in my dry mouth that will help me form the right words. Instead, a rasping noise escapes me. 'That's great!' I swallow, breathe and try again. 'The scouts came through then?' Almost even, almost neutral.

He laughs again, that nervous, jittery thing he seems to have only recently learnt. Where's the cocky Josh

I know? 'Yeah, they did. It is. It's great.' But he's frowning again, with confusion or disappointment.

I'm meant to be happier. I wind it all back in my head. I *am* happy. I refuse not to be happy. This is good, I tell myself. Brilliant, even. It's just not what I expected. But I won't lose this moment to celebrate with him. I've lost too many of them already. 'Seriously, I thought you were going to say something else,' I admit, realising too late that I've left myself wide open. 'It really is fantastic,' I gush, trying to cover my blunder. 'I mean, I knew they'd want you. I always said so, didn't I?'

'What did you think I was going to say?'

My face burns. I struggle to think of a single believable answer that doesn't involve my inevitable humiliation, but come up with nothing. I shake my head, study my toes and glance over at the halo of light outside the clubhouse.

'Are you still mad about that Ginnie Perkins thing? I told you I didn't say anything – she knows a lot of the players here. You said you believed me.'

Ginnie Perkins is so far from my mind right now that it's almost funny. 'I believe you,' I say, feeling a sudden urge to laugh. I don't know if it's fear or embarrassment, frustration or stupidity, but a bubble of laughter rises up in my throat. I kill it quickly, but maybe not quickly enough.

He shakes his head in disbelief.

'What? You're being weird again.'

He doesn't answer. For a moment, I think I've ruined everything forever. And then he kisses me. It's gentle and shy but it's right on my lips, so there's nothing brotherly or friendly about it.

I freeze, his lips still pressed against mine. My mouth won't move. My mind won't move. *I* can't move.

He stops and frowns. 'Jesus, Shell. You don't give an inch, do you?' And then I see that his face is, mercifully, as red as mine.

For a long second my heart seems to stop beating. Time halts. It's now or never. I close my eyes and my whole body relaxes, as though I've been holding on to something for ages and now, finally, I can let it go. I open my eyes again and look at him – right into him – and smile. 'No, I don't.' Before I can change my mind, I kiss him back. Our lips touch softly, then less softly, warm and familiar but also completely new. I can see that mouth in my mind's eye, having seen it a million times before: the rise and curve of it, the shape it makes when he smiles.

We kiss for a long time. And soon, neither of us is blushing from embarrassment.

CHAPTER 30

IN TRAINING

School has been lonely without Tara, but I've been making an effort to talk to girls I didn't spend much time with before. Elena Irving is funny and smart, and likes a lot of the same music as me. She's also fiercely loyal, like Josh. Rose DeLillo from my Italian class makes me laugh out loud. She's shy and speaks really quietly, so you have to listen hard, but it's always worth hearing. Mum was like that too – she didn't talk a lot, or force people to notice her, but as soon as she opened her mouth, people would lean forward to listen.

I'm sitting next to Elena in Australian History when Sister Brigid starts handing our essays back. I notice that Ginnie Perkins got a B, possibly her first ever, but otherwise all the usual names are at the top of the class.

I wait for Sister Brigid to give me mine, but she tells me to see her after class. After everyone files out, Sister Brigid hands me my essay with a big red A++ marked on the front of it.

'Thanks. Wow. I've never had a double-A plus before.' I'm blushing again, but I mind less and less now. Mum once told me that you can really trust someone who blushes because you always know what they're thinking. What they're feeling. I'd forgotten she said that.

'I hope it's okay,' Sister Brigid says, as I scan her comments to see what it was that she liked so much, 'but I gave your essay to Andrew.'

I blink a moment, wondering who Andrew is.

'My cousin,' she adds.

'Oh right. At Glenthorn.'

She nods, smiling. 'There's an internship starting at *The Falcon's Nest*, the newsletter. It's like a work-experience placement but for the whole year – on and off season. One afternoon a week, after school.'

Heat rushes from my toes to my head, then back again. The world does that slanting thing it does when I'm not expecting something good to happen.

I shake my head. 'I can't do it.'

Sister Brigid smiles and places her hand on my shoulder, looking me dead in the eyes with that steely gaze that usually ends up with me or Tara being sent to Siberia. 'Yes, you can,' she says simply, and lets go.

The thing is, I think she's right.

I cross the street to the tram stop, still buzzing from Sister Brigid's news. At the lights, I see Ginnie Perkins and her dad standing by their car. He's yelling at her and shaking what looks like Ginnie's History essay in his fist. Ginnie is leaning against the car, half turned away, as though ready to run if given the chance.

'Not acceptable!' Mr Perkins' voice cuts across the gap in traffic noise, disappearing again as the lights change and engines rev. Ginnie looks over just as her father disappears into the car. For a long second it's just Ginnie and me, studying each other. There's a hint of something unspoken in her eyes – not an apology, or even regret. But something like understanding.

The lights beep their warning not to cross, startling me out of the exchange. I've missed my chance and have to wait for another cycle.

I look back at Ginnie, but she's in the car now, and it's heading towards me with the surging traffic. Through the windscreen I can see Mr Perkins still berating her, while her eyes remain firmly ahead. Unwavering. Despite all those clingy friends, the boys who adore her and having more success than any one person should enjoy, Ginnie looks suddenly, painfully, alone.

Maybe our worlds aren't as far apart as I thought they were.

CHAPTER 31

THE PRE-SEASON DRAFT

Ever since Mum and Angus died, I've hated Sundays. Especially during the footy season. For most people it's Mondays. But for me, Monday is a day closer to the weekend, while on Sunday, the weekend – the bit about it that I love, anyway – is already over. And there's something so quiet about them, when the relief and excitement of a day at the footy has passed and I'm left alone with the worry and the dread and the quiet of our house.

That was before. I like Sundays now. Sometimes I go to Josh's for lunch, or he comes here. I've been at the McGuire house a lot lately. It was weird at first with Mrs McGuire knowing that Josh is my boyfriend. I'm not really sure what I expected her to say or do that first time I saw her after he told them. In the end, I stood in their kitchen, flushed and frowning, thinking hard about what I should say, if I should say anything different or special. But she didn't wait for me to work it out. Before I had time to adjust to this new situation, she took me in her arms and kissed my forehead like she does with Josh. 'I'm so happy we're going to see more of you now, Shelley,' she said. 'We really missed you.' And that was the end of it. Everything went back to exactly the way it was all those years before.

Well, not *exactly*. Not with Josh anyway.

So after Josh's on Sunday afternoon I usually work on my articles for *The Falcon's Nest*. I'm learning a lot, and the editor there, Mrs Evangeline, is nice. She's a bit bossy and really hates it when anyone's late, but she loves writing and she wants the paper to be great. No second prize. No room for carelessness. She says that if you're going to do something, you might as well do your best or why bother. I like her a lot, although I'm not sure everyone else does.

Fernlee Park is deserted when I go there. It's off-season so the players aren't around, and the cheersquad has no reason to show up. I haven't seen anyone since the grand final, but two months after my internship starts, I run into Lisa on Fernlee Park Road on my way to work. She looks so different without make-up, her hair pulled back into a tight ponytail; the flat school shoes and the square, sack-like school uniform changing her whole shape and even the way she walks. I almost walk past her without realising until she stops me and says hello. She says she's on her way to the Glenthorn library, and I explain about the internship.

'That sounds like fun. Must be weird, though, being there off-season.'

'Yeah. It's quiet. They'll be back, though,' I say.

'What about you? Will you be back next year?' she asks.

'The internship lasts for a year,' I say, without really answering her question. She means the cheersquad. And training. Will I be back? Honestly, I don't know the answer, though I know it won't be the same, no matter what I decide. 'You?' I ask.

She shrugs. 'I'll be doing my HSC. Doubt I'll have time,' she says, laughingly. 'Renee won't be happy. She said she'll have to go back to Carringbush now, since we're all so boring.'

I shake my head in disbelief. 'How's Kimberly?'

'Fine. She's seeing Danny now. Think it's serious. I doubt they'll be back next year either.'

'Not going to be many left,' I say, not really believing it. Red will be there – I don't even have to ask about her. Sharon and Jim-Bob and their endlessly bickering kids will be there too. Even David and the committee members who always get the best seats. Or someone just like them. There's always someone to fill their spot. That's how it works.

Lisa asks about Tara and I tell her the basics. Nothing about her parents, just about changing schools and moving house.

'She looked pretty wasted on grand final night – and pissed off too,' Lisa says. It's meant to be a question and I realise then that she doesn't know what happened later.

'Yeah, she was pretty drunk. We all were,' I say. 'Nothing serious, though.' Some lies are good. The ones that don't hurt anyone or don't fester inside you. The kind that can save your friend from humiliation.

I'm not sure she believes me, but I don't care.

'Good luck next year,' I say, meaning it. I have to start thinking about Year 12 too. And about what happens after that. I have some ideas about what I want to do, but nothing for sure. One week at a time, I tell myself. One week at a time. I'm about to cross the road when I remember someone else. 'Hey – Lisa! Do you see Bear at all?'

She stops mid-step, almost slamming into a woman with a pram. She apologises to the woman and turns around, her face flushed and a funny smile on her face. 'Er, yeah.'

I stand there, waiting.

'He's fine,' she says.

But there's more. I can hear it in her voice. 'Wait . . . He's mates with Danny. So you'd see him a bit, wouldn't you?'

She does something cute with her shoulders before she nods. 'Yeah. He's . . . good. Jason is really good.'

Jason? No one calls him that. 'Are you and Bear together?'

She blushes furiously, smiling. She doesn't quite nod. It's more of a shrug.

'Wow,' I say, then wish I could take it right back. But when I try to picture this pretty, slim girl hand in hand with the huge, tattooed Bear, the only thing that can come out is another *wow*.

'He's enrolling in TAFE,' she says, her blush fading, her smile widening. 'He's getting fit and losing weight,' she says quickly. 'It was the job – all that crappy food on building sites. But he looks great now.'

I realise she's defending him to me. 'No. Hey. Bear – Jason – is *great*. Really, really great. I think you make a perfect couple,' I add, meaning it. 'Say hi to him for me, will you?'

'Yeah. And say hi to Tara for me.'

'I will,' I say, and decide to call Tara that night. We could catch up for a movie or a concert – something that has nothing to do with football.

There's a first time for everything.

———

366

The next Sunday, I'm sitting in our lounge room, having just finished my final draft for the week's article – a summary of the new players and what we can expect from them over the next few years. Dad has already given it the nod of approval, and we're both watching the TV. The news is halfway over. There are still footy stories occasionally – the Warriors' end of year trip, that kind of thing. But it's faded out with the cricket season starting up. 'And the big news in footy tonight is the trading of Mick Edwards from Glenthorn to Sydney in what's seen to be the beginning of the fallout after Glenthorn's surprise loss in this year's grand final.'

I knew it was coming, but I thought he'd go back to South Perth, to be honest, back to those beautiful beaches. Either way, I knew he was leaving Glenthorn, and I thought I was okay with that. Except now, as I sit here in the quiet living room, the words ring in my ears like a siren, announcing the end of something important.

I can't look at Dad. He's been so good with everything that's happened – with Josh and me, with the McGuires being back in our lives, and with my new job at Fernlee Park. Over the weeks, I've noticed some of the photographs from the Arnotts tin appear in brand-new frames on the wall: one of Mum and Dad at their wedding, another of the four of us at the beach – Rosebud, I think, or maybe Rye. And another of Angus and me when we were babies, both of us looking so different to each other – him dark-skinned and dark-eyed like Mum, and me fairer with blonde stringy hair and eyes that look like a mix of Mum's and Dad's – that you wouldn't think we were related, let alone twins.

Dad has even bought a standalone frame for his bedside table, and in it he's slipped a photo of him and Mum, taken when they were young, both dressed for a formal dinner or party. Right next to it is a matching photo of them taken right before Mum and Angus died, their clothes from a different time, but there's the same shiny happiness in their eyes. I think that one's my favourite.

I blink at the TV, surprised that seeing Mick still hurts. I don't brave a look at Dad, but I can feel his worry and discomfort like they're physical things, standing beside him, dwarfing us both. I'm a little ashamed of myself that it still matters, so I force a smile – which comes out more like a grimace – but Dad seems to take something from it, because he smiles back.

After the news item finishes and the weather report begins, Dad breaks the awkward silence. 'I taped the game,' he says.

It takes me a moment to work out what he means. There are no games on right now. It's almost summer.

'The grand final,' Dad clarifies, sensing my hesitation. 'I taped it for you.'

Of course he did. Through all our silences and our

difficult moments, Dad always did what he said he'd do. I asked him to tape the match because I thought we'd win. I wanted to sit in the lounge room and relive our success over and over. To revel in Mick's win – *our* win – blow by blow, goal by goal, and analyse it all until I knew it by heart. Except we lost and Mick has gone. And nothing will be the same again.

But I'm still here and this is now, and I refuse to let these moments defeat me. *Pick myself up, dust myself off and get back to position.*

I widen my smile and nod at the TV. 'What are you waiting for? Put it on.' My voice sounds unnaturally bright, even to me, but it doesn't crack, and the tears that prick the back of my eyes don't spill.

Dad sits on the couch beside me, places his legs on the footrest and smiles gently. He suddenly looks strong to me. Bigger than when I was a little, but more distant, too. And I understand that I will never feel as safe as I did back when I was a small child in my dad's arms, back when I had a mother and a twin brother, all of us taking care of each other, being a piece of a whole, the whole being better than the sum of its parts, the champion team always better than a team of champions. But that's okay. There's still Dad and me. It's not perfect, but it's okay. We'll be okay.

The Falcons theme song kicks in and we watch the boys burst through the cheersquad's amazing run-through banner, the house-sized image of Killer Compton tearing through the middle, and for a second I'm right back there, the roar of the crowd in my ears, the buzz in the air. One hundred thousand people united in the singular hope that today they'll come out on top. The sun shines with that delicious September clarity and the commentators remind us that this is the biggest day on the Melbourne calendar.

I settle back into the couch and rest my feet on the ottoman beside Dad's. 'You never know,' I say, the beginnings of a real smile starting somewhere inside me, rising up to touch my eyes. 'We just might get up and win this time.'

ACKNOWLEDGEMENTS

I am and always have been a huge AFL fan. Much like Shelley, and to the chagrin of my twin brother, I 'played' for the local footy club during my primary school years. Because of how girls were viewed back then, this was limited to training with them religiously and wandering wistfully along the boundary line, hoping I might one day get a game. There was a lot of talk that I would, too. This lasted until, following an appeal by my coach to the competition tribunal, the administrators officially banned me from playing, on the grounds that the game wasn't safe for girls to participate. Although this ban was lifted for girls under 14 only a couple of years later, it was too late for me. By then I was ensconced in secondary school and had already found my way to the steps of Glenferrie Oval, where I deposited myself for a good chunk of my teenage years. There were many times that the only solace I could find from that endless ache that is adolescence was in the shape of a muddied red Sherrin and those impossible-to-accessorise brown-and-gold stripes. So before I thank the *people* in my life, I'd like to acknowledge my first real love in that oft-cited, heartfelt cry: '*Carn the Hawks!*'

That you are reading this book is largely due to my agent and friend, Elizabeth Troyeur, and her unwavering support and limitless patience. (She said this was the one and she was right. As usual.) Special thanks to the brilliant team at Random House Australia, especially Zoe Walton and Catriona Murdie for their gentle guidance and boundless wisdom. I am confident they now know more about AFL than either of them ever dreamed of – or wanted to. Now if I can just drag them along to a game . . .

A huge thank-you to my long-suffering writing partner, fellow author, first reader and dear friend, Melanie Benjamin, for reading more drafts of this manuscript than anyone should have to and never once complaining. Her feedback, encouragement and insight into the publishing world has been critical to my development as a writer. To Jacqueline Tomlins and Sarah Nichols for their excellent feedback and unbridled enthusiasm for this story, despite having a healthy antipathy for all things football. To PD Martin, crime writer extraordinaire and friend, for her practical, no-nonsense critique and her laser-sharp editorial eye. To Eliza Graham for reading a late draft at short notice in record time and still managing to offer brilliant feedback. To my oldest friends, Rose Giannone and Elena Christie, who have been spurring me on and inspiring me to write since our schooldays. (And thanks for the feedback, Rose.) To Anna for keeping me company on the boundary line on those bleak and wintry afternoons at Glenferrie. And to my reader, friend, babysitter, sounding board and personal cheersquad, Veronica Pardo, who was also happy to beat me upside of the head any time I suggested this book might not happen.

Peter Bishop and the Eleanor Dark Foundation gave me the time and space to revise early drafts of this novel at Varuna, more than a decade ago. Guiding me in the battle was Mark McLeod, who nailed it from the start, and my talented friends and fellow writers in the trenches, Steven O'Connor, Meg McKinlay, Ian Trevaskis, Gillian Wadds and Kylie Stevenson. Their company, enthusiasm and certainty that this would happen, despite all evidence to the contrary, drove me onwards at those darkest of moments.

To the Writerscave dwellers, to Karen Dionne and the crowd at Backspace, as well as the team at Done

Deal Pro, especially Will Plyler and Craig Mazin – you have all taught me about story, craft and collegiality, demonstrating a generosity of spirit that I can only hope to emulate.

To the Phoenix Park Writers and staff – thank you for sharing your stories and wisdom. And to the talented women of Tuesday Writers – you're next!

A very special thank-you to my family: the Webbs and Dunstons in New Jersey, who are supposed to be the 'dreaded in-laws' but have turned out to be great friends and the most devoted fans, especially Madeline, Allan and Joanne, who I could hear cheering for me all the way from America. To my sisters, Ryse and Amanda, their kids Ellyahne and Liam, Jessica and Kirsty, for their support, encouragement and unwavering loyalty, and to my twin brother, Damien, for letting me steal from our lives. (The good bits, anyway.) To my mother, Linda (Yolanda) Hayes, for never doubting – not for a second – that this would happen, and to my much missed father, Geoffrey Hayes, for so eloquently showing me the power of language and the poetry in football. We miss you, Dad.

But most of all to Frank, Hannah and Emily for letting me close the door and write. There would be no novel without you. And, frankly, no point.